THE HUNTED SERIES

Eruption

THE HUNTED SERIES - BOOK 3

THE HUNTED SERIES

Eruption

IVY SMOAK

ISBN: 9781942381099

To everyone I've ever hated.
My inspiration for Isabella.

PART 1

CHAPTER 1
Saturday

I walked up to the stage, being careful not to trip. Falling in front of thousands of people was something I wanted to avoid at all costs. I took a deep breath and stared at the dean who was announcing everyone's names. I felt like I had come such a long way. My whole life I had focused on doing well in school. And now that I was about to graduate, I had no idea what I actually wanted to do. I wanted to be excited about this moment, but I was so nervous.

"Penny Taylor," Dean Mullins said.

I slowly walked across the stage, grabbed my diploma, and shook a bunch of people's hands that I didn't know. I smiled as I walked down the stairs on the opposite end of the stage. *I did it. I graduated!* It didn't matter that I had no idea what I wanted to do. Graduating was a huge accomplishment. I moved the tassel on my cap to the left and smiled for the cameraman that was waiting there to capture the moment. Now it was official.

My eyes scanned the crowd as I walked back to my seat. I didn't see any familiar faces. It was going to be almost impossible to find anyone after the ceremony with all these people. I sat down in my seat and listened to the rest of the graduates' names being called. I only recognized a few. The campus was so much bigger than the University of New Castle's. And coming in halfway through sophomore year hadn't made it any easier to meet people. I hadn't thought much about it until this moment, seeing all the people walk by that I had never met.

This chapter of my life was closing forever, and it suddenly felt like I hadn't really experienced it. I quickly shook away the thought. Just because I didn't recognize hundreds of the names that the dean announced, didn't mean I didn't have a fulfilling college experience. These past few years had been amazing. I wouldn't have changed a thing. I looked to the left and searched the crowd again. *Where is he?*

"Congratulations to the class of 2018!"

Everyone around me stood up. I followed their lead and clapped my hands together. As soon as people started moving around, I squeezed past everyone in the row I was in and made my way toward the entrance hall. I knew they were serving refreshments out there, and if I didn't get in there early, I would never be able to find anyone.

When I opened up the doors, there were already hundreds of people in the room. I made my way through the sea of people celebrating.

"Penny! Over here!"

I smiled and turned toward the familiar voice. "Tyler!" I ran over to him and threw my arms around his neck.

He laughed and lifted me off my feet, twirling me through the air for a second. "Congratulations, Penny," he said and kissed my cheek as he set me back down on my feet.

"Thanks, Tyler. I'm so glad that you could come."

"I wouldn't have missed it," he said and let go of my waist.

"I can't believe I'm actually done. I'm officially an adult."

He laughed. "I'm pretty sure you need a job in order to be considered an adult."

"I'm working on that. Not everyone can graduate with a full time gig lined up, Mr. Hotshot."

He laughed and put his hands in his pockets.

"Where is everyone else?"

"I had to go to the bathroom, so I cut out right after I saw you walk. They'll all be down in a minute."

"Did Melissa make it?"

"Yeah, she's here." Tyler scratched the back of his neck. "Actually, Penny, I wanted to talk to you about..."

Before he could finish his sentence I felt someone attack me with a huge hug.

"Penny!" Melissa yelled.

I laughed. "Welcome to New York!"

"Thank you." Melissa released me from her embrace.

"Did you move everything in okay? When I left and you still weren't there I was worried something happened to you."

She laughed. "No, no, I'm good. My stuff is all moved in...just not at your place."

"What do you mean?"

"I just decided that it would be easier to crash at Tyler's place until I find something. I dropped my stuff off there this morning."

"Oh." I felt my heart sink. "I was excited to be roommates with you again."

"I know." She smiled and gave me another hug. "But it was only going to be for a couple days anyway. I'm going to find my own place really fast."

"Are you sure Tyler doesn't mind?"

Melissa laughed. "No, he practically begged me. Isn't that right, Tyler?"

Tyler made a weird face and looked away from us.

Melissa laughed again. "I heard about your new job. It sounds really exciting."

"Geez, he's trying to convince you it's a good idea too? It's not. You know that I'm not taking that job."

"Why not?"

"Because Penny doesn't want to work with me," James said.

I smiled and turned around. "You know that's not it."

"Hmm." He put his hand on the side of my face. "We can talk about that more later. Congratulations, Penny." He leaned down and placed a soft kiss against my lips. I wrapped my arms around the back of his neck.

My dad cleared his throat. I could feel my face turning red.

"Hi, Dad!" I immediately stepped away from James, gave my dad a quick hug, and then gave one to my mom too. "Hi, Mom."

"Congratulations, sweetie," My mom said. "We're so proud of you. And we're so excited about meeting your parents, James. We've been looking forward to it."

"About that." James put his arm around my shoulders and looked down at me. "They had to cancel."

I pressed my lips together. *God.* I had let myself get my hopes up this time. Who was I kidding? I always got my hopes up. I thought maybe now that I had graduated, though, they might actually want to meet me. So it wasn't my age. It was starting to seem like they had no intention of ever meeting me. I swallowed hard.

James squeezed my shoulder. "I'm sorry, Penny."

"That's fine," my dad said. "Let's go out to lunch anyway. My treat."

I put on a smile. "That sounds perfect."

"We're going to head out," Melissa said.

"You're both welcome to lunch" my mom said.

"I still have a lot to unpack, so I should probably get started. Bye, Mr. and Mrs. Taylor." Melissa gave them each a quick hug.

"You're coming with us tomorrow, right, Melissa?" My mom asked.

"I wouldn't miss it." She winked at me.

It was hard to even think about shopping for a wedding dress right now. James' parents clearly didn't want me to be a part of their family. Every time they canceled plans to finally meet me, James told me not to worry about it. But how could I not worry about it? We were getting married at the end of the month. And at this rate it didn't even seem like his parents were going to come.

"Congrats again, Penny." Tyler smiled at me and then followed Melissa through the crowd.

***

I rested my head on James' shoulder. Lunch had been so much fun. I loved catching up with my parents and all the goings-on in Delaware. It helped me feel connected to the life I had left behind. At least, I thought I had left it behind. I wanted to fit into James' life. I didn't want to cause him unnecessary stress. But that's exactly what I was doing. I didn't know what to do in order for his parents to like me. Liking me was far off, though. James and I had been dating for two and a half years and they still hadn't even met me.

I closed my eyes and listened to the sounds of the city as our driver, Ian, expertly sped us through the city streets. The cars honking now seemed to relax me instead of unsettling me. This was my home now. I just wished I fit in a little better.

"Hey." James grabbed my chin and tilted my face up to his. "You've been awfully quiet."

I bit my lip.

"Penny, we're supposed to be celebrating."

I felt a lump building in my throat. "They're not going to come to our wedding, are they?"

He sighed and pressed his forehead against mine. "I think maybe that's for the best."

I pulled back. "How can you say that? They're your parents. They should be there."

"I love you. That's all that matters."

"I'm going dress shopping tomorrow."

He smiled. "I know."

"Your mom should be there."

"You don't want her fashion advice, trust me." He placed a soft kiss against my neck. "How about we focus on something else?" He kissed my neck again and placed his hand on my thigh, running his fingers along the hem of my dress.

I laughed and grabbed his hand. "We're almost back to our place."

"Your point is?" He kissed my collarbone, making a moan escape from my lips.

"My point is that Ian will know that we're having sex back here if we don't come out when he parks."

James laughed. "You're acting like we haven't done it before. Ian doesn't care. Being discreet is in his job description."

I ran my hand through James' hair. "We'll be back in five minutes."

He sighed and moved his hand off my thigh. "Well, if you insist on talking, I'd like to revisit the internship idea."

"I'm still thinking about it."

"That's not what you said to Melissa." He grabbed my hand and ran his thumb along my palm.

"I know." I looked down at his hand. "What would people think?"

"Is that really the reason? You've never seemed that worried about what other people think."

I looked back up at him. He was right. That wasn't the real reason. "I didn't earn it, James."

"You just graduated with honors from NYCU. You're just as qualified as all the other interns we've already hired. I wanted to give you an actual job, but you shot that down right away. If you insist on proving yourself, this is the way to do it."

"I don't know."

"You don't have to accept it. I'm not going to force you to work with me. You don't have to work at all. You know that."

I laughed. "Of course I have to work. I already owe you so much."

"You don't owe me anything." He lowered his eyebrows slightly. "I hope you don't really feel that way."

"I owe you everything."

"Penny..."

"I'm not talking about money. You know that. I'm talking about you. Where would I be without you?"

"Jobless, for one."

"You're not going to let this go, are you?"

"Not a chance."

"If I don't hear back from anywhere by next week, I'll do it."

He smiled. "This is going to be so much fun."

"I said *if*. It's not a done deal yet."

"I'm pretty sure you'll be working with me."

I laughed. "When I asked you not to interfere with my apply-ing for jobs, I never imagined you'd be telling places not to hire me."

"What, you think I called all the places you interviewed with and told them how awful you are?"

"I'd hope not. Maybe that's what you did with your parents too. Is that why they don't want to meet me? You told them about all my flaws and scared them away?"

"I love all your flaws."

The car came to a stop.

"What do you think my flaws are?" I asked.

He smiled at me and got out of the car. I quickly climbed out of the car and grabbed his hand.

"James, what are my flaws?"

He squeezed my hand and typed in the code for the elevators. The doors immediately opened and he pulled me inside.

I stared up at him and pursed my lips.

"There's just too many to name," he said. "The list is end-less."

I lightly pushed his shoulder. "Just tell me the biggest then."

"Hmm." The elevator came to a stop and he swiped his ac-cess card against the reader. The doors opened behind us.

"You know how good I am at getting information out of you." I trailed my hand down the front of his dress shirt, stop-ping at his belt.

He grabbed my hand and smiled. "Turn around, Penny."

I looked over my shoulder. There were tons of people stand-ing in the living room of our apartment.

"Surprise!" Melissa yelled. Everyone else quickly yelled sur-prise too.

I could feel my face turning red. Had they all heard what I just said? I quickly turned back around to look up at James.

He smiled down at me. "For one, you're very bad at telling when you're being thrown a surprise party. Congratulations, baby."

CHAPTER 2

Saturday

"Well that wasn't awkward at all," Rob said as he leaned down and hugged me.

"So everyone did hear?" I asked. I had talked to almost everyone and escaped to the kitchen to catch my breath. I wasn't as good at parties as James was. Networking wasn't something I was good at. And I had just embarrassed myself in front of all my friends and a few people I'd probably consider more of acquaintances. They'd probably remain acquaintances now.

"That you were about to give James head to extract information from him? Oh, yeah, everyone heard that," he said as he let me out of his embrace and handed me a drink.

I laughed. "Well, no one's mentioned it but you. Not everyone has as dirty of a mind as you."

"Or you." He winked at me. "How was lunch with my parents?"

"They canceled again."

"You're kidding. They're really holding out."

"Holding out for what?"

"James to change his mind, I guess."

Right. My biggest fear was that they'd just start throwing women at James that were way more suitable to be their daughter in law. I looked down at the drink Rob had given me. "What is this?"

"Trust me, you'll like it."

"You're not roofieing me, are you?"

He laughed. "The girl my brother is about to marry? I would never."

"I never believe anything you say, you know."

"That's how I prefer it. But it's just a sex on the beach. If you'd prefer the actual thing, I think we could arrange that, though."

"I'll take the drink. Are you still enjoying living on campus?" I took a sip of my drink. It was sweet, but very strong.

"Of course. That's a ridiculous question. I'm living the dream."

"Taking advantage of innocent young women?"

"What, like you?" He smiled at me. "Shagging your professor wasn't so innocent, Penny."

"Is Rob harassing you again?" Bee said and leaned against the kitchen counter next to me.

Rob laughed and looked down at his watch. "Is it time for me to move on to you already?"

"You can focus on Penny tonight," Bee said. "It's her big day. Congrats, again," she said and squeezed my arm.

"Thanks, Bee."

"And congrats on the new job too. James just told us about it."

"Did he?" I looked over at James. He was sitting on the couch next to Mason. As if he could feel my stare, he turned away from Mason and smiled at me. He raised his left eyebrow and lifted his glass slightly. Mason laughed beside him and gestured for Rob to join them.

"I've been summoned," Rob said. "I'll let you two ladies talk. I'll be back when you're done that drink, Penny. You won't even be able to resist me." He walked over to the couch and plopped himself between Mason and James.

I looked down at the drink. He was joking right? "On a scale of one to ten, how likely is it that this drink has a roofie in it?"

Bee laughed. "Like fifty."

"That's what I thought." I pushed it aside and grabbed a glass of champagne off a tray that a waiter was walking around with. "Okay, so I have a question for you. What's it like working with Mason?"

Bee smiled. "Wonderful."

"Really? It doesn't make it hard to keep your work and personal life separate?"

Her cheeks turned slightly red. "We don't really keep it that separate."

I laughed. "I'm guessing the blurred line doesn't mean you go over reports in bed at night?"

"Not exactly. We share an office, though. What do you expect?"

"Right. But it's not going to be like that if I work with James. Or, for him, I guess is a better way to put it." Bee and Mason were an amazing power couple. They had grown their advertising firm to seven figures within just a couple months after their launch. Now it was one of the top agencies in the city. And even though they worked a lot, they still looked at each other in that way that made your heart melt.

"I doubt he's going to make it feel like you're working for him. And either way, it'll look great on your resume. You still have different last names, you can take advantage of that. Use it as a stepping stone. And your next employer doesn't have to be any the wiser when you use James as a reference."

I laughed. "I'm pretty sure he's sabotaging me from getting any other jobs."

"I'm sure that isn't true."

"You have no idea." I took a sip of my champagne.

Bee laughed. "I think he and Mason are pretty similar. They're both used to getting whatever they want. I'm not sure they understand the word no."

I laughed. "Shh, they're coming over here."

Bee smiled as Mason wrapped his arms around her. "What are you two talking about?"

"How stubborn you are," Bee said. "What were you two talking about?"

"James' bachelor party," Mason said. "Rob and I have so many good ideas."

"Trust me," Bee said and grabbed my arm. "You do not want Mason planning James' bachelor party."

I laughed even though she didn't look like she was kidding. "I'd rather him plan it than Rob. Whenever Rob and James get together they always do something stupid."

"You have nothing to worry about," James said and wrapped his arm around my shoulders. "I'm not having a bachelor party."

"Of course you are," Mason said. "I already bought the tickets. It's going to be awesome."

Bee frowned. "Where exactly are you guys going?"

"I can't say," Mason said. "It's a surprise."

Bee shook her head.

"We're not going anywhere," James said. "Don't worry about it."

"You should have a bachelor party," I said and looked up at him. "Isn't that like a rite of passage?"

"Yeah, but I've already had one."

Every now and then I let myself forget about his past. I downed the rest of my champagne and picked up the sex on the beach. I kind of hoped it was laced with something. I hated thinking about finding a job. I hated thinking about James' parents not wanting to meet me. But most of all I hated being reminded of Isabella. I took a huge sip of the drink. "You should still go, James. You'll have fun."

"See," Mason said. "She wants you to go."

James squeezed my shoulder. "I'll think about it."

"Are you ready to get going, Bee?" Mason asked and removed his arms from around her. He whispered something in her ear and she laughed.

"I guess we need to get going," she said. "Bye, James." She gave him a quick hug. "See you tomorrow, Penny," Bee said as she hugged me. "Don't encourage them, Penny," she whispered. "You seriously don't want Mason to plan it. Trust me." She pulled back. "Congratulations." She gave me a small smile

Weird. "Thanks, Bee. See you tomorrow."

Mason hugged me. "Congratulations on finally graduating. I guess I can't really make fun of James for being with someone so young now."

"I'm sure you'll find something else to tease him about."

Mason laughed and released me from his hug. "It's going to be a blast, man," Mason said and slapped James on the back. "Maybe not as much fun as you guys are about to have when everyone clears out of here, though, right, Penny?" He winked at me.

Oh God. Everyone really did hear. I put my hand over my face as they left the apartment. "I'm mortified."

James laughed. "It gave everyone something to talk about all night." He put his hand on the small of my back and pulled me into him.

"You could have stopped me two seconds earlier, you know. Usually when someone throws a surprise party they don't let the guest of honor say something embarrassing in front of a room full of people."

"I don't know. How many surprise parties have you been thrown?"

"Well, none, but..."

"So I'm pretty sure this was exactly how it's supposed to go." He leaned down and lightly nipped my earlobe. "I had considered letting you keep going. So you're welcome."

I laughed and looked into the living room. There were only a few people left. Melissa and Tyler were sitting on the couch, laughing about something. "Did you say something to Melissa? To make her not want to stay with us? I was really looking forward to it."

"Although I am excited that I get to keep you all to myself, I don't think her not wanting to stay with us has anything to do with me." James nodded back over to them.

"What do you mean?"

James laughed. "They're obviously sleeping together."

"No they aren't." Tyler and Melissa were definitely not hooking up. That was ridiculous. I looked back up at James.

"What, does that upset you?" He lowered his eyebrows slightly.

"Of course not. But they're not sleeping together." Tyler was sweet and kind and Melissa was my best friend, but she was Melissa. They weren't a good fit.

James laughed. "I'm pretty sure they are."

"Melissa would have told me. Tyler would have told me."

"Maybe they thought it would be awkward."

I laughed. "Why would that be awkward?" I swallowed hard and looked back over at them. They were just friends. All three of us were just friends. Melissa laughed and lightly pushed Tyler's shoulder. *They are just friends, right?*

James kissed my cheek. "Let's go try to subtly get rid of everyone. I want to give you your present in private."

"I told you not to get me anything. You already paid for..."

He silenced my protests with a kiss. "My fiancée just graduated. Of course I got you something." He grabbed my hand and guided me back toward the living room.

The only people left were Melissa, Tyler, Rob, and Mason's little brother, Matt. James sat down in the only empty chair and pulled me onto his lap.

"How'd you like the rest of that drink?" Rob asked. "Are you feeling frisky yet?"

I laughed. "I didn't finish it." I was feeling a little frisky, but not at all toward Rob. The man with his arms wrapped around me was the only guy I ever wanted.

"Now what am I going to do with the rest of my night?" Rob said and leaned back in his chair.

"Stop being gross, Rob," Melissa said.

"I thought you liked when I was gross?" he said and smiled at her.

I looked over at Tyler, but he didn't seem to have any reaction to what Rob had just said. After I had moved to New York, Rob and Melissa had a short fling. Tyler knew about it because we had talked about how weird it was. If Melissa and him were dating now, it would make him uncomfortable to hear about it again. Tyler didn't seem to care at all that Rob wanted to do gross things to Melissa, though. And I didn't doubt at all that they'd be gross.

"I have an idea," James cut in. "You could call it a night and go to bed early."

"That wasn't subtle at all, James," I said.

Matt laughed. "What, do you two need to finish whatever it was you were about to do before Penny realized there was a whole room of people watching?"

"I wasn't about to do anything," I said. "That was a complete misunderstanding. I was just making sure James' outfit looked good. Checking his buttons and stuff." *Worst excuse ever.*

"That's not what it sounded like," Tyler said. "I'm pretty sure we were all just a few seconds away from witnessing quite the graduation celebration."

Melissa glared at him. I couldn't tell if she looked jealous or if she was just mad at him for further embarrassing me. I couldn't read either of them tonight.

"Well, as much fun as this has been, we should probably get going," Melissa said and put her hand on Tyler's knee.

I looked at her hand on Tyler's knee and then back at her face. She immediately moved her hand. *Oh God, they are sleeping together.* Why didn't she tell me? I bit the inside of my lip.

"Yeah, we probably should head out." Tyler stood up.

Melissa immediately stood up beside him. "I'll see you tomorrow, Penny."

"Sounds good. Thanks for coming tonight."

"Of course. Great party, James."

"Are you not even going to say goodbye to me?" Rob asked.

Melissa rolled her eyes. "As if you deserve a goodbye. Bye, Matt. It was great seeing you again."

"Bye, Melissa," he said with a laugh. "See you around, Tyler,"

Tyler nodded and they both went over to the elevator.

I wanted Melissa and Tyler to be happy. Why did she think I'd be upset about them dating? I looked down at my lap. My first thought had been that they weren't a good fit. Maybe she was right for not telling me.

"I think you're right," I whispered to James.

"About what?" Matt asked.

I looked over my shoulder. Tyler and Melissa were gone. "Am I terrible at whispering or something?" I asked.

"You're always really loud," Rob said with a wink.

I felt my face turning red.

"She was talking about how Melissa and Tyler are sleeping together," James said.

Matt laughed. "There's no way those two are banging. Don't you see the way he looks at you, Penny? He probably wants you even more than Rob does."

I felt James' arms tense around me. *Damn it, Matt.* "Tyler and I are just friends."

"And I don't want Penny," Rob said. "She wants me."

I laughed. "Yeah, right."

"You're all in denial," Matt said. He stood up and yawned. "Okay, I think I'm going to head out too. Are you crashing here?" he asked Rob.

Rob looked over at me. "Well, that depends on if Penny wants me to stay."

I sighed. "I think maybe you should spend the night at Matt's. You've gotten me all wound up from that cocktail, so now I have to do super inappropriate things to your brother. And we don't want to keep you up all night."

James laughed. "That sounds fantastic." His body seemed to relax at my words.

"Yuck. Okay, let's get out of here," Rob said and slapped Matt on the back.

"Congrats, Penny," Matt said. "My parents wanted me to give this to you." He handed me an envelope.

"What is it?"

He shrugged. "A gift I guess. Later, James," he said as they did one of their weird handshakes.

"Are you going to open it?" James asked as Rob and Matt left our apartment.

"Do you know what it is?"

He shook his head.

I ripped open the envelope and pulled out the card.

Penny,

We have known James his whole life. He was at our house growing up almost as much as Mason and Matthew were. He's like a son to us. And we can't think of someone more perfect for him than you, Penny. We would be honored if you'd let us throw you a late engagement party at our house. Just something small, to officially welcome you to the family. Call us so we can arrange a date. And congratulations on your graduation!
-Mr. & Mrs. Caldwell

I could feel the tears welling in my eyes. James' parents didn't want to meet me. But I already knew the Caldwells. I had spent a lot of time with them since moving to New York. Every time they saw me they always asked if I had gotten to meet Mr. and Mrs. Hunter yet. I tried to act as optimistic as I could, but every-one knew I was upset about it. Mr. and Mrs. Caldwell clearly cared about me and James. Maybe it was okay that James' parents didn't want me to be a part of their family. Maybe everything I had was enough.

I looked up at James. "That's really sweet, isn't it?"

"I didn't know they thought of me like that." He had a weird look on his face. It wasn't confusion exactly. He almost looked sad.

I moved so that I was straddling him. "James, I love you so much. You are the sweetest man I have ever met. But you are just terrible at telling when people care about you."

He smiled at me. "I know that you care about me."

"Mhm. And all the people that came tonight. And Mason and Matt's parents," I said and held up the letter.

"I think everyone just likes you."

I shook my head. "I don't think so."

"Like Tyler."

I laughed. "Oh God. You know that's not true."

He shrugged. "Now that I'm friends with him, I don't think it matters one way or the other. He's a good guy. He won't try to steal you away now."

"Apparently he likes Melissa. So you have nothing to worry about."

"I wasn't worried." He kissed my cheek and then the side of my neck. "Let me go get your present."

I reluctantly moved off his lap. I had only been half joking when I was talking to Rob earlier. I was definitely planning on enjoying James tonight. When he disappeared into his office, I looked back down at the note. They wanted to welcome me to the family. My body felt warm, and not just because of the mixed drink Rob had made me. I had tried so hard to fit in here in New York. But at first I had really missed the suburbs. I had missed passing strangers on the sidewalk that were nice, having grass everywhere, and not being worried I was going to be mugged if I stepped outside at night. It was a hard adjustment. I wasn't sure when it had happened, but suddenly I fit. James' friends had become my new family. And New York had become my home. James' parents not wanting to meet me was the last thing that made me feel like I shouldn't be here, like I didn't belong in this new life.

But this could be enough. I stared at the note in my hands. It was going to have to be.

CHAPTER 3

Saturday

James sat down on the rug in front of the chair I was in and handed me a manila envelope. He put his hand on my knee, rubbing the inside of my knee with his thumb, not looking at my face.

I had gotten pretty good at reading him. Whenever he did something he knew I wouldn't like, he rarely ever looked me in the eyes. Whatever was in the envelope, he thought I wasn't going to like it. My heart started to beat faster. "What is this?"

"Your present." He tore his eyes away from my knee and looked up at me. "Open it." He leaned down and kissed my kneecap.

I moved my leg away from his hand. Now he was just trying to distract me. I tore open the top of the envelope and pulled out a small stack of photos. They were pictures of really beautiful rooms. Really beautiful, huge rooms. Each room was elegant, yet modern at the same time. It was exactly James' style. Which had become my preference as well. I let my eyes meet his.

"Now, before you say anything..."

"I don't want to move." We had discussed this in length. And I thought we had agreed to stay here for at least a while longer. Graduating, starting a new job, getting married, it was all too much at once. I didn't want to move on top of everything else.

"Baby," he said and grabbed my hand. "When we get married, we're going to need a bigger place."

"This place is big. It's way too big actually."

James laughed. "It's cozy. That's why we picked it."

"I think I remember telling you that it was too big to be cozy, but this was the place you wanted. So I said yes."

"And now you love it here."

"Exactly. So I don't want to move."

"But we're going to be a family."

I stared back at him. We rarely ever talked about having kids. Whenever I brought it up, he not so subtly diverted our conversation to a safer topic. Was he changing his mind? I squeezed his hand. "James, I thought you didn't..."

"You're going to be my wife." He cleared his throat. "We're going to be a family."

Oh. Me and him. Of course that's what he meant. And that's all I wanted. He was always all that I had ever wanted. "Since we're going to be married, you want more space to escape from me?" I smiled at him.

James laughed. "No, not exactly." He grabbed my waist and pulled me to the edge of the chair. "More rooms to have you in, maybe." His hand slid up my thigh.

I laughed. "Are you sure that you don't want to just run away from me because I have so many flaws?"

"Hmm." He leaned down and kissed the inside of my thigh.

God was he good at distracting me.

He slowly pushed up the bottom of my dress, following his fingertips with a trail of kisses. He hooked his thumbs in the sides of my thong. "Baby, you don't have any flaws."

And he knew exactly what to say to wear me down. I lifted my hips and let him remove my thong. "Okay, fine. We can make an appointment with your realtor and go look at it together. Happy?"

He smiled. "We don't need to make an appointment. I already bought it."

"James!" My exclamation quickly changed to a moan as he thrust his tongue deep inside of me. *Fuck*. "James, you can't...God!" I let my head drop back against the cushion as he spread my legs farther apart. I couldn't possibly think straight like this. *Damn it.*

He pushed the bottom of my dress up over my waist and I quickly pulled it over my head. My anger had been replaced by a more primal need, somehow making my want for him even stronger. I unhooked my bra as his mouth moved to my clit, sucking on it hard.

"Yes!"

His fingers replaced his tongue, plunging deep inside my aching pussy. His tongue on my clit matched the rhythm of his fingers, pushing me closer and closer to release. Why did I always give into him? Why did I always let him manipulate me with sex? He curved his fingers, hitting that spot that always made me lose control.

Oh God. My whole body felt warm from the combination of the alcohol coursing through me and the building desire in my stomach. I moaned again as his hand slid up, pinching one of my nipples. The sensation had a direct line to my groin.

I grabbed the back of his head as he sucked hard on my clit again. "James!" My orgasm crashed down on me. But the high didn't last long. The reality of what he had just done quickly returned. *Jesus.* I pushed on his shoulders.

After one last stroke against my wetness, he pulled back and stared at me.

I knew why I always let him have what he wanted. Because I could never resist him. Not when he looked at me like that. Who was I kidding? I could never resist him.

He started to unbutton his shirt.

My chest rose and fell as I tried to catch my breath. I stood up and pointed my finger at him. "You can't just buy a new apartment and not tell me about it. We're getting married. We need to make these kind of decisions together. And we had already discussed this. It's too much change, too fast."

He stood up too.

"I'm really mad at you," I added, when he didn't say anything.

Ignoring me, he slowly removed his belt and unzipped his pants, letting his erection spring free.

I quickly looked back up at his face. "What are you doing? James, we need to talk about this."

His eyes were ablaze. "I like when you're mad at me."

Fuck it. I grabbed the back of his head and pulled his mouth to mine. He was always right. When I was mad at him, it just made me want him even more.

***

James propped his head up on his hand and looked down at me. "I think I know what you like, Penny."

I tried to suppress my smile and shook my head. After everything he had just done to me, I didn't have any energy left to talk about this right now. I winced slightly as I turned to face him. The odds that I didn't have rug burn on my ass were slim to none. "It still would have been nice to be part of the decision."

"I'm sorry."

I smiled up at him.

"But it was a present and I..."

I put my finger against his lips. "Don't ruin your apology."

He grabbed my hand and kissed each of my knuckles. "You're going to love it. I promise."

"As long as you're in it, I will." I ran my fingers through the contours of his six pack. "So where is it?"

"Closer to where we'll both be working."

"You're impossible. You do realize that, right?"

He shrugged and smiled down at me. "We can walk to work together every day. And we can walk to our new home together every night. We can make detours through Central Park whenever you're missing the suburbs. It's going to be wonderful."

"Thank you, James."

He tucked a loose strand of hair behind my ear. "Why does it feel like you aren't thanking me for the new place?"

"I am. But it's not just that. Thank you for not getting annoyed when I stayed up late studying so many nights. And for waiting to get married until after I graduated. For putting your life on hold here while I finished school. And for not getting mad at me when I'm stubborn for no reason. And for just being you."

"You're awfully sentimental tonight." He pulled me into his chest.

I'd never get enough of the sweet scent of his skin. "You've given up so much to be with me."

He ran his fingers through my hair. "That's not the way I see it."

I knew it wasn't how he saw it, but that's how it was. The past few years I had been a burden. "There is no other way to see it, James. I just want you to know how much I appreciate everything you've done. Everything you've given me and everything you've given up."

"Penny, it goes both ways. What's mine is yours. And what's yours is mine."

"But I don't have anything."

He rolled over, pinning my back to the rug. "You're everything that I've ever wanted. These past two and a half years have been the happiest of my life. We're getting married in a few weeks. You're the one giving me everything."

"I'm worried that I'll always be a burden. I don't know what I want to do now that I've graduated. I don't know what I want to be."

He smiled down at me. "Well, you can start by working with me at Hunter Technologies. And by becoming my wife. Does that really sound so bad?"

I pursed my lips. Of course he was right. Even if I just worked there until I figured out what I really wanted to do. He knew me better than I knew myself. "It sounds perfect." I put my hand on the side of his face, running my palm along the scruff on his jaw line. "I can't wait to be Penny Hunter."

"God I love the sound of that."

CHAPTER 4
Sunday

My phone buzzed just as the car pulled up to the J.F.K. Airport. I quickly pulled my phone out of my purse, expecting to see James' sister, Jen, calling me. Instead, I saw Melissa's name. I swiped my finger across the screen. "Hey, Melissa. I just got to the airport to pick up Jen. It'll be at least forty minutes before we get to you."

"Actually, that's why I'm calling. I'm just going to meet you there if that's okay?"

"Yeah, of course."

"Great. I might be a little late. I just have a bunch of errands to run first. Trying to get everything settled." Tyler said something in the background, but I couldn't hear what it was.

"The appointment is in an hour," I said. "How late are you going to be?"

"Not very. I gotta go, I'll see you all there."

"Melissa?" I said, but she had already hung up the phone. It didn't sound like she wanted to come at all. I couldn't force her to tell me whether or not she was dating Tyler. But now it felt like she was trying to avoid spending time with me altogether. We'd have to have this conversation eventually. The longer we waited the more awkward it seemed.

My phone buzzed again and this time it was Jen. "Hey, Jen!"

"I'm coming out now. Are you already here? Never mind, I see Ian. See you in a sec." She hung up the phone.

I looked out the window. She was already running over to the car. She dropped her bags, threw her arms around Ian, and kissed his cheek as I stepped out of the car. Ian always looked happiest whenever Jen was in town. It was pretty clear to me that he had a crush on her. I just didn't know if it was apparent to Jen. I waited a second before getting out of the car, letting them enjoy their moment.

Jen squealed and threw her arms around me. "I can't believe you're marrying my brother in less than a month! We really should have looked for dresses sooner, you know. The consultants are going to have a fit."

Ian opened up the door to the car for us and we both climbed back in.

"I know," I said. "I was just hoping I'd get to meet your mother before I went dress shopping. I pictured her coming, you know?"

Jen waived her hand through the air. "She'll come around. Don't let her ruin this for you. This is going to be so much fun." She squeezed my hand.

"I know, I am excited. I just have absolutely no idea what kind of dress to get."

"And that's why I'm here."

We were heading to Kleinfeld's. Jen swore it was the place I had to get my dress from. Melissa usually gave me all my fashion advice, but Jen knew elegance better than anyone else. I needed her help making this decision, because I had no idea what James expected me to wear.

"How's the west coast been treating you?" I asked. She looked tan and much more content than the last time I had seen her a few months ago. She had just called it off with her boyfriend and was debating whether to buy a ticket to escape to the other side of the country. I had my doubts, but it looked like it was working for her.

"Amazing. I've been working on a new book, and there is literally nothing better than writing when you have a view of the ocean."

"That does sound amazing. I miss the beach. I used to go every summer with my family."

"Tell James to take you. God knows he needs a vacation." She shifted in her seat. "How is he by the way? Is he getting nervous?"

"For the wedding? I don't think so. We're both just really excited. Why? Did he say something to you?"

She laughed. "No, no, don't worry. I just know how much he worries about everything. This thing with my parents has been just as upsetting for him."

"I know. I think I'm finally at peace with it, though. I can't force them to meet me. So I'm just going to try and not think about it."

"They're being so ridiculous. I bet they're going to love you when they meet you too. Maybe I can do some nagging of my own while I'm in town."

"It's fine. Please don't on my account. I'm not sure James even wants them to come to our wedding at this point. So I'm done dwelling on it. Actually, Mr. and Mrs. Caldwell are going to throw us a late engagement party thing at their house on Friday." James and I had called them this morning to set up the date.

"Really?"

"Yeah. So I'm just focusing on being excited about that. I hope you'll stay for it."

"I wouldn't miss it."

***

I sat down on a velvety couch and looked up at the chandelier above my head. Everything about this place screamed elegance. It was going to be ridiculously expensive. I don't think I was ever going to get used to spending exorbitant amounts of money like James liked to do. Our wedding alone was going to cost more than my tuition at NYCU.

"When's the maid of honor getting here?" Bee asked with a smile as she sat down beside me.

I had picked up my mother and Bee after getting Jen. "She's running late, but I'm sure she'll be here soon." I hoped Melissa would be here any minute. I didn't want whatever weirdness was going on between us to continue. She knew how important it was that she helped me pick out a dress. I couldn't even think about doing this without her. She was my best friend.

A young woman in a black dress walked up to us. "Hi, I'm Anna, and I'll be your bridal consultant today. Which one of you is the bride?"

I raised my hand awkwardly. I was still used to being in a classroom. "That would be me," I said and immediately dropped my hand. "I'm Penny," I said as I stood up and shook her hand.

"And who is with you today?"

"This is my mom and my two bridesmaids, Bee and Jen."

"Nice to meet all of you," Anna said.

I looked over Anna's shoulder to the door. Where was Melissa?

"Are you ready to get started?" Anna asked.

I pressed my lips together.

"We were waiting for one more person," my mom said. "But I guess we might as well get started, right Penny? We don't know when Melissa will get here."

"Yeah." I sat back down on the couch. "Let's do this."

Anna laughed. "Okay, well, what silhouette were you going for?"

"I don't really know. What are the different options?"

"How about we try one of each kind to give you a feel for what you like?" Anna said and gave me a sympathetic smile.

"That sounds great."

"When is your wedding?"

"June 30th."

Anna stared at me for a second. "Wait, you mean *this* June 30th?"

"Yes?" I wasn't sure why I said it as a question.

"That's less than three weeks away!"

"I mean, just one day less than three weeks. So pretty much three weeks."

She just stared at me, not at all affected by the particulars. "I'm so sorry, but I don't know if we're going to be able to help you."

"What? Don't you have anything? Couldn't I buy a sample dress or something?" *Shit.* I had waited too long to look.

Jen laughed. "You're not buying a sample dress, Penny. That's ridiculous. Anna, your designers always make exceptions under certain circumstances, right?"

Anna looked at Jen and then back at me. "Yes, under very limited circumstances. But what is your budget? Rush orders start at..."

"She doesn't have one," Jen said.

I could feel Anna's eyes on me. I was wearing a simple blue sundress and sandals. She was probably thinking there was no way I could afford a rush delivery. She probably didn't even think I could afford to be here to begin with.

"It's not an issue," Jen said.

Anna turned back to her. "Okay, well there will only be a few designers that will be willing to work with us. Let me talk to my manager real quick." She looked slightly embarrassed as she rushed away from us.

"I don't know," I said, turning toward Jen. "Maybe we should go look somewhere else? I don't want to spend a fortune on a dress I'm only going to wear once."

"No way, Penny. I'm under strict instructions to make sure you get whatever dress you like the best here, regardless of the price. He said to just put it on the credit card he gave you. It's fine." Jen waived her hand through the air like it wasn't an issue at all.

I bit my lip. James had given me a credit card when I moved to New York with him. I had only ever used it a few times to buy fancy dresses for functions that I attended with him. I didn't even know what the credit limit on it was. And I certainly didn't want to reach it. "You talked to James?"

"Yes, I talked to James."

Bee laughed. "I feel for you, Penny, but I'm pretty sure there's no way James is going to budge on this. Geez, I can just picture this happening to me too."

"Wait, Bee," I said. "Did Mason propose?" I could feel the huge smile spread across my face and I hoped I didn't look like a lunatic.

She immediately blushed. "No. I mean, we've talked about the future. I think he will at some point, but not yet."

I loved Mason and Bee. They were perfect together. When I had first met Mason, I wasn't really sure what to think of him. He had this edge that I couldn't quite explain. Since he was James' friend, I had pushed that thought aside and become good friends with him too. But when he had started dating Bee, he seemed different. She balanced him out somehow. It reminded me that I really needed to talk to her about what she meant about Mason planning James' bachelor party. Because I was almost positive that he had taken the wheel for the plans. It would be better if I talked to her about it in private though. "I know he will, Bee. And when he does, you think he'll make you buy a dress that is as expensive as a new car?"

Bee laughed. "I wouldn't put it past him."

"Well, maybe there aren't any other options," I said. "I waited too long."

My mom ran her hand up and down my arm.

"I heard about the party that Mason's parents are throwing you next weekend," Bee said, trying to lighten the mood. "That's going to be so much fun."

"It's going to be a blast. They're both so sweet. I really wish you could come though, Mom."

"Your father and I already took off time this week to come up. And time off for the wedding at the end of month. I'm so sorry that we have to miss it."

"It's okay, you'll meet them at the wedding."

Anna walked back over with a smile on her face. "Okay, I'm sorry about that. How about you come back with me and we can get started?"

I looked over her shoulder once more but Melissa was still nowhere in sight. "Sounds good." I stood up.

"And if you ladies would like to look around for dresses you think Penny will like, please feel free."

Jen was up, searching through the racks before I even took a few steps to follow Anna. I wound my way past some of the dresses and followed her into a fitting room.

Anna closed the door and gestured for me to sit down. She jotted something down on the clipboard she was holding. "Do you know what size you are, Penny?"

I tried to think of the most recent event I went to. "A two I believe?"

"Okay, you'll probably be a four in wedding dresses then. Don't ask me why they make the sizes smaller. It seems like the absolute worst time to do that to someone."

I laughed. "Designers don't want you to feel good on your wedding day?"

"Apparently not." She smiled at me. "So, I know you don't know exactly what style you want, but are you opposed to anything in particular?"

"I really have no idea."

"Like poofy, shiny, lacy..." her voice trailed off when I didn't have any reaction.

"I'm sorry, we're probably going to be here forever. I'm just so indecisive."

"It's okay, dear. Let me go grab a few dresses to get us started. And what is your bra size?"

"32 B."

"Great, I'll be right back."

As soon as she left, I pulled my phone out of my purse and clicked on Melissa's name. The phone rang a few times and then went to voicemail. "Hey, Melissa, it's me. I know you said you'd be a little late, but I'm about to start trying on dresses." I paused.

Maybe I should just confront the issue. "I feel like you're upset with me, and I don't really know what I did," I said, chickening out. "I want to fix whatever it is. But right now I need you. Please don't make me do this without you." I paused again. "Hopefully I'll see you soon." I hung up before I could say anything stupid. I had this urge to go all bridezilla on her and demand she come because she was my maid of honor. That was probably not the right way to go. If it really was that she felt uncomfortable telling me about her and Tyler, that was ridiculous. Tyler and I had been together one night two and a half years ago. We were over before we even really had a chance to begin. I didn't see how that could be the issue.

Anna came back in with a few dresses in her arms and hung them up. "Are you ready to get started?" she said with a huge smile.

"I guess so."

She laughed. "There's nothing to be nervous about. We're going to find the perfect dress, I promise. Is there one in particular that you wanted to try first?"

"Let's start with this one," I said and pointed to the one that was the most simple.

"Good place to start. I'll help you get into it. Do you want me to step outside while you undress?"

"Oh, no, it's fine." I turned away from her and pulled off my sundress. She handed me something that almost looked like a corset.

"Trust me, it does wonders," she said as she got all the small hooks together on the back.

I looked down at my breasts. She was right. They looked amazing. I wanted to wear one of these all the time. Minus the fact that it was super uncomfortable.

"Now, how did you meet your fiancé?" she asked as she helped me step into the first dress.

I hadn't really been expecting the question. And I never really knew how to answer it. "Um, in school. We ran into each other in a coffee shop right before classes started." I smiled, remembering the first time I had ever seen him. "He bumped into me and spilled coffee down the front of my shirt."

Anna laughed. "That's quite the meet cute."

"It was." I stared at my reflection in the mirror as she zipped up the back. She added a few clips to the back, drawing the fabric against my skin. It was tight down to my hips, and then the fabric was a little looser against my legs. I thought I'd be used to the idea of getting married after being engaged for so long. But for some reason it hit me the most right now as I stared at my reflection. It made my pulse quicken. I didn't want a simple dress like this. I wanted something that would make James' jaw drop when he saw me.

"What do you think?" Anna asked.

"I want something a little...more."

Anna smiled. "There are barely any embellishments on this one. Would you still like to show everyone?"

"Yeah. It's a good starting point."

Anna opened the door and I followed her back to my mom and friends. She said something about the designer as I stepped up onto the elevated platform.

"Penny, you look amazing," my mom said.

"Gorgeous," Bee said.

"It's a little simple, don't you think?" Jen cut in. Jen was always honest. I was so glad she was here. Especially since Melissa wasn't.

"Penny was thinking the same thing," Anna said. "A jeweled belt would add some character though." She grabbed one off a display nearby and wrapped it around my waist. "What do you think?"

I turned to the mirror that was behind me. It did help, but it still wasn't perfect.

"I think maybe you should try the next one," Jen said.

"What do you think, Penny?" my mom asked.

"I think it's missing a wow factor."

Bee laughed. "Just wait until you see the one that Jen picked out."

"Okay, let's go try on the next one," Anna said.

I followed her back toward the dressing rooms.

"Would you like to finish the dresses I picked out so that you can get a feel for the different styles? Or would you like to jump into the ones your friends picked out?"

"Let's finish the ones you brought first," I said and entered the dressing room.

Anna unzipped my dress and helped me step out of it. "So was your fiancé the same year as you in school?" She grabbed the next dress off the hook.

I ran my thumb along the band of my engagement ring. I wasn't ashamed of how I had met James. Why did I always skirt around the truth when people asked? "No, not exactly."

Anna whistled as she pulled the next dress up my waist. "Older or younger?"

"Older." I shouldn't have to beat around the bush anymore. I wasn't embarrassed of how we met. *Screw it.* "Actually, he was my professor."

Anna met my eyes in the reflection in the mirror as her fingers stopped mid-zip of the dress. "You're not talking about James Hunter?"

The scandal had followed us to New York. I just thought that it had been so long ago that no one really remembered anymore. "Yeah, that's him."

"Oh my God, you're engaged to James Hunter?"

"Yes."

She finished zipping up the dress. "He is quite the catch. I remember hearing about you two. I thought your story was so sweet."

For some reason, that hadn't been what I thought she was going to say. I turned toward her. "Thank you for saying that."

She smiled back at me. "Love has no age limit. Now, what do you think about this one?"

The dress was beautiful. It was strapless and the bottom of the dress was huge and poofy. I felt like a princess. "It's gorgeous." I stared at my reflection for another second. "I think I want something a little more sophisticated though."

She nodded. "Should we show them?"

"Yeah, let's see what they have to say about this one." I lifted up the huge skirt and walked back toward the group.

"Oh, God no," Melissa said as I stepped up onto the platform.

I laughed and turned around.

"Sorry I'm late," she said and sat down next to my mom on the couch.

"What, is this one that bad?"

"It makes you look so young," she said. "Which you've been trying to not be ever since you met James."

I pressed my lips together and looked back at the mirror. I didn't want simple and I didn't want poofy.

"What you need is an elegant dress that is classy and sexy at the same time," Jen said.

"I think you look absolutely beautiful," my mom said. She looked a little teary eyed.

I smiled. When I was little I had pictured a big poofy dress. But Melissa and Jen were right. I had tried so hard to seem older and more mature the past few years. I wanted to look like a bride worthy of James. I wasn't a student anymore and he wasn't my professor.

"What do you think, Bee?" I asked.

"Sexy and classy seem to go against each other. You look beautiful in that one, though, not cute."

I smiled.

"Oh, please just try on the dress I picked out already," Jen said. "It's perfect."

I shrugged. "Okay, I'll try yours next." I followed Anna back to the dressing room. She grabbed a lace dress with some diamonds embroidered into the design. It had elegant thin straps that were just wide enough to accommodate the diamonds embellished on them. And the front looked like it plunged way past where my breasts would be. There was a tan material behind the lace at the top, which gave it an even sexier look.

"I'm not sure I'm going to be able to pull this one off," I said as Anna unzipped the poofy dress.

"I think this really might be exactly what you're looking for. The lace is so delicate and it has just the right amount of sparkle. And the top is indeed sexy. Plus this one is actually in your size, so you get to see how it would really fit."

I stepped out of the poofy dress and into the other one. "I guess we'll see."

"The top goes down too much in the middle for you to wear this, though," she said as she unhooked the corset.

I instantly felt more relaxed as she began to pull the dress up. I wanted to be comfortable on my wedding day. There was going to be enough stress without the added element of not being able to breathe. There was a layer of silk underneath the dress that felt soft against my skin. I closed my eyes as Anna zipped up the back.

"You look beautiful, Penny," she said as soon as she let go of the zipper.

I opened my eyes and swallowed hard. I don't think I had ever looked this good. The dress hugged my waist and thighs and was a little looser past my knees. Even though it was tight, it didn't look raunchy. It looked elegant yet casual. And the top made it sexy. There must have been some kind of built in bra, because it had pushed up my breasts despite the fact that I had ditched the corset. The V down the front stopped a few inches above my belly button, but it didn't look over the top. It was very narrow and the lace made it look fancy.

"What do you think?" Anna asked.

"He'd love this." My voice came out as a whisper. There was a lump in my throat, and I wasn't sure why. I felt like I wanted to cry. I was always so worried about disappointing him. There wasn't a chance I could do that in this dress. I'd look like I actually belonged beside him.

"Let's go show everyone." Anna opened the door and I slowly followed her out, holding up the delicate lace so I wouldn't step on it.

Everyone stopped talking when I stepped up on the platform. I dropped the fabric so it pooled perfectly around my legs.

"Penny," Melissa said. "You look like a movie star."

I laughed.

"Seriously," Bee said. "You look like a million bucks."

I turned and looked in the mirror. I felt like a million bucks. It was hard to believe it was me in the mirror.

"That's the one," Jen said. "It was made for your body."

"Do you think James will like it?" I asked.

"James won't be able to keep it in his pants," Melissa said.

I laughed and turned back around to face them.

"Ew." Jen smacked her arm. "Don't be gross. That's my brother. But yes, he'll love it."

Melissa laughed and stood up. She grabbed my hand and squeezed it. "Penny, this is definitely your dress. Look at yourself." She spun me back around to look in the mirror.

I felt like I wanted to cry again.

"Here," Anna said and clipped a veil into my hair. She spread it across my shoulders. The diamonds in the clip matched the ones on the straps of the dress. I could picture it all. Walking down the aisle. James' smile.

"Mom?" I turned around to look at her. She was the only one that hadn't said anything.

She had grabbed a tissue out of her purse and was blotting her eyes. "You look so grown up, sweetie. You're absolutely stunning."

I could feel my own tears welling in my eyes. "Do you think it's the one?"

They all said yes at the same time.

I ran my fingers under my eye where a tear had rolled down. "You don't think it's too sexy?" I looked down at the rather revealing front.

"It's sexy, but it seems more elegant than anything else," Melissa said.

"And it's so fancy, but you look so much more comfortable in this one," Bee said.

"And happier," Jen added.

"That's because I'm not wearing that corset thing anymore." I laughed and turned back to the mirror. I thought I'd be here all afternoon. But they were right. And I knew it before they had said anything. This was the dress that I wanted James to see me in when I said I do. There wasn't a doubt in my mind.

CHAPTER 5
Sunday

"So, what do you think?" James asked. He was staring at me intently.

"It seems so...cold." It didn't feel like a home. And I didn't mean that the air conditioner seemed to be at full force.

He laughed. "That's because none of our stuff is here yet. Use your imagination." He stepped past the foyer into the main room. "Our couch can go here. And the picture of the beach we have can go on the wall there." He pointed to the one spot of wall along the far side that wasn't a window. He looked so excited. As if he could picture our life here together. "And you have to come see the view. It looks right out onto Central Park. It won't even feel like we're in the city."

I walked over to him and kissed his cheek. "I love it."

"You didn't even see the view, though."

"I like my view right now."

He laughed and pulled me into his arms. "You really like it?"

"I'm happy wherever we are, as long as we're together. Aren't you?"

He raised his eyebrow as he looked down at me. "Is that why you're upset? Baby, I didn't buy this place because I wasn't happy in our old apartment. You know that. I just want a fresh start."

"From what exactly?"

"We moved to New York to get away from all the rumors. But it was hard to put it all to rest while you were still in school."

My stomach churned. I was a burden.

"Now you're not. Your graduating puts it all in the past. I want to start our life together."

"James, we already have."

"You know what I mean. As husband and wife."

"We could have just rearranged the furniture or something."

He laughed and pulled me toward the wall of windows. "But then we wouldn't have this view."

I could feel my jaw drop. Dusk was just settling over the city. A few lights had already turned on in Central Park. We were so close that it almost seemed like the building was in the middle of the park. I could see the Tavern on the Green in the distance. That was where we were getting married. Every day, I was going to be able to look outside and remember our wedding.

I knew that James didn't care about having this view. He had picked out this apartment because he knew it would make me happy. I felt him wrap his arms around me and kiss the side of my neck. I leaned my head back against his chest. Maybe we did need a fresh start. It was time to brush off the chip on my shoulder whenever people snickered about how we met. I was ready to let it all go. "When did you want to move our stuff in?"

He rested his chin on top of my head. "I took the whole week off."

"What are your employees going to think? A whole week off now and then time off for our wedding and honeymoon at the end of the month?"

"They're going to think that my fiancée isn't starting her internship until next Monday and I wanted time off to spend with her."

"If I don't get a different position."

"Of course. Although, I really only want you in one position right now."

I laughed and turned around, clasping my hands behind his neck. "Aren't you going to give me a tour of the rest of the house?"

His hands slid to my ass. "Is that really what you want to do right now?"

I bit my lip and shook my head.

Before his lips met mine, his phone started vibrating.

"Don't answer it," I said.

"It's probably work."

"I thought you had off this week?"

He squeezed my ass before putting his hand in his pocket and pulling out his phone. He turned around without even looking at the caller I.D. "Hunter."

His body seemed to stiffen. He cleared his throat. "Hi, Mom." He turned to me, put his finger in the air to signal he'd just be a minute, and then quickly walked back toward the foyer.

I folded my arms across my chest and turned back to look down at Central Park. The apartment suddenly seemed even colder. I closed my eyes, picturing myself in my wedding dress. All that mattered was that he wanted to marry me. His parents didn't have to be there. They didn't have to ever even meet me. James' love was enough.

I opened my eyes and stared down at the Tavern on the Green. The lights hanging in the trees outside the restaurant were shimmering, dancing in the summer breeze. James' love was all that I needed. But Jen said that their parents not wanting to meet me was weighing on James too. It was hurting him. Which meant

I was hurting him. And it killed me. I ran my hands up and down my arms. It was freezing.

A few months ago, I had found their address and gotten a taxi to their house. I had stood outside the gate for several minutes before retreating. I had wanted to barge in on them and tell them they were being ridiculous. That they were horrible for treating their own son like this. I hated them for making him feel like he was unlovable. They had hurt him, in more ways than James would ever admit. But my telling them that wasn't going to help. They didn't respect me, so they wouldn't care about my opinions. I couldn't force it.

What it came down to was that they didn't want him to be happy. They put their own wants in front of his. And that wasn't what parents were supposed to do. It certainly wasn't what I was going to do with my own kids. I shook the thought away. That was just another reason to despise them. James said he was scared to have kids because of his problems. But really, it was their fault. He was worried he'd be a horrible parent because they were so awful.

"So, that was my mother."

I jumped. I hadn't heard him come back over to me. "Oh?" I used to get so excited whenever she would call, hoping that it meant she had changed her mind. Now I knew better.

He smiled. "They want to meet you."

"Sure." I laughed. "Let's set a date so they can cancel at the last minute. Can we not talk about this right now?"

"Apparently they found out the Caldwells were throwing us an engagement party. They've decided to commandeer it."

"What?"

"Jen told them about it or something. The party is being thrown at their house now. Apparently they just needed to feel like they were being cast aside." He shrugged.

"I think that's awfully rude to the Caldwells when they've been so nice."

"Yeah." He ran his hand through his hair. "That's what I said. She assured me the Caldwells were fine with it."

Now that it finally seemed like it was happening, I wasn't sure why I felt so hesitant. "What are the odds that they'll cancel a whole party?"

"It wouldn't look good. So, not very high."

"Does that mean they're coming to the wedding?"

"She didn't say. She just said we have a lot to talk about."

"You don't look very excited."

"Because you don't look very happy."

"I'm sorry." I took a deep breath. "They've just canceled plans with us so many times that..."

"She sounded serious this time. I think they're finally coming around. She said she was excited to meet you. She's never said that before."

I bit my lip.

"And she said to tell you congratulations on graduating."

"That was nice of her." I tried to dismiss all my negative thoughts from earlier. "I'm so disappointed that my parents won't be there. They were really looking forward to meeting your parents."

"They can't change their plans?"

"My parents aren't their own bosses like you." I smiled at him. "I guess they'll just have to meet your parents at the rehearsal dinner."

"It's probably best if you meet my parents by yourself first anyway. They can be rather intimidating."

"Do you think they're going to try to scare me away?" I laughed.

He lowered his eyebrows for a second. But the worried look was fleeting. "No, they wouldn't do that. We should have set Jen on them awhile ago. They rarely ever say no to her."

"I should have known she'd interfere when she told me she wouldn't."

He laughed.

"Does this mean I get to see where you grew up?"

"You can make fun of my old bedroom." He smiled and pulled me back into his arms. "But like I told you before, there really aren't tons of embarrassing photos of me or anything. My parents aren't like your parents."

I closed my eyes as I pressed my face against his chest. I knew he didn't mean that as an insult. He meant that his parents didn't care for him like my parents cared about me. I didn't want to go into meeting them feeling like this. But I wasn't sure if I could ever like them. Not after everything they had put James through.

CHAPTER 6
Thursday

We had almost moved everything in and I was completely exhausted. I pulled my hair up into a ponytail as I looked around at all the boxes. The living room and kitchen were a complete disaster. Luckily Ellen was going to help me organize everything in the morning.

"Your ass looks amazing when you do that," James said.

I laughed and turned around as I finished putting the elastic in my hair. "You think?" I arched my back slightly before letting go of my hair.

He smiled at me as he dropped a box down next to my feet. "Why was it again that you wouldn't let me hire movers?" He was wearing athletic shorts and a fitted t-shirt. There was a v-shaped sweat stain down the front of his shirt, and I found it unbelievably sexy.

"Because I love how you look when you're all sweaty."

"Is that so?"

"Mhm." I traced my finger down his chest. "So hot."

He gave me that smile that always made me feel overheated. It was playful and sexy and I knew exactly what was on his mind. "It actually is a little hot in here, don't you think?" He grabbed his shirt by the collar and pulled it off over his head. His abs glistened from sweat.

"Scorching."

He smiled. "That's better. Are you ready for a break?"

I had gotten the perfect idea. "I'm going to give you to the count of ten, James."

"To get you into bed with me? Done." He leaned forward to kiss me, but I put my hand on his chest.

God. Seeing him like this always turned me on. "To hide." I ran my fingers down his muscular stomach.

"What?"

"Let's play hide and go seek."

"I'd rather christen the new..."

"Ten. Nine."

"Shit."

I put my hand over my eyes as James jumped over a box and sprinted out of the living room. When I finished counting down from ten I opened my eyes. I had only walked around the apartment a few times. But there was barely any furniture in any of the rooms. He'd only be able to hide behind doors and other fixtures.

I wove my way through the boxes on the floor in the living room and through the kitchen. I hadn't heard him run upstairs, so I assumed he wasn't in any of the bedrooms. My eyes gravitated toward the balcony above me, just to check. This place really was amazing. It was an apartment that was probably designed for a big family, not just two people. It must have cost him a fortune. I didn't even know apartments in New York could have an upstairs.

A creaking noise made me turn my head. I peered around the column into the dining room. Nothing. The downstairs was mostly an open floor plan. There weren't that many places he could hide. I walked toward the bathroom. The reflection in the mirror made it easy to tell that he wasn't hiding behind the door.

Another creaking noise made me jump.

"James?" I whispered. The sun was beginning to set, casting eerie shadows in the room. I tried not to think about it as I made my way through the archway toward a few of the closed off rooms. There was an office and a small library back here. I turned into the library. The blinds were all drawn, and it was almost pitch black. I switched on the light and looked around. The built-in shelves were all empty. Soon they'd be filled with all of James' books. I thought about my bookshelf back at home, filled with Harry Potter novels. They didn't seem sophisticated enough to be in here. But there was something charming about the idea.

There was a grand stone fireplace in the center of the wall. I could just imagine curling up in front of it with a good book. This apartment was amazing. I'd have to tell James whenever I found him. It could be awhile. I still had a lot of rooms to check. I turned around just as the lights cut out.

I made a small squealing noise as the door slammed shut. "James?" I couldn't see anything. "James?" I said a little louder.

A clicking noise made me turn around again. A small blue flame had spread across the fireplace.

"James?" My eyes were still adjusting to the lack of light.

His arms wrapped around me before he said anything and I screamed again. His laugh in my ear calmed me right down, though. "I found you," he whispered in my ear, as he wrapped his arms even tighter around me, pressing his chest against my back.

"I was the one that was supposed to be finding you."

He kissed the side of my neck and trailed his fingers down the sides of my torso. "You were taking too long." His fingers skimmed the bottom of my tank top as he lightly pushed it up. His palms were hot against my stomach. He smelled like sweat and that wonderful scent that was all his own.

I could feel his erection through his athletic shorts. I arched my back slightly, pressing my ass more firmly against him.

The low groan in his throat was my favorite sound in the world. I lifted my arms up in the air. He immediately pulled off my shirt and sports bra and threw them onto the ground. His hands slowly trailed back down my arms and shoulders, stopping on my breasts. He massaged them gently and soon I was the one moaning.

His torso was sticky against my back and I loved the sensation. I reached up behind me and ran my hand down his neck. I wanted to be as close to him as possible.

"I want to savor this moment," he whispered. He pulled my hair tie out. My hair falling against the back of my neck made me shiver. Everything he did in moments like this somehow seemed sexy.

"I need you."

He pushed my spandex shorts and thong over my hips and down my thighs as he ran his fingers gently across my wetness. "I know you do."

I moaned and pressed my ass against him again.

"I need you too, baby." He gently massaged my clit before thrusting a finger inside of me. "I always need you."

"James," I moaned as he slipped another finger inside of me. I rested my head against his shoulder as he slowly moved his fingers in and out of me. He began to tease my nipple with his free hand, matching the steady pace of his other fingers.

"You're always so wet for me, baby."

Oh God.

His fingers moved even faster.

"Please fuck me."

He lightly bit my earlobe. "Not tonight."

"Please." My voice sounded desperate.

"I want to make love to you, Penny." His fingers thrust farther inside of me. "I want to make sure we always remember our first night here."

His words sent chills down my spine, despite how hot the fire was in the room. I began to feel like I was melting into him. "Please make love to me."

I laughed as he quickly lifted me up in both his arms. He laid me down in front of the fire and my laughter disappeared as soon as he kissed me. My whole body felt hot and I wasn't sure if it was from the fire or him. He leaned back to remove his shorts. But my eyes were captivated by his face. James was the most handsome man I had ever met. And the firelight just made him look even sexier.

"It's so hot in here," I said breathlessly.

He grabbed both my hands and placed them on the back of his neck. The fire in his eyes seemed even hotter than the flames in the fireplace. "You said you liked when I was sweaty," James said as he pressed the tip of his rock hard cock against my wetness.

I spread my legs even farther apart, but James didn't move an inch.

"I love you."

I wasn't sure why, but the sincerity in his voice made me want to cry. Like it was the only fact in the world that he was certain of. "James, I love you too. I'll always love you."

He immediately thrust inside of me.

Yes! I pressed my fingers down on his shoulders. All I could do was revel in how complete I felt with his cock inside of me.

His strokes were slow and full, driving me crazy. He gently kissed the side of my neck and left a trail of kisses across my collarbone. "You're all I need, Penny."

He was all I needed too. I ran my fingers down his shoulders and strong biceps. Every time he thrust inside of me, I felt this fire inside of me intensify. But he continued to slowly make love to me. The torturous rhythm just made me want more. What was he waiting for? I tilted my hips up, inviting him to go even deeper.

"Always so eager." His breath was hot against my neck.

"Please, James."

He grabbed my hips with one hand and rolled over, pulling me on top of him. "Show me exactly what you want." He had a challenging look in his eyes.

James rarely ever let me take control. He knew I got distracted when I was setting the pace. Staring down at his chiseled abs always made me forget what I was doing. He knew what I needed better than I did. And we were both aware of that.

He smiled up at me and put his hands behind his head, ready for me to admit defeat already.

I leaned forward, moving my hips slowly up and down, matching the rhythm he had set before. He groaned as I lightly kissed his chest. His skin was salty from sweat. He was my favorite taste, sight, sound, touch, and scent. I wanted to savor him too. I moved my hips even faster as I left a trail of feathery kisses everywhere I could reach. Tonight I wanted to be the one that made him lose control.

"Don't stop," he said as I pulled away from him.

Instead of listening, I stood up. He said he liked my ass in my spandex shorts. He'd like this view even more. I turned around, straddling him in the opposite direction and slid back onto his length.

"Fuck," he groaned as I slid his length back inside of me. His hands were immediately on my back, trailing down to my hips and ass.

I moved my hips faster and faster as his fingertips dug into my skin.

"You're so sexy, baby." His voice sounded husky. Even though I could only see his legs, it was still getting harder and harder to focus. His hands on me were suddenly all I could think about. I loved the way he loved me. I couldn't set the pace anymore. I couldn't even think straight. As if he knew, his hands on my hips slowly started guiding me more than I was guiding myself.

"James," I moaned.

He moved my hips faster and faster, slamming me down on top of him. It seemed like he was moving me way faster than I could myself. He put his arms around my waist as he sat up and pushed me forward so that I was suddenly on all fours.

"I'll always give you what you want." He grabbed my hips hard and thrust himself deep inside of me.

"Yes!" My palms were a little sweaty and they slid slightly on the wood floor.

He kept one hand on my hip and his other found my clit. He slid his length in and out of me faster and faster.

"Say my name when you come, Penny." He slammed into me and pressed down hard on my clit.

"James!" The fire in my stomach seemed to spread out in a million different directions. I would have melted into the ground if he wasn't holding me up. "James!" I moaned again as I felt his cum shoot up inside of me.

The rest of his strokes were slow but rough, his hips slamming hard against my ass. He sighed behind me as he finished. I couldn't remember the last time I felt this exhausted. James leaned forward and lightly kissed my shoulder blade. He pushed my hair to the side and kissed the back of my neck. Even though I had ended up asking him to be rough with me, I still felt cherished. He had still made love to me. James always made me know how much he loved me.

"Was that memorable enough for you?" I panted. I was completely out of breath.

He ran his hands down my back and over my ass. "Every moment is memorable with you." He slowly pulled out of me. I was about to turn around, but felt his lips against the small of my back. He left a trail of soft kisses down my right ass cheek and thigh. "How about we continue making memories in the shower?"

A ringing noise sounded through the apartment, making me jump.

"It's just the doorbell, baby," James said and kissed my thigh once more before standing up. "I'll get rid of whoever it is." He turned off the fireplace and pulled on his shorts before disappearing out the door.

"I was going to say congrats on the new place, but instead I'm going with why are you so sweaty?" Mason's voice could be heard clearly through the open floor plan.

"Crap," I mumbled and tried to find my clothes in the dark.

"Hey, Mason and Bee!" James said way too loudly, probably hoping for me to hear.

I quickly got dressed and walked out the door to greet our first house guests.

"Why are you yelling at us?" Mason asked.

"I'm not yelling," James said a little quieter. "And I'm super sweaty because Penny wouldn't let us hire movers."

Bee laughed.

I was pulling my hair back in a ponytail when I came into the living room. "Hey guys. And we did hire movers for all the super heavy things. Like the couch, the bed, the..."

"Are you insinuating that I can't lift heavy things?" James asked with a smile.

I laughed and opened up the last box that he had carried up. It was filled with sheets.

"Well, that one wasn't heavy." He put his arm around me as I joined him in the foyer next to Bee and Mason.

"And it's really hot in here, don't you think?" Mason asked. "Do you even have the air conditioning on?" He was staring directly at me. It was pretty clear he knew what we had just been doing. Especially since James hadn't even bothered to put his shirt back on. I couldn't exactly say we had started a fire in the library, in more ways than one.

"I can turn it up if you want," I said instead. "I'm a little overheated too. We were doing hot yoga." *Why the hell did I just say that?* "Oh you brought pizza and champagne? I'm starving." I had never been very good at segues.

James laughed.

"Hot yoga?" Mason winked and slapped James on the back as he walked past us into the living room. "Gross, you're so fucking sweaty." I looked over my shoulder to see him wiping his hand off on his jeans.

"I'm just going to pretend you two were actually doing hot yoga," Bee said and smiled at me. "Your new place looks amazing. Should we eat while the pizza's still hot and then go on the tour? Mason, don't go through their stuff!"

"What? I'm just trying to find the champagne flutes." He was holding an attachment to a vacuum cleaner. "Is this some weird sex thing that I don't know about?" He held it farther away from himself as he inspected it.

Bee laughed. "Of course you wouldn't have any idea what that is."

"I honestly have no idea what that thing is either," James said.

"You two are hopeless, you know," I said to James and Mason. "What on earth would you do without me and Bee?"

"Do hot yoga alone and cry ourselves to sleep," Mason said and tossed the vacuum cleaner attachment back in its box.

Bee and I both laughed.

James kissed my temple and whispered, "I couldn't live without you."

I smiled up at him. I didn't have to say it back. He knew. Just like I knew how he was feeling by looking into his intoxicating brown eyes.

He kissed my temple again. "I think I know where the glasses are," he said and walked over toward Mason.

"And seriously, turn up the AC, or I'm going to take my shirt off next," Mason said.

Bee laughed. "I'm not going to complain about that."

A few minutes later we were sitting at the dining room table drinking champagne out of coffee mugs and eating pizza off of napkins.

"Are you two getting nervous?" Mason asked and grabbed another slice of pizza.

"About what?" I said.

"What do you mean about what? About marrying him." He pointed his pizza at James.

I put my chin in my hand and looked over at James, pretending to scrutinize him.

He raised his left eyebrow at me. He actually looked curious about my answer.

"I'm terrified."

James immediately frowned and Mason laughed.

"I'm just kidding." I put my hand on James' thigh and squeezed it. "I'm not nervous about our wedding at all. The only thing I'm nervous about is meeting his parents tomorrow. After that, I'm just going to be excited."

"You should be nervous about that," Mason said.

I reluctantly tore my eyes away from James to look at Mason. "Why do you say that?" Maybe it would be better if I knew exactly what to expect.

Mason shrugged. "They've avoided you like the plague ever since you moved to New York. Clearly they don't want to meet you."

James put his hand on top my mine. Mason was just saying what I already knew, but it was still hard to hear.

"It's like they're in denial," Mason continued when no one said anything. "They still want Isabella to be their daughter in law. I don't even know why you want to meet them. Besides, James basically grew up at my house. His parents are horrible. I'm sure you already know you're going to hate them. What's the point? There are so many better things that we could do tomorrow night."

"They're perfectly nice," Bee said. "You have nothing to worry about."

"Wait, you've met them?" I couldn't believe it. Bee had never mentioned meeting James' parents before.

Bee took a sip of champagne from her mug and then cleared her throat. "I mean, yeah. At their annual New Year's Eve party."

"You never told me that you had met them."

She took another sip of champagne to avoid answering me.

I looked over at James. "Annual New Year's Eve party?" James had never mentioned that party to me. We always went out to dinner on New Year's Eve and walked around Central Park before the clock struck twelve. Last year it had started to snow right before midnight and I could still picture the snow falling around us as we shared our first kiss of the new year. It was romantic and perfect. But had we only done it because his parents had told him I couldn't come to their exclusive party?

"It's not that big of a thing," James said.

I looked over at Mason and Bee. "How many people were there last year?"

Mason shrugged. "Not that many. And it's not even fun. I doubt Bee and I will even go next year. We only go because my parents go." Bee was busy pouring herself more champagne, still avoiding eye contact with me.

"Did they invite you?" I asked James.

"I haven't gone since I broke it off with Isabella."

I just stared at him. That didn't answer my question.

He sighed and ran his hand through his hair. "Yes, they invite me every year. But they never extended the invitation to you."

"See, they're the worst," Mason said. "They try to control everything James does. They're just pissed that he chose you without their approval first. If I was you, I'd skip the party tomorrow night just to spite them. Throw the whole thing in their faces."

"Mason, you're not really helping," Bee said. "And I'm sorry I didn't tell you, Penny. I just didn't know what to say. The whole situation sucks. I didn't think telling you I had met them would help anything."

"It's okay, I get it." I hated the way I was feeling right now. "So, they're perfectly nice?"

"I don't know," Bee said. "They were polite to me. I don't really know them, though. Well, besides for the fact that Mason doesn't like them and they refuse to meet one of my best friends. I was just trying to make you feel more optimistic. But clearly they're the worst. Sorry, James," she quickly added.

James laughed. "You all already know how I feel about this. As far as I'm concerned, you guys are my real family."

I smiled. That's what Mason's parents had said in their letter to me. Our friends in New York had become part of our family. I loved that James had taken that to heart. He wasn't good at letting people in. But he was opening his heart so much easier recently. When we had first met he seemed so cold. I liked this new warmer side of him.

Mason lifted up his mug. "Here's to the start of a new chapter in our lives."

"Didn't you already start that chapter when you turned 30?" James said and clinked his glass against Mason's.

"I'm only a few months older than you, asshole. Next month you'll know how it feels."

James laughed and took a sip of champagne. "Well, right now, I'm still in my 20s, so I get to tease you for another month, old man."

Mason sighed.

"Speaking of new chapters in our lives, does that mean the two of you have news?" James and I always joked around with Bee and Mason about getting engaged. They had been dating for almost as long as James and I were engaged.

"Unfortunately, Bee has major commitment issues," Mason said.

Bee lightly nudged his shoulder. "Yeah right."

Mason smiled at her. "I'm sure we'll make it official soon."

Bee's cheeks turned even rosier.

"Well, you're not getting any younger," James said.

"Ha. Ha. Let's talk about your bachelor party. We're running out of time, so we need to decide soon. If you want something more traditional, we could do Vegas. Strippers, sex, cocaine, that empty feeling you get inside when you..."

"Whoa," Bee said. "Nope. Mason, you're not planning his bachelor party. There is a zero percent chance that's happening."

James laughed. "Really, none of that sounds appealing."

"What empty feeling are you talking about?" I asked.

"You know...like when you hook up with someone and the next day you wake up realizing how depressed you are that you have nothing real in your life."

"No, I don't know about that."

"You've never had meaningless sex?"

"No?"

Mason shrugged. "Girls from Delaware are so tight laced. Well, until you awaken them."

"Mason!" Bee lightly shoved his arm again.

"He's not wrong," James said.

"Both of you are ridiculous." My face was probably even redder than Bee's. "And both of you have full lives. So you wouldn't get an empty feeling. Unless we broke up with you after you cheated on us."

"Here's to that," Bee said. I clinked my glass against the one she had raised.

"Well, I know that," Mason said. "But James already vetoed my first several ideas."

"Which were way worse," James said.

"I really don't understand the whole bachelor party thing," Bee said. "It's your last night as a single guy before you marry the girl you *chose* to marry. That shouldn't be a big deal."

"Exactly," James said. "Which is why I don't want one."

"Fine, we'll just go with the first idea I had. I already have the place booked anyway," Mason said.

James laughed. "I don't think so."

"It's not like we have to participate in everything. Obviously." He gestured to Bee and me.

"Is that supposed to make me feel better?" Bee asked.

"Yes." Mason kissed her cheek and put his arm around her shoulders. "Wait, does this mean you don't want me to have a bachelor party before our wedding?"

"Um...yeah."

"I need to rethink everything now."

Bee laughed as Mason pulled her onto his lap and wrapped his arms tightly around her.

"Never mind, you're worth it."

James squeezed my hand and I looked up at him. We had an ongoing bet for when the two of them would get engaged. He had guessed Mason would pop the question sometime this summer. It was looking like he was going to win. He usually did win our bets. But I was always willing to give him the rewards he requested. I shrugged my shoulders and smiled at him.

"How about that tour?" James asked.

"Sounds good. What did this place set you back? I honestly didn't know apartments could be this big this close to Central Park," Mason said.

"It was actually two apartments that we had to combine. So we got everything custom done, which was great."

It was cute that he said we, even though he had kept it a secret from me until it was already done. I hadn't even known it had been two apartments before. But that made sense. I had just been thinking that I hadn't seen an apartment with a second story before.

Recently James and Mason had gotten really into talking about real estate. I was pretty sure the two of them were trying to buy up all the prime real estate in the city. Their conversation quickly turned into discussing copper versus aluminum wire and different light fixtures.

"Do you want a normal person tour?" I asked Bee.

"Absolutely." She stood up and followed me into the kitchen. "They lost me at light fixtures."

CHAPTER 7
Friday

I opened up one of the last boxes. On top was a small frame. I smiled and turned it over. It was a picture of James and Rob. James was smiling brightly and Rob was giving the middle finger to the camera. I couldn't believe this had been taken two and a half years ago. James didn't look any different than he did in the picture. I wasn't sure if I looked any older either, but I felt older.

Rob joked around with me all the time, but I knew he didn't mean it. He had become one of my best friends. He was like the brother I never had. He teased me enough to make it true. And James' sister was like the sister I never had. I truly did fit into James' life. With everyone but his parents, that was.

"Do you need help finishing up?" Ellen asked and sat down next to me on the couch.

"No, that's okay." I set the picture down on the couch, leaned back, and smiled. It was crazy how James and I could pick up our whole lives and move within a few days. Ellen had been wonderful helping us pack and unpack everything. I relied on her as much as James did now.

"Shouldn't you be getting ready?" Ellen asked.

I ran the back of my hand against my forehead. I knew I was a mess. All day I had been delaying getting ready to go to James' parents. Just thinking about it made me unbelievably nervous.

"Dear, I know you're worried. Just be yourself." Ellen put her hand on my forearm.

"If they wanted to know me, they would have done it months ago. No, years ago. They don't want me to be me. They want me to be someone else." *Isabella.*

Ellen squeezed my arm and then stood up. "I laid out a dress on your bed. How about you go get ready and I'll finish unpacking. James will be back soon and he won't want to be late."

I knew that better than anyone. It was strange how quickly the apartment had been transformed into our home. I already felt comfortable here. James had been right. And I'd never tire of seeing the new view. Our first apartment had been between his office and NYCU. We didn't need to be near my school now. And it was really nice to be so close to Central Park. I sighed and stood up. "You're right. Thanks for all your help this week. I don't know what we'd do without you." It was strange going to meet James' mother when Ellen really seemed to fill that role.

"Go on and get ready." She waived her hand in the air, shooing me away.

***

I drummed my fingers against the kitchen counter. When I had come back out after my shower, Ellen was gone. She had picked out a sundress that was a little more sophisticated than the other ones I owned. It was white with a modest neckline and a lacy skirt that stopped a few inches above my knees. I had put on the diamond necklace James had gotten me last Valentine's Day, which made the outfit look even fancier. And I chose white heels instead of sandals. Hopefully it would be fancy enough. I looked around the kitchen at the shiny stainless steel appliances. It was odd being here alone.

I looked down at my phone. Normally when I was nervous about something, I'd call Melissa. But she had avoided me all week. She hadn't even stopped by to see the new apartment even though I kept asking. When she'd decided to move to New York after graduating, I had pictured spending a lot of time with her. I thought I'd be getting my best friend back. I hadn't even gotten to spend any time alone with her to talk about her dating Tyler. Hopefully I'd be able to pull her aside tonight.

James had said there wouldn't be more than 30 people or so at the party. It was just supposed to be close friends and family, and I'd know most of them. I was pretty sure his parents were the last people in his life I hadn't met. The thought just made me more nervous. And I couldn't stop thinking about all the things Mason had said last night.

I quickly answered my phone as soon as it buzzed. "Hey, James."

"We just pulled into the parking garage. Do you want to come down?" He sounded tense.

"Yeah, I'll be right down." I was in the elevator before I even hung up the phone.

The car was waiting near the elevator door. James was standing by the open door, staring down at his phone. He was dressed in a navy blue suit with a white dress shirt underneath. The top few buttons were undone and he wasn't wearing a tie. He looked casual and I instantly felt more relaxed. I'd need to thank Ellen for picking me out a perfect outfit for the occasion.

He smiled when he saw me and put his phone back in his pocket.

"So they haven't canceled yet?" I asked.

"Not yet." He kissed my cheek and gestured for me to get in.

I climbed in, scooting to the middle seat so he could slide in next to me. As soon as our seatbelts were buckled, he wrapped his arm around my shoulders.

"I like this," he said, running his opposite hand along the lace of my dress.

I smiled to myself. If he liked the lace on this dress, he was going to love the wedding dress I had picked out. "It's okay for tonight?"

"Absolutely." He grabbed my hand and ran his thumb along my palm. "Are you nervous?"

I looked up at him. Even if I tried to sugarcoat it, he'd be able to read how I was feeling. "Yes."

"Don't be." He gave me a small smile. "It's going to be fine, I promise."

"What if they don't like me?" I laughed awkwardly. "That's a stupid question. They already don't like me."

"It won't change anything."

"Yes it will. I don't want to be the reason that you're not close to your parents, James."

He lowered his eyebrows. "They're the reason I'm not close to them. Just be yourself. I fell in love with you. If they don't like you, it's their loss, not the other way around."

I took a deep breath. I couldn't go into this with preconceived notions about them if I expected them not to have them either. I just needed to pretend them avoiding me for the past couple years hadn't happened. This was a fresh start, just like the new apartment. They were going to be my family.

My knuckles brushing against James' lips pulled me out of my own head. I smiled up at him. "I'm sorry about how much this has been weighing on you. I know that I was annoying you, pushing your parents to meet me."

He kissed the back of my hand again. "Nothing you do annoys me. I just want you to be happy."

"I am." I rested my head against his shoulder. And nervous, excited, angry, and anxious. I needed to calm down. James' cologne always seemed to soothe me. He continued to stroke his thumb against my palm. It didn't take long for me to calm down.

As soon as we pulled up to his parents' house on the outskirts of the city, though, I could feel myself getting tense again.

"I thought it started at seven." James looked at his watch.

We were half an hour early, but the gate was already open and there were tons of cars parked along the long driveway. It looked like there were going to be way more than 30 people inside. I had already seen the outside of the house. It was more of a mansion than a house really. And I had been nervous about what I was going to say when it came into view because James didn't know I had come here one day and seen it already. At least I could still be surprised when we got inside. Luckily he was too distracted to notice my silence. It was hard not to stare at the immense building though. It was made up completely of gray stone and reminded me of an estate that had been turned into a museum back home. No wonder James wanted a bigger place if this is what he was used to. Our new apartment would make him feel claustrophobic soon enough as well.

"They said they wanted to meet you one on one first, without everyone else around." Now James sounded tense too. "Maybe I got the time wrong."

That was doubtful. James was rarely ever wrong. And even if he was, he never admitted it. I pulled my eyes away from the house. "It's okay. I'm sure I'll still have plenty of time to talk to them." But my heart wasn't in my words. Maybe they had told us the wrong time so they wouldn't have to talk to me at all.

Ian pulled the car around to the front. James quickly got out of the car and put his hand out for me. He didn't look tense anymore. He just looked pissed. I grabbed his hand and he pulled me to my feet.

"James." I grabbed both sides of his face. "It's okay. But please, please don't leave me alone in there."

He smiled and gave me a quick kiss. "I don't know what my parents are up to. I'm not letting you out of my sight."

I laughed. "You make it seem like they're planning something evil."

"We should get inside." He interlaced his fingers with mine and walked me toward the door.

His words made my heart beat even faster. I knew his parents didn't really want to know me. But it didn't seem like they were trying to get rid of me. They were throwing a party for us. We had just gotten the time wrong. Everything was going to be fine.

We walked up the front steps, which were a matching gray stone. A man standing outside the front doors grabbed the door handle, but paused before opening the door when he saw us. A huge smile spread over his face. He let go of the door handle. "You must be Penny," he said.

James squeezed my hand. "Eric, this is Penny. Penny, this is Eric. He's worked for my parents for as long as I can remember. And he's a good friend."

Eric walked down the few steps that separated us and stuck out his hand.

I immediately shook it. "It's so nice to meet you."

"The pleasure is all mine, Penny. James has told me so much about you. You are just as lovely as he said."

"Thank you, Eric." If everyone was this friendly inside, I had nothing to worry about.

James clapped Eric on the back. "The party was supposed to start at seven right?"

"No, it started at six. A last minute change. You didn't know?"

James laughed, but it wasn't his normal contagious one. It sounded forced. "I must not have gotten the memo."

"Well, you two better get inside. Everyone's waiting for you." Eric ran back up the steps and opened up the door for us.

I heard classical music playing as we stepped into the foyer. The floor was marble and it lead toward an ornate twisted staircase. It really did feel like I was in a museum. There were even old portraits hung up on the walls around us. I looked up the ceiling, where an enormous chandelier hung. "I can't believe this is where you grew up." I almost tripped when I felt the resistance of James' hand on mine. He had stopped directly in the middle of the foyer.

"What's wrong?"

James was just staring straight ahead. I turned to see what he was looking at.

"You can't be serious." Rob was standing by an older couple in the foyer. Someone else was directly in front of him, but he was blocking my view. "He'll never forgive you. You do realize that right? You can't do this. Please don't do this."

"She's still part of this family, whether you like it or not. I believe James knows that better than anyone," the woman I didn't recognize said.

"Won't you just listen to me for one second? You haven't even met Penny. Is this really how you want to meet your future daughter in law? This is supposed to be the start of your relationship, not the end."

"Enough," the older man said. He looked a little like James. He must be his father. "You will not treat a guest in our house like this."

The woman, who I assumed was his mother, cleared her throat and nodded toward James.

Rob's face was red when he turned around. He looked directly at me. He looked more sad than upset. His eyes landed on James and he shook his head.

James' grip tightened around my hand.

A hand wrapped around Rob's arm, pushing him to the side. Isabella was standing there with a smug look on her face. She looked me up and down and then whispered something to James' mother. Both women laughed.

"Hippopotamus," I whispered. When we had first moved to New York, James had always made me promise to tell him if I was ever uncomfortable. That was our word. Whenever I said that, he knew I wanted to leave. I had never used it before. When we had chosen it, we thought that whatever the situation, it would make us laugh. Neither one of us was laughing now.

CHAPTER 8
Friday

Rob quickly walked over to us. "Penny, I'm so sorry. If I had known I would have told you guys."

I didn't even know what to say.

James dropped my hand. "Can you take Penny into the main room? I need to talk to our parents."

"James, please..." I said.

But he didn't seem to hear me. He had already started walking toward his parents and Isabella.

My whole body felt cold. I couldn't do this. I didn't belong here. I turned around so I could walk out the door, but Rob caught my hand.

"It's okay," he said. "Hey, it's okay. There's a bunch of people in the other room that actually want to see you."

"I can't do this, Rob. They don't want me here."

"Well, I want you here." He linked his arm in mine. "Come on, don't let my parents ruin tonight. Everyone is here to celebrate you and James." He pulled me past them and through a long hallway.

I could hear James raising his voice. It echoed in the large foyer, making it impossible to hear what he was saying. Rob picked up his pace, trying to put distance between them and me.

I breathed in through my nose, not even trying to hide the sniffling noise.

"Oh, geez." Rob looked down at me and stopped. "Don't cry." He pulled me to his chest. "Don't show them that they won. That's the last thing you want."

"They did win. They didn't even give me a chance."

He put his hands on my shoulders. "Part of being in this family is learning how to ignore my parents. You have to have thick skin. You can't let stuff like this bother you."

"They invited his ex wife to our engagement party."

"Yeah, my parents suck. That can't come as a surprise to you. They're the fucking worst."

I laughed and wiped away a few tears that had fallen down my cheeks.

"You're going to be my little sister. I'm going to help watch out for you. But you can't let them get under your skin. Show them that you don't care. That's what the three of us do."

I took a deep breath. Rob always joked around with me. It was nice to hear that he truly cared.

"And they're not even doing this because of you. They're mad at James. And trust me, not having their approval makes us all like you even more. So cheer up." He lightly bumped my chin with his fist.

I laughed. "I'm sorry, I'm still focused on the fact that you said I was going to be your little sister."

"Ugh. Don't hold that against me. I mean, if you're looking for less drama, I don't have an ex wife." He winked at me.

"You can't take it back now. I always thought it would be nice to have a brother."

He rolled his eyes. "Don't let it go to your head. I was just being nice."

"Mhm."

He removed his hand from my shoulder. "So, are you okay?"

"The brotherly pep talk definitely helped. Thanks, Rob." I looked down the hallway toward the foyer. I wanted James to walk into the party with me. I didn't want him to be fighting with his parents. And I definitely didn't want him to talk to Isabella. I just wanted him by my side.

"Come on," Rob said and held his arm back out for me. "I'm supposed to be escorting you to the party. Not letting you mope around in the hallway."

"I'd rather just hide somewhere and not see anyone."

"Just bottle up all your emotions and try not to think about them. That's what becoming a Hunter truly is. Why do you think we're all so messed up?"

I laughed as he walked with me down the hallway.

"Welcome to the family, Penny." He winked at me again as he turned the corner. We walked through a marble archway into a room filled with at least a hundred people. And I didn't recognize any of them.

"Shouldn't we wait for James?"

"I don't know. He said to bring you in here." He looked over his shoulder. "How about I go grab you a drink to calm your nerves. What's your poison?"

"Don't leave me."

He laughed. "Jen's over there. I'm sure she'd love to introduce you to some of the family."

I nodded. "Get me something strong."

"I'll do my worst." His arm fell from mine.

It felt like everyone was staring at me. I smiled awkwardly and walked over to Jen.

"What took you two so long?" she said as she gave me a quick hug. "Wait, where's James?"

"Talking to your parents." I didn't want to think about what he was doing. "Rob said you might introduce me to some of your family members. I thought this was going to be a small thing. Why are there so many people here?"

"Well, your wedding is going to be so small that Mom and Dad insisted that everyone come down to meet you now. They're all so excited to meet you."

So this was basically everyone we hadn't invited to the wedding? *Oh God.* I swallowed hard. They all probably hated me too.

"You okay?" Jen asked. "You look really pale."

"I'm fine. Do I know anyone here?"

"I think the invites got a little confusing. Most of your friends are arriving around seven I think. But come on, I'll introduce you to everyone."

***

It was just a blur of faces and names. I gave up trying to remember who everyone was. It seemed like hours before I felt James' hand on my waist.

"Let's go. I've already made our excuses," he said.

"But I haven't even met your parents yet."

"And you're not going to. Let's go. Now."

I wasn't sure I had ever seen him this upset. All I wanted to do was grab his hand and run out of there. But Rob's advice was stuck in my head. I didn't want his parents to think they could scare me away. I wasn't going anywhere. "Our friends are coming any minute. We can't leave now."

"Oh, there you are, James," Jen said. The smile on her face instantly disappeared. "What's wrong?"

"Did you know Isabella was going to be here?" James said in a stern voice.

"Don't snap at her." I put my hand on his chest. "This isn't her fault."

"Is she really?" Jen asked. Her voice sounded small.

"Dad said you're the one that convinced them to throw this thing. You must have known. You set us up."

"Of course I didn't," Jen said. She sounded like her normal self again. "You know I wouldn't do that."

James ran his hand through his hair. "Please let me get you out of here, Penny." There was so much pain in his eyes. And it killed me.

"I have to meet them." I put my glass in his hand. "Hold this for me, please."

I started to walk away before he had time to react.

"Penny!" he hissed.

I ignored him and walked over to the archway. His parents had just entered the room with Isabella in tow. She smiled as I approached. She probably thought that I was about to embarrass myself, but she was dead wrong. I went straight up to them and smiled. "Hi, you must be Mr. and Mrs. Hunter. I'm Penny Taylor, your son's fiancée. I'm so sorry that it took us this long to meet. We had such conflicting schedules." I gave them as genuine of a smile as I could. "But I'm glad we finally get a chance to meet now, before the wedding. And thank you so much for throwing this wonderful party to celebrate our engagement. It's been quite lovely. Your whole family has been so kind."

James' mother raised her left eyebrow. The expression reminded me of one that James made so often. Maybe the two of them had some similarities after all.

Isabella made a weird noise with her throat, clearly disapproving of what I had just said.

"Oh, and Isabella, it's so nice to see you again. I wasn't sure I would get the pleasure. I'm so glad you could make it."

"Unfortunately we can't stay," James said and wrapped his arm firmly around my waist, almost making me jump. "Something has come up and we really must go."

"Don't be ridiculous, James," Isabella said with a huge smile. "The party has only just begun. Let me get you a scotch. That's your favorite, right?" Her voice was oozing with so much fake sweetness that I wanted to throw up.

"Not anymore, no." His grip tightened on my waist.

"How about we go make a few phone calls?" I said and smiled up at him. "I'm sure whatever urgent thing that has come up can be handled by someone else. If you'll excuse us for just a moment." I smiled politely at all three of them and grabbed James' arm.

He followed me into the hallway. I stopped right past the archway, but he grabbed my hand, pulling me farther down the hall.

"James?"

He didn't say anything, he just kept walking.

"James, stop." I pulled my hand out of his grip.

"We're going. Now."

"We're not going anywhere. Your parents threw us this party and I'm not going to make a bad first impression by leaving early."

"You're joking right? They invited..."

"No. I'm not joking. Would you calm down for one second?"

He lowered his eyebrows.

"If I'm going to be a part of this family, then I need to learn how to deal with them. And if that means I have to be civil around Isabella too, so be it."

"I'm not asking you to do that."

"I know that you're not asking. I'm offering."

"And I'm rejecting your offer. I don't want to be here. I'm never stepping foot in this fucking house again. I already told them as much. I'm done. With all of them."

"You don't mean that."

"I do mean it. Don't you see what they're doing? They're trying to force Isabella back on me. They don't want me to marry you. They won't even give you a chance. They want me to be miserable. They don't care about me."

"They do care. They think that's what's best for you. But I'm going to wear them down. I'm going to make them see."

"They're not like your parents, Penny. I'm not having a fight with them over something small and insignificant. This isn't just a misunderstanding. They're torturing me. They're trying to break me. Again."

It wasn't like I couldn't see the pain in his eyes. I knew. I just never realized quite how bad it was. I wanted to think the whole thing was a misunderstanding. No one's parents could act this way without an important reason behind it. They had to be doing it because they thought Isabella was what was best for him. But maybe I was wrong. Maybe they were torturing him on purpose because he wasn't doing the things they wanted him to be doing. And there was a huge difference between the two. It didn't seem like they wanted him to be happy. I had been nice to them and they hadn't said a word.

"I just want to fix it," I whispered. I put my hand on the side of his face. "Please let me try."

"You can't make them love me." His Adam's apple rose and fell. He shook his head, making my hand fall from his face. "I need some air."

CHAPTER 9
Friday

I downed another glass of wine. This party was a complete disaster. James was missing. His parents were always talking to someone, so I couldn't catch them alone. And Isabella was walking around like she owned the place. All of James' family members seemed to adore her. I should have just left with James. I knew he needed me right now. But I wasn't calm enough to console him. All I wanted to do was set the house on fire.

"You okay?" Melissa asked as she walked up to me. "You look pissed."

"I'm fine." It was so nice to finally see someone I recognized. I took a deep breath and set my glass down on the bar. I was trying to calm my nerves before I potentially made a scene. I just wished I had the courage to do it without alcohol.

"This place is almost as big as Tyler's apartment building," she said.

I laughed. "Yeah, it's crazy." Maybe a distraction was what I needed. And I could really use someone on my side right now. "Actually, Melissa, I was hoping I could talk to you about Tyler. I just want you to know that if you two are dating, I'm totally okay with it."

"I don't need your permission to date someone, Penny."

"I know, that's not what I meant. I just thought that maybe because of our history, you thought..."

Melissa laughed and placed her glass of wine down on the bar beside mine. "Thought that it would be awkward because you've slept with him? Yeah, well you have nothing to worry about. I would never date Tyler Stevens. I'm sorry, I need to use the bathroom."

"Melissa?"

She was already quickly walking away.

What the hell was that? I glanced over at Tyler. He was staring at us, but he quickly looked away when he caught my gaze and started walking after Melissa.

Not only was I in a room full of people that preferred James' ex wife to me, but now two of my closest friends seemed to be mad at me. *Fuck this.*

I walked over to Rob who was playing some drinking game with Matt and Mason. Hopefully they weren't taking shots whenever Isabella gave me a death stare, because they'd be totally wasted. And I needed Rob's help.

I put my hand on his shoulder. "I'm going to talk to your parents. Could you go find James so we can leave when I'm done? He said he was going to get some air, but he's not answering his phone. And I..."

"Say no more, gorgeous. I'll find him." Rob downed his shot and stood up. "Don't play without me," he said and disappeared into the crowd of people in the room.

"Are you okay, Penny?" Mason asked. He looked truly concerned and it made me feel a little better. I just needed to remember that James' friends were the true family I was gaining. If his parents weren't going to accept me, then I wasn't going to keep pretending everything was alright.

"Besides for the fact that James' parents want him to get back with Isabella? Yeah, I'm great." I looked over toward his parents.

They were talking to a group of people about their age. It didn't really matter if I was rude and interrupted them. They deserved it.

Matt laughed. "You don't have anything to worry about. James is completely addicted to you. You're like the only sustenance he needs. Ow, fuck! What is wrong with you?"

I turned back to them.

Matt was grabbing his shin under the table and giving Mason a dirty look. Had Mason just kicked him?

Mason cleared his throat. "Do you need help getting James' parents alone to tell them off? I think we're both up to the challenge."

"No. I'll do it myself. I'm kind of looking forward to embarrassing them. Have fun with your game." I walked away from their table toward Mr. and Mrs. Hunter. They were still talking to the same group of people. "Excuse me," I said when I reached them. "I was hoping to have a word alone with Mr. and Mrs. Hunter."

"Of course, dear," said a woman who I recognized as one of James' aunts who I had met earlier.

James' mother turned toward me reluctantly. "I didn't realize you were still here."

Yeah, fuck you too. "Can the three of us go talk somewhere in private?"

"We're hosting a party. We can't just..."

Mrs. Hunter was cut off by her husband. "Of course, Miss Taylor. We thought you might request a word. Let's discuss this in my office."

I instantly liked Mr. Hunter a little more than Mrs. Hunter. He didn't seem nearly as cold. They started walking away and I quickly caught up to the them. It felt like I was about to be scolded as I followed them out of the room and into the main hallway, though. I wondered what they thought I was about to talk to them about as Mr. Hunter stopped in front of a door. He pulled out a key from his pocket and put it into the door. He pushed it open, letting Mrs. Hunter walk in first. He continued to hold the door open and gestured for me to go in as well. Maybe he wasn't so bad.

I stepped in and turned around in a circle. The room looked more like a small library than an office. I suddenly felt weird for not knowing what his parents did. James never talked about them. So I really knew nothing about them at all. Except that they were hurting James. That was all that I needed to know.

His father cleared his throat and I turned toward him. "Miss Taylor, let me apologize for inviting Isabella to this event."

James' mother crossed her arms in front of her chest and didn't say a word.

"Thank you for saying that." I sighed with relief. I had every intention of yelling at them as soon as we were alone, but I bit my tongue. This whole thing was just a huge misunderstanding. I could still fix this.

"We realize that option should have been presented to James at a different time."

"A different time?" *You mean not at all?*

"Yes. Once we settle this," he said.

"Settle what?" I asked.

James' mother shook her head. "There's no reason to be formal, Jonathan. We all know why we're here." She stared at me for a second like I was completely dense and walked over to the desk. She opened up a drawer and pulled out a checkbook.

You've got to be kidding me. "I don't want your money. That's not what I wanted to talk about. I wanted to talk about the way you've been treating your son."

She tore a check out of the booklet and stuck her hand out to me.

I bit my lip, trying to prevent myself from crying. How could they think that's why I was dating their son? "I'm in love with James."

"Of course." She sounded disgusted as she pulled out another check. She set them both down on the desk and slid them toward me.

I looked down. Both checks were already made out to me. And they were each for one million dollars. They had already written them. They never had any intention of getting to know me. This had been their plan the whole time. "Don't you want him to be happy?" My voice sounded small and sad.

"That's really no concern of yours," his mother snapped.

"Yes it is. I'm his fiancée. All I care about is his happiness."

"This charade has gone on long enough. I thought it would sizzle out on its own, but now I see that we need to step in before it's too late. So that's what we're doing. Because we do care about his happiness. And we won't let him ruin his life over some girl. It's just a matter of time before he comes to his senses. We're just helping it along. Now take the money and disappear from his life. That's the offer."

"I don't want your money." I had clenched my hands into fists. "You think this is showing him that you care? Instead of accepting him how he is? Your son is sweet and caring and..."

"And he doesn't know what's best for him. You think marrying a middle class girl is helping him? Pulling him down to your level?" She made the same noise with her throat that Isabella had made earlier. "He's a Hunter." She picked up the checks and threw them at me.

Her words made me shiver. "He may be a Hunter, but he's in love with me."

"He doesn't love you." She looked me up and down. "He's attracted to you for some reason. And I don't even see why. You're quite common. Isabella and him have a real bond. Our families are connected. And they're going to work it out."

"There's nothing to work out. They're divorced."

"Which was a mistake. They both realize that. And they're working on fixing it."

She made it seem like it was already happening. I wasn't going to let her crawl under my skin. That was nonsense. "He doesn't love her."

"Again, that is none of your business. You'll never be one of us. Even if you have conned our son into living in sin with you for the past two years. Enough is enough."

"I don't want to be one of you." I tried to keep my head up high even though all her words seemed to cut through me like a knife. "I'm glad I never will be." I leaned down and picked up the checks off the floor.

James' mother smiled. "What a relief."

"Because James and I want nothing to do with you." I tore up the checks and let the pieces flutter to the ground. "I was hoping that we could come to an understanding, but it's clear that you're not interested in listening to me. Or your son. So you're officially uninvited to the wedding. Not that you ever accepted the invitation in the first place. And you're uninvited to be a part of the rest of our lives as well. You won't even get to hold your grandchildren. So congratulations to both of you. You've lost your eldest son. I hope you're happy."

James' father cleared his throat. "Miss Taylor, you seem like a smart girl. We hope that you'll make the right decision. Please let yourself out when you've calmed down." He took a step toward the door.

"I'm not done. I came here trying to give you both the benefit of the doubt. But do you have any idea how much you've hurt him? Forcing him to marry Isabella even though he didn't love her? He would have done anything to make you happy. Don't you see that? He's tried so hard to please both of you. But you're impossible. Do you even know what he's been through? He was depressed. And it's your fault. You made him an addict."

"Enough!" yelled his dad. "Our son's shortcomings are no one's fault but his own. He's never known what's best for him. He chose to find solace in vices because he's weak. He's always been weak." His father's words made tears come to my eyes.

"James is the strongest person I know. Strong enough to walk away from his own parents. And thank goodness, because the thought of ever being in the same room as either of you again makes me feel sick to my stomach. You're both pretentious snobs. And you don't deserve his love."

"Is that quite all?" his father asked. "Are you done insulting us in our own house?"

"If you give me more time, I'm sure I can think of something else to say." I glared back at him. I knew I was being childish. But it was better than punching him in the face, which is what I really wanted to do.

"There is one more check in the check book. We're willing to pay you five million dollars total to walk away from our family. I suggest you take it."

"Or what?"

"You may think that we don't love our son, but we're willing to do anything to protect him."

"He doesn't need your protection. What he needs is your love. What is wrong with you?"

His father frowned. "We need to get back to our guests." He walked out of the room without another word. James' mother stared at me for a second before following her husband out of the office.

I sunk into one of the chairs in front of the desk and put my face in my hands, finally letting my tears free. Why hadn't I just left with James when he told me to? I hadn't believed him. I didn't think there was any way that his parents were as bad as he said. But he was right. They were absolutely horrid. And now James was out somewhere alone. I thought about earlier in the week when his mother called. He had seemed so happy that they were finally willing to meet me. He let himself get his hopes up, just to be crushed by them again. And I had put him in that situation. He was probably furious with me. The thought just made me cry even harder.

"Oh my. I'm guessing your little conversation didn't go so well?"

My whole body felt cold. I quickly wiped my tears away and looked up at Isabella. "Please, Isabella. Not right now."

She walked into the room, closing the door behind her. "I have a few things to say myself."

"Mr. and Mrs. Hunter have already filled me in on their plans to get you two back together. I don't want to hear about it."

"You poor thing. You really had no idea why Jonathan and Susan invited you here?" She looked down at the scattered pieces of the checks on the ground.

If she thought that her being on a first name basis with them bothered me, she was dead wrong. I never wanted to be that close to them. Not now that I knew what they were like.

"I believe James was thrilled to see me. It's been much too long since we were close. And I'm excited to change that."

"Why can't you just leave him alone?"

"I let him have his fling. I gave him the distance he needed. It's time for us to work things out."

"You loathe each other. What on earth are you talking about?"

"Just because he's not addicted to me doesn't mean he doesn't love me. It's a sickness. If you want what's best for him, you'll let him go. I'm the only one who knows what he needs. I can help him."

"He doesn't need your help." I stood up. "And he's not addicted to me. He loves me."

"It's a fine line. And I'm afraid it's a little blurry for him."

"All he needs from you is to be left alone. Please, just leave us both alone."

"I'm trying to help you. I'm giving you the chance to walk away from all of this. You still have your whole life ahead of you. You don't want to spend time taking care of..."

"He doesn't need to be taken care of. We've been together for two and a half years and I've seen nothing. He's fine. He's over whatever it is you're talking about. We're both fine."

"He's not fine. He's addicted to you."

"Stop saying that." I knew she was just trying to make me paranoid. But James was fine. He wasn't like that anymore.

"You're rewarding his behavior."

"Are you so blind that you can't see the difference? Just because no one has ever loved you doesn't mean you have to take it out on me."

"You don't think James loved me? He really does like to keep you in the dark, doesn't he? His affection lasted for a few years and then it was gone. The same thing will happen to you."

"Stop living in the past. It's pathetic."

"Stop living in denial."

"Don't you ever come near him again, Isabella. Leave us alone."

"Or what?"

"You don't want to find out."

She laughed. "I'm so unbelievably scared." She smiled at me. "There's two weeks until your wedding. Which means I have two weeks to make James see the light. It's plenty of time. I just have to remind him about what he's missing. I'll only need a few minutes alone with him. Until he's screaming my name instead of yours."

"You bitch."

She slapped me hard across the face.

I grabbed my cheek. No one had ever slapped me before. I hadn't been expecting that at all. She was wearing a few rings on her hand and I could feel the small bruises already forming on my face.

She put her hand on her cheek and made a fake shocked look. "Sorry, did I hurt you?" She removed her hand from her own cheek and smiled. "I didn't think you'd mind. I know how aggressive James can be. I figured you liked to be smacked around."

"You don't know him, Isabella. I know you wish you did. I know you're upset that he left you. But it's not my fault. Stop blaming me for your shortcomings."

"My shortcomings? He slept with you while he was still married to me. You're a slut."

"Look, you can keep his parents. I know you have them wrapped around your finger. And I want nothing to do with them. But you can't have him. He's mine." I walked past her and out of the room. I looked to the right toward the party. There was still light classical music pouring through the hallway. I turned to the left and walked as quickly as I could away from everyone else.

I pulled out my phone and called James. There was still no answer. I stopped in the middle of the foyer, unsure of where to go. I heard voices outside and the front door started to open. I couldn't face anyone else right now. I turned and ran up the stairs.

CHAPTER 10
Friday

I felt like I was trespassing as I made my way down the corridor. I just needed to find a bathroom to hide in until James picked up his phone. When I turned the corner, I saw a door with a nameplate on it. *Robert.* My heart skipped a beat and I looked farther down the hall. A door with James' name was on the opposite side of the corridor. I looked behind me. It didn't matter if I was sneaking around. There was never going to be another opportunity to see James' childhood room.

Before I could change my mind, I walked over to the door and went inside, quickly closing it behind me. Moonlight shown in through the sides of the closed blinds, casting eerie shadows along the floor. I ran my hand along the wall until my fingers found the light, and I quickly switched it on.

Everything in the room was a pale blue. The walls, the carpet in the center of the room, the comforter on the bed. His parent's must have been thrilled to have a boy. There were a few posters pinned to the walls of who I assumed were old quarterbacks for the Giants. The only one I had ever known of was Eli Manning, and neither poster was of him. Besides for those, there was nothing that seemed very personal in the room. Actually, there wasn't much in the room at all except for the extensive library along one wall. I walked over to the shelves and let my eyes wander the titles. There were tons of classics that had been on my school reading lists growing up, like Lord of the Flies, To Kill a Mockingbird, and Huckleberry Finn.

It was almost like he had put them in order of when he had read them. The later shelves seemed to be filled with books from college. Books about website coding, marketing, management, and any kind of business imaginable. I only recognized one title in the marketing section, and I was glad that my education shared at least one similarity with his at Harvard. Unless he had just read Marketing Principles in Foreign Markets on a whim one summer.

I smiled when my eyes fell on all the books in the Harry Potter series. When he had seen my room, he had teased me about Harry Potter. I thought he had been joking when he said he read the series, that he was just trying to make me feel less immature for having children's things in my room. It was sometimes so hard to tell whether or not he was serious. Either way, I was glad he liked Harry Potter as much as I did. I tilted my head as my eyes wandered across the titles in the series. He didn't have all of them, actually. He was missing the first one. I scanned the rest of the shelves to try and find it.

I laughed to myself as I ran my finger along the spine of a Boy Scouts handbook. For the life of me, I couldn't quite picture him in one of those cute little uniforms. Actually, I couldn't really picture him as a child at all. And there hadn't been any pictures of him on the walls downstairs like I'd hope there'd be either. I turned away from the bookshelf and saw a picture tucked into the side of the mirror above his dresser. But it wasn't of him. I walked over, staring at the girl in the picture, and pulled it off the mirror.

I didn't need to turn it over to know who it was. It had to be his high school girlfriend, Rachel. Young love. It was something I knew nothing about. James was my first real boyfriend. I guess I was young when I first met him. I didn't feel young anymore though. And compared to the girl in the picture, I doubted I looked young either.

James must have kept her picture hanging here all through college too. The only reason that they had broken up was because his parents thought she wasn't suitable for him. If they had liked her, would they still be together? Would he have had a happier life?

When I had first met Isabella, she had told me I wasn't his type. Rachel had brunette hair like Isabella and brown eyes like her too. Isabella and James weren't compatible, but he must have been attracted to her if she looked like Rachel. Maybe they really were his type. Which meant I wasn't.

I turned the picture over. There was just one line scrawled on the back: Forever and always.

I had the eerie feeling that Rachel had given this to him after they had broken up. Maybe she thought he'd go back to her after college when he no longer needed his parents money. Maybe she was still waiting for him.

I tried to shake the thought away as I stuck the image back on the mirror. She was part of James' past, just like Isabella. I was his present and future. There was no reason to dwell over either of them. I pulled out my phone and saw that there were still no messages from James. Hopefully Rob would find him soon.

As I sat down on James' bed to wait for him, I noticed the copy of Harry Potter and the Sorcerer's Stone that had been missing from his bookshelf. It was sitting on his night stand. I pulled it onto my lap and let it fall open to a random page. The copy was really worn and felt oddly comforting in my hands, similar to my own copy. I skimmed the words that I had read half a dozen times and froze.

James hadn't read these books for the cute little redheaded girl. That part had been a tease. He read them because he needed an escape. He felt trapped here. I looked up at the very blue room. Living up to his parents' expectations must have been stifling. He dumped the girl that he loved and married a girl he never would. But that's all I really knew. And that wasn't his childhood. What horrible things had they made him do before that?

I loved the man that I knew. But I didn't know everything about him. All I knew about his childhood now was that he escaped to this very blue room to read. He must have felt so alone. There were hundreds of books on those shelves. I had told him I was nerdy growing up, preferring a book over socializing, but he had never told me that he was the same. Maybe we had more in common than I ever realized.

I started flipping through the book and saw a folded piece of paper lying between the pages. I pulled it out and unfolded it. The writing was faint, either faded from age or he hadn't had as sure of a hand back then. But I could make out the words. It was a list of criteria for emancipation. James had crossed out each line, probably because none of them applied to him. A permanent escape was unattainable.

So where had this boy gone? Why had he tried to become independent from his family only to do whatever they wanted for the next ten years of his life? What had changed? It couldn't have just been the issue of money. His parents were plenty generous with that. Offering me five million dollars to disappear to supposedly protect their son. They would never have really cut him off, would they? It didn't make any sense. There must have been something James hadn't told me.

I put the piece of paper back and closed the book. I didn't need to ask myself all those questions. His parents had taken away the love of his life, and I knew better than anyone how strongly James loved. So he had given up on life. He realized he was destined to be miserable and just seemed to accept it. James wasn't weak. He was the exact opposite. He was stoic. His parents repeatedly tried to break him and he just took it. Anyone would have needed an escape. A book, a bottle of scotch, sex. His escapes had matured with him.

I set the book back down on the nightstand. He wasn't addicted to me. We were both an escape for each other from our normal lives. We were each other's happy endings. The fairy tales in the books that lined his shelves really did exist. It wasn't an addiction. It was our reality. We were the lucky ones because we had found each other. No one could ever convince me otherwise.

The door squeaked but I didn't turn around. I could feel that it was him. "You really did like Harry Potter?" I put my palm down on top of the book on the nightstand.

"I've been looking everywhere for you," he said, ignoring my comment. He sounded on edge, like he really had searched through the whole house for me.

"I texted you to tell you I was in your room." I stood up but kept my face turned to the ground. I knew there was a bruise forming on my cheek and I didn't want him to see it. Not until we were far away from this awful party.

"There's no cell reception in this stupid house."

"Oh. Is it okay if I take this?" I asked and picked up the book. "We don't have a copy at our place."

"No." He cleared his throat. "We'll buy a new copy for us."

He hadn't wanted me to see the paper inside. I shouldn't have come in here. I had invaded his privacy. I put the book back down. "Okay, let's go then." I pretended to scratch my cheek and I walked past him so that he wouldn't be able to see my face.

"Penny?" He grabbed my wrist, moving my hand away from my face. "What the hell happened?" His words were harsh, but his thumb tracing over the bruise on my cheekbone was soft and delicate. "Are you okay?" His touch felt even gentler than it had a second ago. It made me feel like crying. But I didn't want him to think it was worse than it was.

"Nothing." I didn't look up at him. "It's fine."

"Baby?" He kept his hand on the side of my face. "Who did this?"

"No one. I was upset and I made a wrong turn. This house is enormous, I just ran into..."

"Why are you lying to me?" He sounded hurt. I still hadn't made eye contact with him.

Why was I lying? We didn't lie to each other. Not anymore. And it didn't matter if he knew the truth. Making him hate Isabella even more was only for the best. I never wanted to see any of these people ever again.

"Penny, tell me."

"Isabella slapped me. It's not a big deal. Can we please just go?"

His hand fell from my face and he grabbed the door handle.

"Don't. Don't you dare walk away from me again."

He let go of the handle and turned back to me. "I didn't walk away from you earlier. I told you it was time to go and you refused to come with me."

"Exactly, James. You told me it was time to go. You didn't ask if I was ready to leave."

"Penny, I couldn't stand there and pretend that everything was alright."

"I know, I'm sorry. Please don't leave me alone in this house again, though. Can't we just leave? You were right about everything. Talking to your parents was pointless."

"You talked to them?"

"They think I just want your money. They offered me five million dollars to walk away from you. They wouldn't even entertain the idea that I actually loved you." I shook my head. They were so disgusting.

"They tried to pay you off?" He lowered his eyebrows slightly and then ran both his hands down his face. It looked like he was understanding something for the first time. Like how evil his parents truly were. "Did you take it?" It came out as a barely audible whisper.

"What?"

He stared at me. He looked defeated and tired. Normally I couldn't see the age difference between us. But as he looked at me now, I could see the small crinkles around the corners of his eyes. They probably weren't laugh lines. The thought made my chest feel tight.

"James..." my throat caught. "How could you think that?" The rollercoaster of emotions from the night suddenly seemed to catch up to me and tears started running down my cheeks. The salty water stung as it slid down my left cheek. One of Isabella's rings must have left a small cut on my face.

He just stood there looking stunned.

I quickly wrapped my arms around him. I winced when I pressed the side of my face into his chest. *Hug me back*. His body seemed to stiffen instead. "James?"

He wrapped his arms around me in response. "I'm sorry. God, I'm so sorry." He put his chin on the top of my head. "I knew better than to bring you here. I don't know what's wrong with me. Nothing's changed. They'll never change. I'm so sorry, Penny."

"Don't apologize, this is what I wanted. You knew I wanted to meet them, so you made it happen. And now I have. It's done. We don't have to see them ever again."

He sighed. "Except for the wedding in two weeks."

"I uninvited them."

He laughed. "What?"

"Oh." I leaned back to look up at him. "Sorry, I mean, it was just in the heat of the moment. Obviously if you want them there..."

"No." He put his hand on the side of my face, gently rubbing his thumb over the bruise on my cheek. "No, I don't want them there. I'm done with them."

"I'm sorry that I forced all this. I just thought if they met me, maybe I could change their minds, you know? I was just trying to help."

"You can't change my parents' minds. Trust me, I've tried my whole life."

I wanted to ask him about the paper in his book, about his relationship with Rachel, about his whole childhood. I wanted him to fill in all the blanks. But right now all I wanted was for him to take me home. I needed to get out of this house, away from all the memories that seemed to upset him.

"But it was really sweet of you to try."

"Or foolish. What a disaster of an engagement party. Can we go home now?"

He smiled down at me. "Let me show you one thing first." He grabbed my hand and pulled me over to the window.

"It wasn't a good night, but I'm not going to fling myself out the window."

He laughed as he pushed the window up. He put his hands on the windowsill and looked back at me. "I used to sneak out of my room all the time. Let's leave this way."

I looked past him toward the lawn. We were really high up. "I'm wearing heels. And I've had too much to drink."

"I dare you."

I smiled. Neither one of us had ever backed down from a dare. "Well, I guess a few more bruises won't hurt me." I took off my shoes and peered out the window. "Did you really just jump?" I tossed my shoes out the window and watched them hit the lawn below. "It seems kind of high."

"Geez, no." He grabbed my arm and started laughing. "Were you seriously going to jump out the window?"

"You said you did it all the time. And you dared me."

"There's a trellis." He stuck his head out the window and pointed to the right. He started laughing again.

"Don't make fun of me for trusting you." I poked him in the middle of the chest.

"I'm lucky you said something before you jumped."

"Mhm." I rolled my eyes at him as I stood up on the ledge. "Who were you running off to see in the middle of the night growing up?"

He held my waist as I grabbed the edge of the trellis. It took every ounce of restraint not to look down. I slowly stepped onto it and was relieved to see it was as sturdy as he remembered it being.

"Not someone. Something," he said. "That's what I want to show you. Don't look at me, watch your footing."

I had slipped slightly when I started my descent, but I quickly regained my footing.

"Are you okay?"

"I'm fine. I'm a jungle gym master, James."

"I don't doubt that at all."

I laughed. I wasn't even sure what he meant by that. A few moments later I heard the creak of the trellis. I didn't look up to see him coming down after me. The last thing I needed was to be distracted by him.

I tried to focus on my hands, but every now and then I looked down at my feet, reminding myself how high I was. When I was finally close enough to the bottom, I jumped. The grass was sleek and I slid as soon as my feet touched the ground, landing hard on my ass. "Shit."

James laughed as he jumped down gracefully beside me. He put his hand out for me, but instead of taking it, I grabbed my shoes, got up by myself, and started running.

"You don't know where we're going!" He called after me.

It was only a matter of seconds before I felt his arms around my waist, lifting me in the air. He twirled me around and then pulled me against his chest.

"You have a huge grass stain on that perfect little ass of yours," he whispered in my ear.

I laughed and put my hand on his chest so I could lean back and see his face. "Why is it that I can't picture you here at all? I mean, I can out here. But this is the first time you've seemed like yourself all night."

"None of this is me. I don't belong here anymore. I'm not sure I ever did."

"Did you spend a lot of time outside when you were younger?"

"I keep trying to show you." He let go of my waist, bent his knees slightly, and tapped his back. "Hop on."

I laughed and jumped onto his back. I never minded running around barefoot, but it was sweet that he didn't want me to have to.

He alternated kissing the crook of my elbow and pointing out things in his mother's garden as we walked farther away from the house. Soon all the lights from the house were barely visible and only the moonlight and stars were guiding us.

"Where are we going?" I whispered.

"You don't have to whisper, we're all alone. There it is," he said, pointing in front of us.

I squinted my eyes. It was hard seeing in the dark. "I don't..." I stopped when I saw it. "Is that a tree house?"

He kissed the crook of my elbow again. "Of all the things here, this was the only thing that was truly mine. Jen and Rob never even came up unless I invited them to." He stopped at the base of the tree trunk and let me slide off his back. "I was barely ever in my room in the house. I used to come here all the time. You have no idea how many times I nagged my parents to let me get a zip line from my window to the tree house."

I laughed. "So why was this your special place?"

"Hmm."

"What? Is this where you used to fantasize about kissing girls and plotting evil little boy pranks?"

He wrapped his arms around me and kissed the back of my neck. "For not having any brothers, you have it spot on."

I laughed. I thought he might say something else, but when he didn't, I looked back up at the tree house. "Am I allowed to come up? Or are no girls allowed?"

He laughed. "Let me see if it's still stable." I watched him climb up the steps that were nailed into the side of the tree. The boards creaked when he stepped up into the house, but nothing broke. He put his hand down. "Penny Taylor, I'm officially invit-ing you up into my tree house."

I laughed and climbed the little ladder. I grabbed his hand and he helped pull me up inside. This was more what I was ex-pecting his room to be like. I laughed as I looked around at all the toys and comic books on the floor. There were actual windows in the little tree house, which had somehow preserved everything despite the hole in the floor. There were even pictures that lined the wall. Photos of James as a happy little boy. He had the same facial features, in an adorable little boy kind of way. "You're so cute. Is this you and Mason?"

James laughed and unpinned the picture from the wall. "Yeah. That was taken at summer camp one year."

I laughed and snatched the picture from him. They both had braces and looked so scrawny, nothing like either of them did now. "I have to show this to Bee." I looked up at him and he was smiling at me. "I'm gaining the best family I could possibly ask for, you know. Not your parents, obviously. But your siblings and your friends. I love all of them so much."

He scratched the scruff along his jaw line. "You have such a positive way of thinking about everything."

"That's what they are. Our family."

He turned away from me and gazed at the other pictures on the walls. I would have perused the other pictures too, but I couldn't tear my eyes away from his face. Even his favorite place growing up seemed to make him sad now. I wanted to joke around with him about how he barely even fit in his old tree house. But I didn't want to push him. It seemed like he had something to say. So I just waited, staring at his perfect features in the moonlight.

He sighed and leaned his head against the wooden boards behind him. "When you asked me why I preferred here over my bedroom, I just..." His voice trailed off. "It was the only place where I felt like I could breathe."

He had said that to me before. That he felt like he could finally breathe again when he was with me. I moved onto his lap, straddling him. "So, now I'm your tree house?"

"I wouldn't put it that way." He placed a soft kiss against my lips, cradling the back of my head in his hand.

"How would you put it?"

He grabbed my lower back and rotated us so that my back was against the wooden floor and he was on top of me. "You're my life, my heart, my soul, my everything."

He was so sweet. But for some reason all I could seem to focus on was how handsome he looked with the moonlight streaming in through the branches of the trees, dancing across his face. I spread my legs even wider and pulled my dress up my thighs.

There was an intensity in his eyes that hadn't been there before. And any trace of sadness had suddenly disappeared.

"You must have had fantasies of bringing girls up here, James." I reached out for the button of his dress pants.

"I never thought I'd be this lucky."

I grabbed the collar of his shirt and pulled his lips down to mine. This was always the best way to know if we were okay. We both had this internal need that was constantly clawing at the surface, ready to escape. And tonight had been a complete disaster. We both needed this.

He pressed down on my clit through my thong and I moaned into his mouth. I needed all of him.

"James," I panted. "I need you. All of you." I reached down and grabbed his erection through his dress pants. I had only managed to unbutton them and my fingers fumbled with the zipper.

I yelped as the elastic in my thong snapped against my hip as he tore it off of me. But the sensation was quickly replaced by pleasure as he thrust himself deep inside of me.

Fuck.

He groaned into my mouth and grabbed my thighs, pulling me even closer to him. He didn't wait for me to adjust to him. His fingers dug into my hips as he fucked me just like I needed him to. Intense. Raw. Perfect.

It felt like I couldn't get close enough to him. I hooked my ankles behind him, drawing him even closer, and wrapped my arms around the back of his neck. I couldn't get enough. "More," I said breathlessly.

He lightly bit my bottom lip and kissed me hard, completely consuming me. His mouth claimed me just like his cock, making me feel full in the most satisfying way.

I moaned again as he tilted his hips, hitting a spot that usually made me lose control. But I wasn't ready to let go. I never wanted to let go of him. I grabbed a fistful of his hair, deepening our kiss.

We should have been clumsy in the darkness, but I knew his body better than I knew my own. I had explored every rippling muscle and every inch of his skin. I felt the fire building in my stomach and I could feel myself clenching around him. *Not yet.* I wasn't done with him.

"God, Penny." He grabbed my hands, pulling them from his neck, and pinned them against the floor of the tree house. He thrust his hips faster and harder, driving himself deep inside of me.

I didn't want to come, but I could no longer think straight. I moaned again, trying to resist the building tension. I could stay in this elevated moment forever.

"Come for me, baby."

And just like that, I lost control. "James!" I felt my back arch and my body shudder beneath his as I came down hard. I immediately felt his warmth spread up into me and heard his satisfied groan. His breath was warm on the side of my neck and the comforting feeling made a lingering chill run down my spine. His chest rose and fell against mine, pressing against my taut nipples. Everything he did was perfect. Everything.

I grabbed his face and held it a few inches above my own. "You're everything to me too. Everything, James. I'll never get enough of you."

He lightly kissed the bruise under my eye. "I hope not."

PART 2

CHAPTER 11

Monday

"Strictly professional, huh?" asked James.

"You know what I mean." I squeezed James' hand as we crossed the street.

He ran his other hand through his hair and looked down at me. "Not really. Will you at least eat lunch with me?" He flashed me a smile.

"Of course I'll eat lunch with you."

"So you're fine with everyone knowing that you're my fiancée?"

"Yes. I've already met a bunch of your employees. But the interns are new. They won't know who I am. Of course they'll find out, but I want them to know me first, you know? So I just mean like, don't make out with me in my cubicle in front of everyone."

He laughed and squeezed my hand back. "I'm the boss. I can do whatever I want."

I shook my head. "Exactly. Which is why I'm asking you not to."

"So you draw the line of professionalism at PDA?"

"Precisely." I smiled up at him.

"But you're holding my hand on the way to work." He raised his left eyebrow.

"I'm allowed to hold your hand outside of work."

"Anyone from the office could see us though. You're sending me mixed signals."

"It's my first day, I'm nervous. I need your hand."

He looked satisfied with my answer.

And I did need his hand. Despite what he said, I knew everyone could see the two small bruises on my cheekbone. Foundation wasn't meant to conceal bruises. Hopefully no one would say anything to me. But it wasn't a great way to start a new job. My only real job before this was at a retail store during summers of high school and my first summer of college. I hadn't worked since I had met James. He had insisted that he wanted my free time to be spent with him. And since I had been so busy during the school year, the summers had quickly become my favorite.

Now when I looked up at the sky rise building in front of me, it suddenly hit me that I'd never have a real summer again. But I didn't dare say that to James. If it was up to him I'd never work. Even just thinking about that made me bored out of my mind. And now I wouldn't even have any friends to hang out with during the days while he was at work like I'd normally have in the summer. Everyone around me was suddenly a grown up and I refused to be left behind.

"You ready?" James asked. He dropped my hand and opened up the door for me.

"As ready as I can be."

I had been inside the building countless times. Lunches, late dinners, just to stop in and say hi. Even a few late night rendezvous, which I hoped he wouldn't want to repeat now that I was going to be coworkers with all these people. James owned the whole building, but he rented it out to lots of businesses. His company was located on the top two stories. At one point I thought his office had the nicest view of the city, but now I thought that title belonged to our apartment.

He smiled at me as he pressed the button for the elevator.

"Stop looking at me like that." I smiled back at him.

"Like what?"

"In that way you do."

He leaned forward. "You mean, in that way where I'm undressing you with my eyes and wishing I was about to fuck you in the elevator?"

My face had turned redder with each word that came out of his mouth.

"I'm not sure this not touching you thing is going to work out so well," he said.

I laughed and quickly stepped onto the elevator.

He leaned against the elevator wall next to me. His arm brushed against mine. "Sorry," he whispered.

He was going to try to be distracting all day. There was no way he was actually going to try and keep things professional. I was starting to wonder why he really hired me.

I followed him out of the elevator and up to the reception desk. His office was to the right. The blinds were drawn along the glass walls. He usually kept them open during the day. I could feel my face blushing again. Now that I thought about it, I was pretty sure the last time I had been here we had to close those blinds. *Geez, no one's going to take me seriously here.*

"Good morning, Mr. Hunter. Good morning, Penny," the receptionist, Nita, said. She was already busy typing something on her computer.

"Good morning, Nita," James said and tapped on the desk. "Penny's joining the marketing team with the new interns. Can you take her over? I need to hop on a conference call."

Nita smiled. "Of course. I didn't realize you accepted the position."

"It was kind of a last minute decision," James said for me. "See you at lunch." He kissed my cheek and walked over to his office.

My face was going to be red all day. I turned around and quickly followed Nita into the expanse of cubicles. Even though there were cubicles, it wasn't like other offices I had seen since moving to New York. It was more laid back, but still professional. The dress code was business casual, but the tech guys pushed it a little. Some of them wore t-shirts underneath their suit jackets. And there was always a hacky sack being kicked around the break room. The first time I had come, I had been surprised. James was always so professional. But maybe he just had to be since he was the boss.

The walls were bright colors and they changed depending on the department. And the smaller departments had desks in quadrants instead of cubicles. Each pod of desks didn't have any separations between them except for the employees' belongings and computers.

The marketing department was huge and its color scheme was lime green. The walls were lime green, the desks were black with lime green chairs, and even the staplers were lime green. It was made up mostly of cubicles, but Nita walked me over to one of the few desk pods.

"This is going to be you." Nita winked at me.

There was nameplate on my desk and beside it was a huge bouquet of flowers. *Oh my God.* It wasn't PDA, but it was still ridiculously inappropriate. And I couldn't even hide them anywhere since my desk was open to everyone. *Crap. Maybe I can put them under my desk?* None of the other interns were there yet.

"Everyone else is in the conference room," Nita said. "You're a few minutes late, but I'm sure they didn't start without you."

Shit. "Thanks, Nita!" I hurried over to the conference room she pointed to and quickly went inside. "Hi, I'm so sorry I'm late, Andy." The three other interns were all staring at me, but my boss smiled.

"It's fine, Penny." He scratched the back of his neck awkwardly. "And most people here call me Anderson."

"Oh, sorry Andy...erson." I coughed awkwardly. James always called him Andy. And when we had met during my interview he hadn't corrected me. This wasn't exactly a great start. I could feel the interns staring at me like I was an alien. I pressed my lips together. Maybe I just shouldn't say anything else.

"Penny, this is Tavon, Zach, and Sierra," Anderson said and pointed to the two guys and one other girl in the room. Tavon had tight braids that ended right above his neck and he seemed really laid back. I would have guessed he belonged in the tech department if I had just run into him in the building. He didn't attempt at all to hide his yawn. Zach was the opposite of him. He looked super intense and super serious. He had dark hair almost buzzed right against his scalp. I could see a tattoo peaking out the top of his dress shirt. And Sierra looked as nervous as I felt. She had curly blonde hair and she was holding her purse like she thought a mugger might snatch it. Maybe she was new to New York. Either way, I thought we might get along pretty well.

"Hi, guys." I waved awkwardly. They all said hi to me.

"So this is our new marketing team, full of fresh ideas. We're going to be bouncing off all our pitches on you guys. And you'll even be getting an account of your own that I'll supervise. I think we can all learn a lot from each other, and hopefully this will be the experience that you've been seeking. Or if you're looking for a more permanent position in the future, this is definitely the way in. There's an orientation meeting in a few minutes. All the new interns from the different departments have to go. Let me show you to your desks so you can drop off your stuff first."

Great. No time to hide the flowers.

Anderson walked us over to our desks. "I'll be right back. I have to grab a few notes for the meeting."

As soon as he walked away, Tavon plopped down in the desk next to mine and put his hands behind his head. "Damn, your boyfriend doesn't wait long to make sure everyone stays away."

"No, he doesn't." I tried not to look embarrassed as I sat down.

"Well, I guess your fiancé," Sierra said. "Your ring is amazing." She sat down on the other side of me. "Can I see?"

God, I didn't want to have to be doing this right now. "Thanks," I said and put my hand out for her to see. "Yeah, we're getting married at the end of the month actually."

"This must have cost a fortune," Sierra said and looked back up at my face.

I just shrugged. I didn't know how much it cost and didn't want to know.

"How old are you?" Tavon asked.

"22. Same as all of you I assume."

"Right. So aren't you a little young to get married? Geez, I can't even imagine dating a girl for more than a few weeks. And you're going to marry someone in a couple of weeks? Aren't you worried you're going to get bored with him?"

"Don't freak her out, Tavon," Zach said. He sat down at the desk diagonally from mine. "I'm sure she's not marrying a guy like you."

"Yeah because I'm not whipped. I wouldn't send a girl flowers on her first day of work. It's kinda desperate."

"I think it's romantic." Sierra gave me a small smile. "I wish a guy would send me flowers."

"Then you probably shouldn't date Tavon," I said.

Sierra and Zach both laughed.

I ran my thumb across my engagement ring. I wanted to think James had given me flowers to be sweet. But I think Tavon's first thought was more accurate. James wanted to make sure no one flirted with me. He didn't have anything to worry about. I don't know why he didn't realize that. Or maybe he was just trying to embarrass me because I was giving him a hard time about the PDA thing.

"So, who's the lucky guy?" Tavon asked.

Before I had a chance to answer, Andy came back over and said it was time to head down to the meeting. *Anderson.* That was going to take some time to get used to.

I didn't want to lie to anyone, but I was glad I didn't have to tell them yet. I wanted to make friends with my coworkers and it was going to be hard once they knew I was engaged to the boss. There was no reason why I should be treated differently just because of my relationship with James.

***

Zach leaned on the armrest and whispered in my ear. "So what happened to your eye?"

I immediately removed my arm from the armrest and nodded to the person standing up in front of the large conference room. It was the head of the human resources department and he was talking about all sorts of rules and regulations. "Pay attention," I whispered back. *Pay attention?* Zach was going to think it was something crazy if I avoided the question. "I mean nothing," I whispered again. "I'm clumsy. I hit my face on a doorknob when I bent over to get something the other day."

"Really? It kind of looks like someone hit you."

"Well, no one did. And what would you even know about that?"

"What, you think I haven't been in my fair share of fights?" He looked back up at the director of human resources.

Just because he had a tattoo and a buzz cut didn't make him a tough guy. He was a marketing intern probably from some prestigious school. I rolled my eyes and tried to listen to the sexual harassment policy. I knew my bruise was still visible despite what James said. I lightly touched my cheek but immediately dropped my hand when I could feel Zach's eyes on me again.

"Oh my God, there he is," Sierra whispered from the other side of me.

I looked over to where she was pointing. James had just walked into the room. As soon as I made eye contact with him he smiled.

"He's so dreamy," Sierra whispered.

Yes, he is. "I'm pretty sure he's engaged," I said instead. I had become just as territorial as him. Other girls thought he was dreamy, but he was mine.

"Of course a guy like him is engaged. Do you think we'll get to meet him?"

I didn't have to answer, because the human resources guy had just introduced James and all the interns had started clapping. There were about four interns for every department in Hunter Tech, which meant there were about 50 of us.

James walked up to the podium and raised his hand to silence everyone. "Welcome to Hunter Technologies," James said. It was strange seeing him up there. It felt like I was back in school listening to one of his lectures. He was completely in his element and I felt a pang of guilt. We hadn't talked about it much since moving here, but I wondered if he missed it.

"Even his voice is sexy," Sierra said.

I wasn't sure how much I liked her anymore. I silently laughed at myself. Surely Sierra wouldn't be saying those things if she knew I was engaged to him. I just needed to ignore her until I finally told them. It wasn't like I hadn't experienced the way other women were around him. He had this magnetism that no one seemed to be immune to. Everyone loved him. If only his parents would open their eyes. I realized I was so in my own head that I was missing his speech.

"Each one of you is going to become a vital part of that. But since each department is part of the whole, I think it's important for us all to work together. We're extremely goal oriented here. And right now our goal is growth. So when working on your individual assignments, make sure to keep the main goal in mind. I know that together we can grow this company to be larger than Blive Tech International.

"And if you have any ideas, don't hesitate to share them. I see so much potential in each and every one of you and I'm not putting a cap on anything. Work between departments. Don't let the colors of the walls fool you, you're allowed to enter a color that your desk isn't in."

Everyone laughed.

"Putting what you learned in school into action is one of the most rewarding feelings. The department heads are meant to foster that experience, so go to them with any questions and insights. I think we have a great new team here and I think we can all learn from each other. And trust me, working in the real world is a lot more than just application of principles. You still have so much to learn. Your education doesn't stop once you throw your cap in the air. Welcome to the real world, class of 2018."

Everyone started clapping. James and I didn't talk about his work very much. He had helped me study so often that his work had taken a spot on the backburner recently. I knew about his current projects in principle, but I didn't really know what he did on a daily basis. I had never thought about myself as being self centered, but I had been recently. I wanted to do something nice for him. To show him how much I appreciated everything he'd done for me.

"You okay, Fight Club?" Zach asked. He was standing up, looking down at me. I hadn't realized that everyone was leaving the room.

"Yeah." I quickly stood up. "And don't call me that. I wasn't in a fight."

"Mhm."

I really hoped that nickname didn't stick. I looked over my shoulder to see James talking to some of the interns in the front row. It was only a few hours until lunch, but it felt like I hadn't gotten to talk to him in forever. Or taste him. *What?* He wasn't an addict. I was.

CHAPTER 12
Monday

I was sitting in James' favorite pizza place, Totonno's Pizzeria, which had become my favorite pizza in the city. It wasn't just that the pizza was amazing, the people were so nice.

"Hi, dear. Where's James today?" Marie, the little old woman who owned the place sat down across from me with a huge smile.

"He's meeting me here any minute."

"I'll go put your usual order in. I just wanted to come over and see how your first day was going."

I smiled. I was glad I was on Marie's good side, because she had seemed suspicious of me the first few times I had come here. That side of her was scary intimidating, but now she was as nice as could be. It was so sweet how much she seemed to care about James. "It's good. Kind of overwhelming."

"You'll be used to it in no time."

"I know. And the other interns seem nice enough." They had invited me to eat with them in the break room, but I had told them I already had plans. Which resulted in Tavon teasing me about my overbearing boyfriend. If only he knew. Maybe tomorrow I should eat lunch with them, though. I wanted to be one of them. But right now all I wanted was a kiss from James and to tell him how much I loved him.

"Let me go put your order in so it's ready when he gets here."

"Thanks, Marie."

My phone started vibrating in my purse a minute after she left. I pulled it out and ran my thumb across the screen. The caller ID said Hunter Technologies. Hopefully I hadn't forgotten about some important meeting for all the interns or something. "Hello?"

"Hi, Penny, it's Nita."

"Hi, Nita. Do you know if James has left for lunch yet?" I looked out the window at the passing cars.

"That's why I'm calling. He had a last minute meeting. He's tied up and can't make it."

"Oh. Okay, thanks for calling, Nita." I hung up and looked down at my phone. I wished he had told me before I had taken the subway all the way here.

***

I stepped out of the subway car with the pizza box in my hand and made my way up the stairs. The sun was blinding as I made my way outside after being underground. I wasn't sure how often I'd be able to go to Totonno's with James during lunch. My break was already almost over and I had quickly eaten a slice in the restaurant because I hated eating alone. I wasn't sure why I thought leisurely lunches were in the job description for interns.

I walked into the building and got onto the elevator. The last thing I wanted was to be late getting back from lunch when I was already late this morning. Hopefully James' meeting would be over and I could drop the pizza off for him real quick. I had five minutes to make my way through the cubicle maze. I quickly got off the elevator and walked up to the reception desk.

Nita wasn't sitting there. Maybe she was on her break. I looked over at James' office. The blinds were closed. I hoped he hadn't left and tried to meet me down there anyway. I walked over and put my face close to the window to see if I could see him through the slants in the blinds.

What the fuck?! I grabbed the handle of his office door.

"Penny?"

I jumped. I released the doorknob and turned around to see Nita staring at me. "Sorry, I wasn't sure if he was in..."

"He's still in his meeting, Penny. He asked me to make sure no one disturbed him. I can give you a call when he's free if you want?"

"No. That's okay, Nita." *What the hell?* I started to walk away but quickly went back over to her. "Could you give him this though?" I put the pizza box down on the reception desk. "Thanks," I said and walked away without waiting for her response.

My heart was beating out of my chest. Maybe I was wrong. It was just the back of her head. *Fuck. No.* It was definitely Isabella. I kept my eyes on the ground as I made my way toward my desk. What was he doing talking to her? Did he seriously stand me up to have lunch with that bitch? I knew there was nothing going on between them, but I couldn't help the jealously that seemed to surge through me. What on earth could they be talking about? After she had slapped me, I thought he'd never speak to her again. Instead they were having a nice, private chat in his office. Why couldn't she just leave us alone?

"You okay, Fight Club?" Tavon asked. "You look like you've seen a ghost."

Had that nickname seriously already spread to him too? I sat down in my chair without looking up. "I'm fine. Are you two seriously going to call me that for the whole summer?"

"That's what happens when you ditch us for lunch," he said. "And when you come to work the first day with a black eye."

"It's just a tiny little bruise, it's not a black eye. You're exaggerating. I just ran into something."

"That's rather vague. Did you run into something like someone's fist?"

"Ignore them," Sierra said. "How was lunch with your fiancé?"

"Great," I lied and turned on my computer. We were supposed to be doing research the rest of the afternoon and I had a feeling that meant all of us were going to be chatting while we did it. I didn't feel like talking. I felt like killing Isabella.

"Where did you go to school?" Sierra asked.

"NYCU," I said. Maybe conversation would help me not explode. "What about you guys?"

"I went there too," Zach said. "I'm surprised we didn't have any classes together."

"It's a big school."

"Yeah but they lump all the freshman into those huge lecture halls. We were probably at least in one of those together and didn't realize it."

"I wasn't there freshman year though."

"Where did you go before that?"

"The University of New Castle."

"Why the switch?" Sierra asked. "I went to my state school in South Dakota and I loved it. Moving here has been quite the transition. I guess it was for you at first too?"

I had been right about her not being from around here. South Dakota was pretty far away. I shrugged my shoulders. "It was at first. I love it now though, you will too. And I wasn't bashing state schools. I loved my old school at first too." I was talking too much.

"So what changed?" she asked.

I turned my attention back to my screen. "Just...personal reasons."

Tavon laughed.

Of all the things to say. I should have just made up something super believable. Like my parents moved. But no, I said personal reasons. I could feel my face turning red.

"Fight Club, you can't just dangle that in front of us and not explain."

My phone started vibrating. *Thank God.* I pulled it out of my purse and saw that James was calling me. I'd talk to him after work. I put it down on my desk, ignoring it. It took me a second to realize that all three of them were staring at me.

"What? I'm sorry, did you say something?"

"Secret fiancé, secret troubled past, a secret black eye..." Tavon had counted off the secrets on his fingers so that he was holding them up in front of me. "You're quite mysterious, Penny."

"Shouldn't we be working?"

"The boss said we're supposed to bond. And the three of us already did while you were sneaking off somewhere secretive for lunch. Yet another secret."

My phone started buzzing again. I didn't bother looking at the caller ID, I just ignored it.

"And you're trying to avoid someone."

"Leave her alone," Zach said. "Clearly she doesn't want to talk about it."

I couldn't help but think he was being nice because he thought I had an abusive fiancé. And he probably thought that I had tried to escape from the abuse by moving to New York. Why had I said personal reasons?

My phone vibrated again. I picked it up. "I'm a little busy right now. Can this wait till after work?"

James sighed. "I figured you saw her when I had pizza waiting for me. I'm sorry about lunch. Can you please come to my office real quick so I can explain?"

I tried to lower my voice. "After work. Please, James."

"You're upset. I just want to tell you why she was here. If you're worried about people knowing, just say you need to go to the bathroom and excuse yourself."

I didn't care why Isabella was there. I didn't care about anything she had to say. What I cared about was why he decided to talk to her and keep me out of the loop. He let me wander off to Brooklyn so I'd be out of the way. It felt dirty and I just needed some time to calm down about it. "Later. Please." I hung up.

All three of my pod mates were staring at me. I glued my eyes to my computer screen and tried to read the article I had found earlier about one of Hunter Tech's competitors.

"Was that your fiancé?" Tavon asked. "Seems a little controlling."

"Nope. Telemarketer."

"The mystery grows."

My phone vibrated again.

"Aren't you going to answer James the telemarketer's phone call?" Tavon asked.

"I'll let it go to voicemail this time," I said and continued to stare at the computer screen without actually reading anything. "Dirty spammers."

"Oh my God, he's coming over here," Sierra said.

I looked over my shoulder. James was walking toward our pod of desks. I looked back at my computer. "I'm sure he's on his way to talk to Anderson or something."

"I think he's coming to talk to us!" Sierra sounded way too excited.

"Chill out, stalker," Tavon said.

"How's the new marketing team getting on?" James asked as he stopped by my desk.

Son of a bitch. I glanced at him from out of the corner of my eye.

"Really great," Sierra said. Her voice oozed with charm.

"And what about you guys?" James asked. "Settling in okay?"

They both nodded their heads. "This place is awesome," Tavon said. "So much cooler than the place I interned at last summer."

"Glad to hear it." James tapped on the top of my desk with the knuckle of his index finger. "Can I have a quick word, Miss Taylor?"

"We have these assignments from Anderson that we really have to get done by the end of the day," I said.

Sierra's jaw visibly dropped.

"Trust me, Anderson won't mind," James said. "It'll just take a minute."

Now he calls him Anderson. "Of course." I got up and followed James away from my desk.

"Fight Club has connections," I heard Tavon say as I walked away.

It felt like everyone's eyes were on me as I followed James to his office. This kind of thing was exactly what I hadn't wanted. The other marketing interns were probably looking me up right now. I'd get back to my desk in a minute and they'd all know. I was going to tell them eventually. But I wanted to make friends with them first. I didn't want them to judge me. Shouldn't they though? The only reason I got this job was because of James.

He opened up his office door for me and I walked in past him. The pizza box was open on his desk and a few slices were missing. My anger and self doubt had made me hungry after barely eating anything for lunch. I grabbed a slice and sat down in one of the chairs by his desk, not making eye contact with him.

"How's your first day going?" James sat down on the edge of his desk directly in front of me. It was the same place he had been sitting when Isabella was there. Luckily she had been standing or I'd want to burn the chair.

"Really great. They're all calling me Fight Club because of my black eye that your lunch date, who you stood me up for, gave me."

He laughed but quickly stopped when he saw my facial expression. "She actually came to apologize about that. And for the surprise appearance at the party."

"Maybe she should have talked to me instead of you then. You seriously couldn't take two seconds to tell me you couldn't make lunch?"

"I thought she came to make a scene. It wouldn't be the first time. And now I have you here to worry about embarrassing too. It seemed like the best option was to hear her out."

"So is that how it's going to be our whole lives? You're just constantly going to put her first?" I knew it wasn't fair. He had talked to her in part to avoid her embarrassing me. But I was pissed. And hadn't he just embarrassed me? He knew I wanted to keep things professional here and he just completely threw that out the window because I asked him if we could wait and talk after work. He hadn't gotten his way so he disregarded everything I had asked him not to do. He was being ridiculous.

"No. She actually came to tell me that she wants me to be happy. She won't be bothering us anymore."

"Well, I'm glad you got the closure you needed. I thought the divorce had handled that. But what do I know?"

"You're seriously upset that I talked to Isabella for a few minutes?" He crossed his arms in front of his chest. "You know how I feel about her. There's no reason to be upset."

"I'm allowed to be upset! You can't control my emotions when you control everything else."

"I don't..."

"Why am I here, James? I applied to dozens of places. How could I not have heard back from a single one? What did you do?"

"I thought you'd want to work with..."

"I would have told you if this was what I wanted. It's not. I know that everyone is going to judge me when they find out we're together. Which you kind of just gave away. I needed to do this on my own. I want to be independent. I don't want to have to rely on you for everything."

"Penny..."

"You don't respect me." I stood up and threw the rest of my pizza slice in the trashcan. "At all. Now can we please just talk about this at home like a normal couple?"

His mouth was set in a straight line. I knew I had hurt him. But for one second I wanted to focus on what I wanted instead of what he did. Ever since we had moved here I had tried to give him everything he needed. I had been hyper focused on making him happy. And I had completely forgotten about what I wanted somewhere along the way. He couldn't always get his way. This was my life too.

CHAPTER 13
Monday

I sat down on a bench outside of the Tavern on the Green. In less than two weeks we'd be saying our vows under the huge tree with the shimmering lanterns that I loved so much. I wasn't having second thoughts. Not for a second. I loved James with every fiber of my being. Sometimes I just wished he could hear me.

During the orientation meeting I had thought about how much I owed him. But I had given up a lot for him too. And sometimes I worried that I lost myself when I moved here. He was complicated and unique and all consuming. And I was just me. It was easy to feel invisible. Which wasn't really fair to say. If anything, James was the first person that had ever truly seen me. How could I feel seen and invisible at the same time?

I closed my eyes and tried to focus on the feeling of the sun on my face. I was just frustrated because school was my thing and Hunter Tech was his thing. And now I didn't have a thing. I didn't want to follow him around like a lost puppy. Maybe I was having an identity crisis.

I pulled my legs up on the bench and hugged my knees to my chest. I took a deep breath and opened my eyes, staring at the big tree again. In twelve days I'd be Mrs. Hunter. That was a new identity. It felt like my heart was beating out my chest. I leaned forward and put my elbows on my knees and my head between them. It felt like I couldn't breathe. It was all too much change too soon. I was never good at change and this was a million things at once. I had tried to tell James that it was too much but he hadn't listened. I put my face in my hands.

"I thought I might find you here."

I lifted my face out of my hands and up at James. He looked so worried. Why did it always seem like I was hurting him?

"Having second thoughts?" He looked over his shoulder at our wedding venue.

"No. Never. James, I'm so sorry about today. I don't know what's wrong with me. I'm so, so sorry, I just..."

"Stop. You don't have anything to apologize about." He sat down and grabbed my hand. "I'm the one that's sorry. I'm still learning about how all this works."

"God." I wiped my tears away with the back of my hand. "Still learning how what works? Me?" I laughed. I didn't even understand myself half the time. How could I expect him to?

"Love. This." He rubbed his thumb along my palm. "Us. Please don't give up on me."

His words made even more tears fall down my cheeks. "I'm not. I'm just so embarrassed. You're allowed to talk to whoever you want. You're allowed to change your lunch plans. I don't know why I even freaked out."

"I didn't want to talk to Isabella. She came to see me. I didn't want her to make a scene..."

"I know. You already explained it. It's fine."

He squeezed my hand. "She asked if we could start over as friends. I told her that we could be civil if we run into each other in public, but nothing more. I told her if she ever stepped foot inside my office ever again I'd have her thrown out. And I said if she ever reached out to you or me I'd get a restraining order against her. I know I can talk to whoever I want, but I don't want to talk to her. Ever again. I have a past. I can't change what's happened, but I will never, ever put someone before you. I can promise you that."

"I know. I didn't mean what I said. It's just...with graduating and moving and planning the wedding, and then meeting your parents and seeing Isabella, and starting this new job..." I let my voice trail off. "Geez, of course no one else wanted to hire me. I needed a week off for our honeymoon almost immediately. But I didn't even get to the interview process to tell anyone about that." I felt so inadequate.

"About that..."

"You knew no one would hire me because of that, didn't you? I'm such an idiot. I was giving you a hard time and you were just being nice and offering me a job because no one else..."

"No." He cleared his throat. "You were right before. I screened your applications."

"What does that mean exactly?"

He shrugged. "I made it clear that you were working at Hunter Tech. I'd rather not go into the specifics."

I started laughing. "You're infuriating. You do realize that, right?" I couldn't seem to stop laughing.

He smiled and wiped one of my tears away with his thumb. I was pretty sure they were tears from laughing now.

When I finally calmed down, I sighed. "I think I've just been really stressed out. For the past few years I've been so focused on finishing school and officially becoming an adult, that I forgot to plan for this point." I had been so eager to graduate. All those extra classes to make up for the semester I had lost switching schools. Maybe I had rushed all of this. Now I was officially an adult and I felt lost.

"That's why I thought fixing you up with a good job..."

"But you should have talked to me about it. Your intentions are always good, but I want my opinion to count."

"It does. And I do respect you. If I made you feel like that wasn't the case, I'm sorry." He cupped my face in his hand. "But I like taking care of you. You can't expect me to just sit here and see you struggling and not try to fix it."

I grabbed his hand and pulled it onto my lap. "Do you ever think sometimes that it was easier when you were my professor?"

He laughed. "No."

"But everything was so clear cut. We each knew where we stood."

"Penny, I never knew where you stood."

I laughed. "Maybe you're right. I just thought this boss/intern thing would be a little easier if we just stuck to those roles and didn't mix in our personal relationship."

"Penny, I don't want to sneak around. I thought we were done with that when we moved here. We're getting married at the end of the month. All I ever want to do is be with you. And when we're not together I want to talk about you. If you're embarrassed..."

"I'm not embarrassed about us. That's not it. I just didn't want all my new coworkers to judge me before they got to know me."

"Knowing that we're together is part of getting to know you."

"I know. You're right. And I'm pretty sure one of the guys I work with thinks I'm in an abusive relationship because I'm being too secretive about everything."

James laughed. "Wait, really?"

"I don't know. I'm a bad liar. It wasn't a terrible conclusion with all the weird stuff I said all day. And I don't recommend starting a new job with a black eye. You told me you couldn't see it."

He shrugged. "You can barely see it."

I lightly shoved his shoulder. "Oh and by the way, Andy prefers being called Anderson. What's up with that? You always call him Andy."

"Well yeah, his employees call him Anderson. His friends call him Andy."

"James! You could have told me that."

He laughed and put his arm around my shoulders, pulling me closer to him. "I know it's a lot of change really fast. But we can figure this out together. If you haven't discovered your passion yet, you have plenty of time. We have our whole lives to figure it out."

His words should have been soothing, but it made me realize what I probably already knew and just didn't know how to admit. I already knew my passion. It was him. And being in love with him wasn't exactly a career path.

"If you want to take some time off to figure it out, you can," he said. "You don't have to jump right into this internship. And if you decide you do want it later, there's always another program in the fall."

"No, I want to do it. I already got special permission from my boss for a week off. It seems mean to flake out now."

"I was hoping you'd say that. And maybe tomorrow you can tell all the new friends you made today that you're shagging the boss."

"Telling them we're engaged sound so much better."

"Going all in right away?"

"Sierra keeps talking about how sexy you are and it makes me extremely uncomfortable."

He laughed. "You sound jealous."

"I'm not jealous." I bit my lip. "Fine, maybe a little. But what about the flowers you sent me? Marking your territory right away?"

"I sent you flowers because I'm an awesome fiancé and I love you."

I stared at him skeptically.

"And I wanted to force you to tell everyone we were together. Like I said, I'm done sneaking around. Besides, I haven't locked you down until you say 'I do.' I'm not going to risk losing you to a younger man at the last minute."

I laughed. "You have absolutely nothing to worry about. Before we know it, we'll be married. Right there." I gestured to the tree in front of us.

He kissed my temple. "I can't wait."

CHAPTER 14
Tuesday

I stepped out of the shower and wrapped a towel around myself. James was watching me through the reflection in the mirror. He had that look in his eyes that instantly made me wet. My eyes gravitated down his body. He was only wearing a pair of boxer briefs and he was clearly just as excited as me. But there was no way he was going to make me late again today. I walked out of the bathroom and tried to focus on what I was going to wear instead.

Before I had even made it to the closet, he grabbed me around the waist and lifted me over his shoulder.

I laughed as he threw me down onto the bed.

"I've been thinking," I said and put my hand on his chest as he leaned down to kiss me. "It's only a couple weeks to the wedding now. Maybe we shouldn't."

"Shouldn't what?" He put his hand on the knot that was holding my towel in place.

"Have sex." I grabbed his hand before he could undo my towel.

"What? Why?"

"I mean, that's a thing that people do. They wait to make the first time after the wedding special."

He laughed. "That's not a thing."

"Yes it is." I smiled up at him.

"Fine, it is. But it's not something we're going to do. You don't really want to, do you?"

"I don't know." I bit my lip.

"We're already indulging in a life of sin." He leaned between my legs, pressing his erection against me, and lightly kissed my neck. "So much sin." He bit my earlobe.

I swallowed down the moan that wanted to escape.

"Besides, you really think you can resist me for two weeks?" He untied my towel and cupped my left breast in his hand, teasing my nipple as he left a trail of kisses down my stomach.

My body squirmed beneath his. He was right. There was no way we'd be able to resist each other for that long.

He kissed my hipbone and then suddenly stopped. He smiled up at me. "Okay, game on. We'll see who breaks first."

"What? You can't just tease me like that."

He laughed. "I'm totally going to win."

"James it's not a game. And let's start tomorrow."

"No way. I have you right where I want you." He kissed my hipbone again and stood up.

"You're not serious?"

"It was your idea. Hurry up, we're going to be late." He disappeared into the closet.

Of course he turned it into a game. And he was right. He probably would win. His ass looked so amazing in those boxers.

***

"Have you told them all about your awesome fiancé that you're withholding sex from yet?"

I laughed. "No, I'm going to tell them after lunch." Today was already going better, although, the nickname Fight Club had seemed to stick. I picked at my salad. I had vowed to eat healthier before the wedding. And Ellen had packed me a lunch that consisted of virtually nothing edible.

James pushed half his sandwich toward me. I didn't hesitate to pick it up and take a huge bite.

"I don't know why you're pretending to go on a diet before the wedding," he said.

"It's the principle of the thing. I'm supposed to look my very best."

"You do."

"Is that so?" I hitched my skirt up a little and watched his eyes wander up my thighs. Maybe I could win this game. I'd have to ask Ellen to pack me a banana in my lunch tomorrow. I could definitely work with that.

"I have a lot of self control, Penny." He grabbed his sandwich back out of my hand.

"Is that why you slept with one of your students?"

He raised his left eyebrow. "The pros outweighed the cons on that one. I could have controlled myself. I just chose not to."

"Sure."

"Mhm. You have something right there." He pointed to the side of my mouth.

I wiped the side of my lip.

"Other side." He leaned forward and slid his thumb along the corner of my mouth, staring into my eyes.

Fuck. Why is that so hot?

I quickly stood up. "Well, I should probably get back to work." I grabbed the rest of my salad and tossed it in the trash, leaning over to make sure he got a good look at my ass.

"You're playing dirty."

I turned around to look at him. "So are you."

He flashed me one of his smiles that always made my knees weak. "Are you still meeting up with Melissa and Tyler tonight?"

Just thinking about it made my stomach churn. "Yeah. I figure the three of us need to talk. I don't want to put it off."

He nodded. "I'll just meet you back home later then. I'm cutting out early today. I have a few errands to run." He stood up, grabbed my waist, and pulled me in close, planting a passionate kiss against my lips.

If I thought my knees were weak before, I didn't even know how to describe this feeling. He squeezed my ass, pressing his body even more firmly against mine. When he pulled back, I was completely breathless.

"I'm totally going to win," he whispered in my ear and released me.

I knew I hadn't wanted it to be a game, but now I was determined to win. "I have a few tricks up my sleeves too."

"Bring it on, baby." He sat back down at his desk chair and turned on his monitor.

I closed the door behind me. I needed to think of something super sexy to do. I was so preoccupied while I walked back to my desk that I'm pretty sure Sierra had called my name a few times before grabbing my elbow.

"Were you just having lunch with James Hunter?" Sierra squealed.

"Umm..."

"I just saw you come out of his office."

We had reached our desks.

"What are you so excited about?" Zach asked Sierra.

"Penny's secret rendezvous with James Hunter during lunch."

"Is that why you keep ditching us for lunch?" Tavon asked. "You're eating with the boss instead? I feel slighted."

"Well, yes and no." Now was as good a time as any. Especially since I had gotten caught red handed. "I..."

"Wait!" Tavon said cutting me off. "Let us all guess what you were doing."

I sat down. "I'm just going to tell you."

"No, this is more fun. Zach, you guess first."

He shook his head. "She was probably complaining about a super annoying new coworker."

Tavon laughed. "I'm sure she was complaining about you. What is your guess, Sierra?"

Sierra stared at me for a second. "Working her way to the top?" She giggled at the thought.

I could feel my face turning red.

"Oh, shit!" Tavon said with a laugh. "You're cheating on your fiancé with your boss, aren't you? Classic."

"No." My voice sounded way more defensive than I intended it to.

"Yes you are! Your face is bright red. How the hell did you pull that one off? He's like the most eligible bachelor in the city."

"Wait, I thought you said he was engaged?" Sierra said.

"This just keeps getting better and better!" Tavon said before I could reply. "You're engaged, he's engaged, and you're both cheating and sleeping with each other. That's pretty fucked up."

"You're such an idiot. Clearly he's her fiancé," Zach said. He was staring at me intently. "James the telemarketer, I'm guessing?"

"Yes. Zach wins."

"Oh my God, what?!" Sierra squealed again. Her voice was starting to hurt my ears. "You're engaged to James Hunter? Are you serious? You're so lucky."

Tavon snickered. "So Sierra was kind of right. You slept your way into this job."

"Dude," Zach said. "You shouldn't be messing with her now. If I remember correctly, you made some pretty shitty hypotheses about her fiancé before you knew who he was."

"Penny," Tavon said. "We're cool right? Obviously James Hunter isn't whipped or desperate or controlling. I didn't mean it."

I laughed. "He actually is controlling. It's fine. I'm not going to tell him you said that."

"Wait, I think I remember reading about this," Sierra said. "James Hunter took a break from corporate America after selling Blive Tech International." She snapped her fingers. "He was a professor at some school for a year or something. And he got fired for sleeping with a few of his students."

"He resigned. And it was just one student." *What is wrong with people?*

"You?"

"I'm going to go get some coffee. Anybody want anything?" When no one said anything, I got up and walked toward the break room. They didn't need any other specifics. Everything they wanted to know was online. I'd hide out here for a few minutes until they were done looking. I grabbed a mug, poured myself a cup, and walked over to the sugar. When I turned around, Zach was standing there with his arms folded in front of his chest.

"So the bruise?" He touched his cheek. "Was that him?"

Oh God. "No." I tried to walked past him, but he blocked my path.

"If you don't want to talk to me about it, you should talk to someone you..."

"No, I actually mean no. It wasn't him."

"Who was it then?"

"Why don't you believe me?"

"Well, for one, you're avoiding the question."

"I'm not. I'm just..."

"So tell me then. If it's not him, it shouldn't matter."

"Fine, you got me. I'm actually in a Fight Club."

Zach laughed.

"Really. And I can't talk about it. The first rule about Fight Club is that you don't talk about Fight Club. I don't want to be kicked out."

He laughed again. "You're too scrawny."

"You wanna bet?"

"Look, if you have a nickname for what your fiancé calls slapping you around, it doesn't make it any better. You can lie to me but you shouldn't lie to yourself."

I tucked a loose strand of hair behind my ear. I didn't want to be talking about this with a stranger. "I'm not lying. And I don't see why this is any of your business."

"It's not." He stared at me for another second before grabbing a cup of coffee for himself. It didn't seem like he believed me at all. "But you admitted that he's controlling and if he's hurting you..."

"He's not. Zach can you please just drop it? You can call me Fight Club as much as you want, but I don't want to talk about this."

"Okay, Fight Club," he said and shrugged his shoulders. "I was just trying to help."

"So why are you such an expert on this anyway?" He had spiked my interest. The tattoos and the tough look seemed to just be a show. He seemed kind and intuitive and for some reason genuinely cared about my safety. Maybe some kind of dark past. Everyone should be asking him questions, not me.

"I don't see why that's any of your business." He winked at me and walked back toward our desks.

I rolled my eyes and followed him out of the break room. I knew he was just trying to be nice, but I didn't appreciate all his prying. Especially if he wasn't willing to give anything away about himself either.

"You have quite the sensational past," Sierra said as I sat back down.

I shrugged my shoulders.

"So let me get this straight," Tavon said. "You fucked your professor. Got caught. Lost your scholarship to the University of New Castle and the respect of your peers. And had to switch schools because of all the scandalous rumors?"

"I chose to transfer to NYCU. We wanted a fresh start."

"So how did you pay for it? NYCU is an expensive college. Especially without instate tuition."

God.

"I'm going to take your silence as confirmation for what I already thought. James Hunter paid for your education. And he obviously got you this job. Everything in your life has been handed to you. This is kind of bullshit. Do you know how hard I had to work to land this internship? How many interviews we all had to do before we got accepted?"

"My transcript is just as good as yours or I wouldn't be here."

"I think we all know that's not true."

"I think you're missing the silver lining here," Zach said.

Tavon sighed and put his hands behind his head. "Which is?"

"Penny has an in with the boss. So if we all play our cards right, we now have a connection that none of the other interns have. You should be happy about this, not pissed off." He gave me a small smile. Having him on my side could be a good thing.

"True," Tavon said. "Maybe the four of us could get drinks one night this week? And you could bring Hunter?"

"Umm..." I let my voice trail off. I didn't know what James would think about hanging out with a bunch of his interns. "I'll ask him. But we're really busy the next few weeks."

"With all the wedding planning?" Sierra asked. "It's probably going to be the most lavish wedding of the year."

I wasn't sure what she wanted me to say. Was she waiting for me to invite her? "I can ask James about getting drinks one night though," I said instead.

"I can't wait!" Sierra said. "I've always wondered what he was like outside of work. It's like hanging out with a celebrity. I'm so jealous of your life."

"If you don't tone it down Fight Club won't even ask him," Tavon said. "We'll be cool, I promise. I'll get Sierra under control."

I laughed. I glanced at Zach, but he was just staring at me skeptically. "Yeah, I'll ask James and let you guys know." I turned my attention to the computer screen. Maybe hanging out outside of work with them would help us bond. And Zach seeing James and me together might get him off my back.

CHAPTER 15
Tuesday

I grabbed the handle as soon as the door buzzed. Tyler had done well for himself in New York. He had aced his first interview and landed the job he had wanted as a business reporter. And he had already gotten a few promotions. Him moving here after he graduated had been wonderful. I think the time we spent apart allowed James to move on from everything that had happened between me and Tyler. They were actually friends now. And I guess it had been good for Tyler and me too. We still talked on the phone every now and then while he was still in Delaware, but we weren't very close anymore. As soon as he moved here, though, it was like we were best friends again. Our friendship had picked up right where it had left off, minus the sexual tension.

I stepped onto the elevator and pressed the button for the fifth floor. Transferring to NYCU had been hard. Everyone had already made friends freshman year, which left me pretty much on my own. Luckily Mason had started dating Bee. She was pretty much the only friend I had made in New York besides for James' friends. And they didn't really count because I couldn't really talk to them about anything personal, despite how inappropriate Rob was all the time. Bee was so great because even though I hadn't known her in Delaware, we could easily talk about home. We even knew a lot of the same people. And the fact that our dating situations were similar made it even easier to confide in her.

I stopped outside of Tyler's apartment. Josh had broken up with Melissa after he graduated. He didn't even want to try to attempt a long distance relationship. Melissa had been devastated. She started coming up and visiting a lot more afterwards. But now I was wondering if she was more interested in seeing Tyler than she had been in spending time with me. How long had this really been going on? How could I have not realized it? And why were they hiding it from me? I knew that Melissa thought Tyler was hot. She had repeatedly talked about his abs and thought I was crazy for not jumping at the opportunity to be with him. Had she liked him that whole time?

And Tyler hadn't dated anyone since moving to New York. At least, not that he told me about. I felt like I could talk to Tyler about anything. It hurt to realize that he didn't feel he could do the same with me. It hurt even more that Melissa wouldn't tell me about their relationship. But I had kept James a secret from both of them for a long time. Maybe I deserved to be kept out of the loop. This whole thing was so weird. I knocked on the door. I didn't want to force them to tell me about their relationship. But if I didn't bring it up, I was worried they never would.

When Tyler opened the door he had a huge smile on his face. He was still wearing a suit from work. For some reason I always expected him to be wearing jeans and a polo like he had in class. But I was the only one that seemed to be having a hard time transitioning into the real world. "Hey, Penny. It's nice getting to hang out with you on a night that isn't Friday."

Tyler and I always watched Shark Tank together on Fridays. It was our thing. James never wanted to watch it with us. We had concluded that he was just bitter that he hadn't been asked to be one of the sharks. And he didn't deny it.

"I thought it would be fun for the three of us to hang out," I said.

"Yeah." He didn't sound quite as convinced, but it could have been my imagination. "I just have to go change. I'll be right back."

I walked into his apartment and sat down on the couch. I hadn't been there since Melissa had moved in. Despite the fact that she claimed it was only temporary, her stuff was everywhere. There was only one bedroom and the couch I was sitting on hadn't been made up with a sheet or pillow or anything. They were definitely sleeping together.

Tyler came out, pulling a t-shirt over his head, and collapsed beside me on the couch. He looked exactly like he did in college when he wasn't in his work clothes. "How's the new job going?"

"It's good, I'm still getting used to..."

"Geez, what happened to your face?"

"Nothing. I'm still getting used to the dynamic at work," I continued. "I just told all my co-workers that I was marrying the boss." I laughed and kept my face turned away from him.

"If you aren't going to tell me, at least let me get you some ice or something."

"No, it's fine. I can't even feel it anymore."

"I guess you've had worse."

"Please don't tell me you still feel bad about that? That was so long ago. And it wasn't your fault."

He scratched the back of his neck. "Yeah, well..." He let his voice trail off. "You're really not going to tell me what happened?"

"I'd rather talk about something else. How's living with Melissa going?" I kicked my shoes off and tucked my legs underneath of me on the couch. I wished I had gone home and changed out of my skirt and blouse before coming over. Maybe Melissa would let me borrow something more comfortable to change into when she got here.

"Do you want a drink?" He stood up and walked toward the kitchen.

I laughed. "That good?"

"I just needed a drink."

"Okay. I'll have whatever you're having."

He grabbed two beers out of the fridge and popped the tops off before handing me one. He sat back down beside me. "No one ever told me how hard it was to live with the opposite sex."

I laughed. "It is kind of an adjustment."

He smiled at me.

"But it's just temporary?"

"I don't know." He took a huge sip of his beer. "It's nice not living alone, I mean."

"I thought you liked having your own place after living in the frat house? You went on and on about it when you moved here."

He shrugged. "People change, Penny."

"I know." I hadn't realized he was lonely. It made sense. He came home every night to an empty apartment. I don't know why I hadn't realized it sooner. If I had made any good friends in New York that were single, I would have tried to set them up with him.

"James' parents' place was really nice," he said. He adjusted himself on the couch so that his back was against the armrest and his feet were resting next to my legs.

"Yeah, I think that was the first and last time I'll ever be invited there."

"I was kind of wondering about that. Was James' ex wife really there? Isabella, right?"

"Yeah."

"Kind of strange to invite their son's ex to celebrate his new relationship."

"They were trying to scare me away. And when that didn't work they tried to pay me off."

"Seriously?" Tyler laughed. "What dicks."

I laughed. "Couldn't have said it better myself."

"And the black eye happened sometime between that night and today. I would have remembered seeing it at the party."

I knew better than to think Tyler would drop it. And it wasn't like Zach prying. Tyler cared about me. "Actually, it was Isabella. She decided to confront me after his parents' bribe, and I was upset and I called her a bitch. So she slapped me."

Tyler laughed.

"It's not funny." I pushed on his foot and he playfully kicked my thigh back.

"It's kind of funny. James sure comes with a lot of baggage."

"Well, he's tossed it all away. His parents aren't even invited to the wedding anymore."

"He's okay with that?"

"I think it's what he wanted the whole time. I was just too stubborn to see it." I bit the inside of my lip. "It was stupid, I just really wanted them to like me."

"That's not too much to ask from your future in laws."

"Apparently in this case it was."

"Are you sure you're okay?" His eyes had gravitated back to my cheek.

"Honestly the clothes I'm in are more uncomfortable than the super small bruise on my face." I moved my legs again, trying to get comfortable on the couch.

He laughed. "I already put a pair of sweats for you in the bathroom. I was wondering when you'd start complaining."

"You know me so well. I'll be right back." I got up and went to the bathroom. Sure enough, there was a pair of sweatpants and one of his University of New Castle t-shirts folded on the shelf. I quickly changed. I loved Tyler's sweatpants. They were big and comfortable. And no matter what I was wearing when I came over, I usually found something to complain about so that I'd get to change into a pair. Eating popcorn in sweats while watching Shark Tank was more accurately our thing.

It was nice to know that just because he was with Melissa now, we could still hang out like this. I made my way back out into the living room. "When is Melissa usually done work?" She had found a summer internship at a law firm nearby. In the fall she'd be going to law school. She was still waiting to hear back from where, but I was hoping it would be in the city.

"She'll be here any minute."

I wasn't sure if it was better to ask him about it now, or wait until they were together. I just wanted to get it over with. "Are you and Melissa dating?" I blurted out, before I could change my mind.

He choked on his sip of beer. "No." He cleared his throat. "I mean, why would you ask that?"

"James thought he saw something going on between you two."

"And that bothered you?" He didn't deny it this time. He wanted to know how I felt about it. That probably meant it was true.

I laughed. "No. I just...I want you both to be happy. You know that."

He didn't say anything, he just took another sip of his beer.

"But you two are my best friends. I guess if you dated...I don't know. I don't want to lose you."

"That's not really fair. You never wanted me to begin with, Penny. You can't lose what you never had."

"I mean our friendship."

He sighed. "I don't really know what to tell you."

"The couch isn't made up. I mean, it's pretty obvious that you guys are sleeping together."

"I don't really think we should be talking about this."

"But we're friends."

"It's weird, Penny. You must realize that. With our history? It's complicated to say the least."

"So, you are then?" I asked.

"This is so awkward."

"Tyler."

"I'm not going to talk about my sex life with you, Penny."

"That's what friends do."

"Not when one of those friends used to be in love with the other friend." He stood up. "Not when we've had sex. Not when I compare every girl I'm with to that night we had." He shook his head.

I didn't know that. My hanging around all the time maybe hadn't been as fun for him as it was for me.

"This is enough for me," he said. "If I can't be with you, I decided being your friend was good enough. And you are my best friend. But I can't talk to you about this. This is where I have to draw the line."

"I'm sorry."

"And I'm not going to feel guilty for hooking up with Melissa. Because I'm allowed to have a life outside of whatever this is. You do. You get to go home to James. And at least Melissa actually likes me. Or liked me. I don't know, it's complicated." He sat down on the couch again and scratched the back of his neck.

He was opening up about it. I didn't want him to close off because of our past. I didn't want to be left in the past too. "Why is it complicated?"

"Because she thinks I'm still in love with you."

I swallowed hard. I didn't want to know the answer, but it felt important to ask. If he was, I shouldn't be coming over here all the time. Or at all. And I definitely shouldn't be wearing his pants. "And?"

"I don't even know anymore. I look forward to Friday nights. I haven't really been trying to meet anyone. I've been stuck. I just wanted something less complicated. And Melissa was easy." He coughed. "Not like that. Sorry, I didn't mean it like that. I just already knew she liked me. It wasn't like it was with you. It wasn't this instant attraction. But, I don't know, our relationship slowly changed into something more. I like having someone to come home to."

"I get that."

He sighed. "I'm friends with James. I wouldn't do anything to mess that up after it took so long for him to be cool with us hanging out. Besides, it's not like how it used to be between us. I still love you, but I'm not in love with you. Melissa doesn't seem to understand the difference."

"Well I do."

"Yeah, that's how you always felt about me." He laughed and looked back up at me.

"Are you in love with her?"

"I don't know. I mean..." he looked uncomfortable. "Honestly, it was just casual hookups. But it was a lot of them. And when she said she was moving here, I offered my place."

"So she wants it to be more than casual?"

"I thought so at first."

"Well, what do you want?"

He laughed. "I'm not good at relationships."

I didn't say anything. His response didn't really answer my question. And usually if I stayed silent, he always confessed what he was hiding. Before this, I didn't think we had many secrets from each other at all.

"It doesn't really matter now. She found an apartment. She's moving out at the end of the month."

"That's plenty of time to change her mind."

"I think I should have never slept with your best friend. What the hell was I thinking?"

"I think it's great. Two of my best friends getting together? What could be better than that?" Even as I said it, I knew it wasn't true. Two of my best friends getting together meant that I could possibly lose both of them. They wouldn't need me anymore.

He finished his beer and put it down on the coffee table. "Yeah, except..."

The front door opening cut him off. Melissa walked in with a huge smile on her face. But as soon as she saw me, it instantly vanished. "Hey, guys. What are you two doing?"

"Waiting for you," I said and smiled at her.

Her eyes traveled down my body. "Penny, if you needed to borrow something to wear, all my clothes are here. You know that."

"Yeah. Sorry. I didn't know when you'd be back and I didn't want to rifle through your stuff. Usually Tyler lets me borrow something comfy when we hang out anyway."

"Mhm." She set her purse down on the kitchen counter. "Of course he does. Well, don't let me bother your guys' time. I'll just get out of your way." She made her way toward the bedroom.

I stood up. "Melissa, I came over to hang out with both of you."

"That's not really what it looks like."

"I'm sorry I borrowed his clothes." *Geez.* "It's just what I'm used to doing. I won't do it anymore if it makes you uncomfortable."

"Why would that make me uncomfortable? Borrowing someone's clothes who you slept with one time isn't weird at all. That's completely normal behavior."

"We're friends."

"I know that! I just don't want to have to come back to my apartment and see you wearing his clothes like you two just banged."

I laughed. "You're being ridiculous."

"I'm being ridiculous? Clearly there's something still going on between you two. You can't even stay out of his pants."

"We're just friends," Tyler said. "Why won't you believe me?"

"Because you're both lying. I should have never moved here." She went into the bedroom and slammed the door.

I was already losing both of them. Neither one of them wanted to talk about these things with me.

"What I was about to say before she came in was that she's super jealous of our relationship," Tyler said. "And it doesn't matter if I love her. I'm not going to choose between you two."

"I should go talk to her."

"Me talking to her sure doesn't help."

I knocked on the bedroom door and slowly opened it. Melissa was tossing some of her clothes into boxes. I closed the door behind me. I had a feeling I didn't want Tyler to overhear our conversation. "Can we talk?"

"About what?" She threw some more clothes into the box.

"About you and Tyler."

"There is no me and Tyler. Don't be weird."

"He told me you guys were hooking up."

She closed one of the lids on the boxes. "Of course he did. I forgot that you two don't have any secrets."

"I didn't think you and I did either. Why didn't you tell me?"

"You know the worst part?" she said, ignoring my question. "I have nowhere to go now. Because I'm mad at you too."

"I don't understand why you're mad at me."

She stood up and pointed at me. "You're wearing his clothes. What the fuck are you doing?"

"I always..."

"Yeah, you always borrow his sweatpants and watch Shark Tank together because that's your thing." She made quote marks with her fingers when she said thing. "And there's no room for me when you're around because he's always going to put you first. God, I never should have slept with him."

"There is absolutely nothing going on between Tyler and me. I'm marrying James in less than two weeks. I don't know what other proof you need."

She looked down at my pants.

"Jesus, Melissa." I pulled them off and tossed them at her. "Tyler and I are friends. I thought we were too. Can you just talk to me for two seconds before throwing a fit?"

She burst into tears.

"Melissa." I went over to her and put my arms around her.

"He's never going to love me like he loved you," she sobbed into my shoulder.

"That isn't true."

"Of course it is. He was obsessed with you for years. He's just settling for me. I don't want to be someone's second choice."

I ran my hand up and down her back. "You're not. He wanted you to move in with him. He looks forward to coming home to you. And he definitely doesn't want you to move out."

She pulled back from me. "Did he say that?"

"Yes."

"When he talks about you it just makes me so mad. It's always Penny this or Penny that. I know you guys are friends. I know you guys talk and hang out all the time. I just...I don't know how to deal with it, knowing that you've been more than friends in the past." She sighed and sat down on the edge of Tyler's bed. The only time I had even been in here was when I had helped him move in. I wasn't interested in sharing a bed with Tyler. I never thought about him like that. He really was just a friend. And I didn't want to be what stood in the way of Tyler and Melissa being happy. I had already done that enough to Tyler. Maybe I should just step back. What it came down to was that Melissa never believed that boys and girls could just be friends. It didn't matter that I had proof with Mason, Matt, and Rob; she'd never understand.

"If you want, I'll give you both some space to figure this thing out. I don't want to be the reason why you guys break up."

"We can't break up. We're not even officially dating."

"You know what I mean. I came over tonight to talk to you guys about this. I didn't want to be kept in the dark. But I realize why you didn't want to talk about it." I grabbed a pair of yoga pants out of the box that Melissa had been packing and pulled them on. "I shouldn't have butted in. But I missed you. I thought when you moved here we'd be hanging out all the time."

"I know. I'm sorry." She was looking down at her lap instead of at me. "I just need some time."

I didn't want her to be mad at me. I wanted to be able to say that she could have as much time as she needed. But I couldn't help but think that my wedding was in less than two weeks and I needed her. "I hope that you two can work it out."

She didn't say anything as I left the room. I closed the door behind me. I didn't even want to make eye contact with Tyler. Melissa had been yelling. He had already heard the whole conversation.

"I'm just going to go. You should probably go talk to her."

"Penny." He stood up and walked toward me. "You don't have to go."

"I think maybe you do have to choose," I whispered. I didn't want Melissa to overhear me. "At least for awhile. If you want to be with her, then she has to come first. You have to tell her how you really feel."

"I feel like she's a lot for me to handle." He gave me a small smile.

"Yeah, she is. And I'm pretty sure you knew that going into it."

He sighed and scratched the back of his neck. "I'm sorry about all this."

"There's nothing to apologize about. I hope that you two can work it out," I said, repeating the same thing I had said to Melissa. I grabbed my shoes off the ground and left as quickly as I could. When I closed the door behind me, it felt so final. Melissa and Tyler were the last parts of my old life I was holding on to. I didn't want to lose them too. But it wasn't my choice.

CHAPTER 16
Tuesday

I wasn't sure when James would be back. He had probably thought I'd be spending most of the evening at Tyler and Melissa's. I flipped through the channels until I found a rerun of New Girl. The T.V. seemed to echo in the empty apartment. Melissa and I always used to watch this show together. I pulled a blanket onto my lap and tried to focus on the T.V. instead of my nagging thoughts. In the show, Winston was currently pulling a prank that was much too small. I had just gotten into the episode when the door to the apartment opened.

"Hey, baby," James said. He tossed his keys on the kitchen counter and draped his suit jacket over the back of one of the chairs.

"Hey," I looked over my shoulder and smiled at him as he walked toward me. "Did you have a good night?"

He lay down on the couch and put his head on my lap. "Yeah. What are we watching?" Instead of looking at the T.V., he was looking up at me.

I ran my fingers through his hair. "New Girl." James was horrible at watching T.V. It was like he didn't have the attention span for it. Which was strange because he could focus on other things for hours or even days. I knew he hadn't watched much T.V. growing up, so maybe he just never got used to it. Even though I wanted to see Winston's reaction to his prank going horribly wrong, I grabbed the remote to turn it off.

"No, I want to watch," James said and turned his face toward the T.V.

I looked over my shoulder toward the door. He hadn't brought any bags in or anything. He had said he had errands to run. Where had he been if he didn't bring anything back with him? "What were you up to tonight?"

"I just had some errands to run." He kept his eyes glued to the T.V. When the show went to commercial, he turned back toward me. "Was I right about Tyler and Melissa?"

"Yeah." I sighed. "Melissa wants me to stay away for awhile so they can figure things out."

"Why?"

"She's uncomfortable with my friendship with Tyler. It's stupid."

"Were you wearing this?" He lifted up the bottom of Tyler's old shirt.

"Yes." I shrugged my shoulders. That was the exact thing that had bothered Melissa.

He laughed. "You two do have a weird relationship."

"We do not."

"I'm not complaining. But I can see how it might make her uncomfortable."

I frowned. "Does it make you uncomfortable?"

"I'm confident in our relationship. Melissa and Tyler just started dating, so she's not confident in their relationship yet. Just different circumstances."

"But does it make you uncomfortable?"

"It used to. But I trust you. And I trust him. Besides, you do look good in baggy t-shirts." He pushed the fabric up my torso and kissed my hipbone.

I laughed.

"Although, you look even better with no shirt at all." He pushed the t-shirt up even farther, kissing the bottom of my ribcage.

"Except we agreed to no funny business until the wedding."

"About that. I was thinking...mouth stuff doesn't really count as sex, does it?"

I laughed. "Yes, it does."

"Are you sure?" He kissed me right above the waistline of my pants. "I've been waiting to taste you all day."

I gulped.

"There's nothing I want more right now than to feel your tight pussy come around my tongue." He pulled down slightly on the waistband of my pants. His warm breath sent chills through my body.

Fuck. He knew how horny I got when he talked like that. I felt my hips rise without my brain's permission.

He kissed my hipbone again. "Let me give you what you want. Just say yes, baby."

I laughed and wiggled away from him. "Mouth stuff is against the rules and you know it. You're not going to win this one, James."

He lowered his eyebrows. "What about hand stuff then? Everyone does that." His palm slipped between my thighs, gently massaging me through my pants.

I half groaned half laughed. "Everyone does that? What do you even mean by that?"

He laughed. "Come on. We both knew we'd cheat a little."

"You mean, like this?" I put my hand on his cock that was pressing against his suit pants.

He locked eyes with me, daring me to take it further.

I moved my hand from his base to his tip and watched him staring intently back at me. There was fire in his eyes. I could get him to give into me. I just needed to give him an extra push. "You know you want me on my knees with my lips around your cock. I want you to come in my mouth." I moved off the couch and kneeled in front of him, trailing my hands up his thighs.

His Adam's apple rose and fell.

"I want to swallow every ounce." I reached for the button of his pants. "How about you say yes?"

He grabbed my hand and raised his left eyebrow. "The only thing I'm saying yes to is a cold shower." He got up off the couch and stretched. "You're welcome to join me if you're ready to throw in the towel. Trust me, the reward will be well worth the defeat." His eyes on me made my whole body feel warm. I didn't doubt that he'd be overly generous if I admitted defeat. But I wanted to be the one that made him cave.

I sighed and sat back down on the couch. "Go take your shower, James." I grabbed the remote and tried to focus on my show.

He laughed and walked out of the living room. He took his shirt off as he walked up the stairs and I almost moaned at the sight of his muscular back. I was in trouble.

***

"The cake tasting is Thursday. And I have a dress fitting on Saturday. Besides that, it's only last minute stuff." My head was on James' bare chest and I was savoring the rise and fall of it beneath my cheek. There was an intimacy about this too. I liked being close to him and talking to him. I had never felt so comfortable around anyone in my life. We just fit so perfectly together.

He absentmindedly ran his fingers through my hair. "What kind of dress did you get?"

I laughed and moved some of my weight to my hand so I could look up at him. "I can't tell you that."

He crossed his hands behind his head and smiled. "Not even a hint?"

"Don't you want to be surprised?" I asked.

"I'll tell you what I'm wearing."

I laughed again. "I already know you're wearing a tux."

He raised his eyebrow. "Maybe not." His grin was contagious.

"What else would you wear?"

"Tell me yours and I'll tell you mine."

I leaned over him and placed a gentle kiss on his lips. "I don't think so. Besides, you could wear meggings and a turtleneck and I'd still marry you."

He laughed. "What the hell are meggings?"

"You know, like leggings for men."

"I didn't know they made leggings for men. Sounds like a good birthday gift." He pressed his lips together to prevent himself from laughing again.

His birthday was next month and he knew I always struggled to think of something to get him. "You know, if you don't give me any other hints about what to get you, I might be forced to buy you a pair."

He laughed. "How about I cash in an early birthday gift right now?"

"James, all you have to do is say you cave."

"My beautiful soon-to-be-wife is ridiculously stubborn."

"I'm stubborn? What about you?"

He shrugged. "Only 10 days, 18 hours, and 15 minutes to go. But who's counting?"

I smiled. I loved that he was counting down the time to our wedding. "You really think you can resist me that long?"

"No. Or else I would have just agreed to wait. But I'm giving it to the end of the week, tops. I should be able to get you to beg me by then." He looked so nonchalant. Like it was a given that I was going to lose.

"We'll see about that." I had just gotten the perfect idea on how to get him to cave. "Goodnight, Professor Hunter."

His throat made a low groaning noise.

I kissed his cheek and rolled onto my side. In a second his arms were wrapped securely around me. When I was little, I couldn't fall asleep without hugging my teddy bear. Every night, James fell asleep with his arms around me. He was my new safety net. I drifted to sleep knowing that I was his equivalent.

CHAPTER 17
Thursday

"Did you ask him yet?" Sierra said when she returned to her desk with a cup of coffee.

I looked up from my computer screen. Earlier this morning I had texted Melissa about hanging out tomorrow night, but I still hadn't heard back. Every day her silence weighed on me more and more. It was getting hard not to think about it. "I'm sorry, Sierra, I keep forgetting. We've been so busy with..."

"Ask him during lunch today."

"Yeah, okay, thanks for reminding me." For the past few days my fellow interns had been nagging me nonstop about meeting up with James and me after work one day this week. And the more they asked me about it, the less I wanted to ask James. It was pretty clear that they didn't care about getting to know me. They just wanted to meet him. But I couldn't really blame them. Who wouldn't want to spend time with James? "What day are you guys all free?"

"I could do tonight," Tavon said and put his hands behind his head. Sometimes he leaned back so far in his chair that it seemed like it was going to tip over.

"Tonight would be great!" Sierra said. "But I'm free pretty much every night." She laughed awkwardly after saying it, which just made me feel bad. She was new to the city. I should be help- ing her out, not avoiding her. What did it matter if she had a crush on James? Every single girl in New York probably had a crush on James.

"We have a cake tasting after work tonight, but maybe tomorrow..."

"How about after the cake tasting tonight?" Zach asked.

"Yeah, I already have plans tomorrow. Come on, let's do it tonight, it'll be so much fun. We promise not to embarrass you," Tavon said.

I laughed. "I guess that could work." I glanced down at the time. It was a little early, but I was already hungry. "I'm going to take an early lunch. And I promise to ask him." Tonight would be the best time to do it this week. Even though I was free tomorrow night since Melissa and Tyler weren't talking to me, James still had plans with his friends. And I'm sure he wasn't going to cancel on them to hang out with a bunch of interns that were obsessed with him. I bit the inside of my lip to prevent myself from laughing. I was an intern that was obsessed with him too. He didn't seem to mind my obsession at all.

Sierra clapped her hands as I walked toward James' office. She probably thought I was out of earshot.

I wove my way through the different departments. Tonight I thought I'd play up the student/professor role playing idea I had come up with. If anything could get James to cave, it was whispering Professor Hunter seductively in his ear. That dynamic between us never got old. It reminded both of us about when we first started our relationship. And no matter what anyone else said, I loved how we met. I could relive our first time together in his office over and over again. I absentmindedly licked my lips. Sex seemed to be the only thing on my mind recently.

The blinds on James' office windows were open, so he saw me approaching before I even knocked. He immediately smiled and waved his hand, gesturing for me to come in. I walked in and closed the door behind me.

"Sounds good," James said into his desk phone. "Reach those numbers and then we can discuss it." He smiled at me as he listened to whatever was being said on the other end of the line. He stood up, eager for the phone call to be over. "Thanks. You too." He immediately hung up the phone and grabbed my waist, pulling me close to him. "I was just thinking about you."

"I'm always thinking about you." I stood on my tiptoes, drawing my face toward his. James' lips were immediately on mine as his palm pressed against the small of my back. The past few days had been filled with the sexiest make out sessions imaginable. Apparently we were both addicted to sex, because not taking it further than a kiss always took all of my restraint. I laced my fingers behind his neck, making the heat between us almost palpable.

He groaned and grabbed my thigh, lifting it around his waist.

I laughed and pulled back, but he kept my thigh in his hand.

"You're killing me," he whispered. "I need you."

"I need you too." I looked up into his eyes and ran my hand down the side of his face. "It's just going to make our wedding night that much better, you know."

He smiled and kissed my forehead. "There's no way you can wait until then."

"There's no way you can wait until then," I said and poked the center of his chest.

"You're right. I can't." He grabbed the back of my neck and kissed me hard. When he pulled back, I was completely breathless. He released my thigh and smoothed my skirt back into place. "And neither can you, baby."

I pressed my lips together and shrugged. "Are you hungry?"

His eyes gravitated down my body. "Starving."

I laughed. "For lunch, James." I sat down in one of the chairs in front of his desk.

"In that case...I guess I could eat." He grabbed our sandwiches out of the small fridge and sat down beside me.

"So, the other marketing interns want to go out for drinks tonight. And they were hoping my fiancé could come too." I smiled at him as I slowly unwrapped my turkey sandwich.

"Should we meet up with them after the cake tasting?" He took a huge bite of his sandwich.

"You actually want to go?"

He shrugged as he finished chewing. "If that's what you want to do. You keep saying you want to bond with them. Wasn't that why you didn't want them to know we were together in the first place?"

"For some reason I thought you were going to say no."

"When do I ever say no to you?"

I smiled at him. "You usually don't say no. You just do whatever you want regardless. Or else I wouldn't even be eating lunch with you right now. I'd have a different internship."

"Fair enough. But I think it'll be fun. I should know all my employees better. It will be good for me too."

"Are you sure?"

James laughed. "If you don't want to, we don't have to."

"No, it's not that." *It's just that Zach jumped to conclusions because of the bruises on my face and Sierra has a crush on you.* "I don't want to force you to do things you don't want to."

James leaned forward and kissed me again. "All I ever want to do is hang out with you. And I'm excited to meet your new friends."

"Just to give you a heads up, I'm pretty sure Sierra is going to try to steal you away."

"I love how jealous you get."

"I'm not jealous."

He smiled back at me. "And maybe after drinks we can go home and reevaluate this whole no sex before the wedding thing?"

"You're incorrigible, James Hunter."

"Is it working?"

I shook my head, but we both knew he was wearing me down.

CHAPTER 18
Thursday

I took another bite of the dark chocolate mousse cake.

"Is that one your favorite?" James asked as he took a bite too.

"I don't know, they're all amazing."

After the pastry chef had reprimanded us for waiting until a week before the wedding to pick a cake, he had laid out an assortment of the most delicious cakes I had ever tasted. It was good we had skipped dinner because I apparently didn't have any self control around wedding cakes.

"You know what this one reminds me of?" James asked.

I nodded. "I was thinking the same thing. Even though it's not lava cake, it tastes like that chocolate cake from your country club."

"Our country club."

I shrugged my shoulders.

"It kind of takes me back to our first date. Our first real date I mean. Not just when I seduced you in my office." He took another bite of the cake.

I smiled up at him. "I seduced you."

He laughed and shook his head.

"You pretended that I was your wife on that date. Do you remember?"

"I remember." He was looking at me in the most loving way.

"Did you ever think we'd be here right now?"

"At that moment?" He ran his hand through his hair. "I think I was just terrified by my own reaction to you."

I knew he was referring to his addiction problem. I looked down at the cake.

"I wasn't really in a good place when we met, Penny."

"I know, I just meant..."

"You saved me."

He had never said that to me before. I swallowed hard. I felt tears welling in my eyes.

"Suddenly the only thing I wanted in life was to see you smile." He reached out and took my hand. "So yeah, I thought we'd eventually be here. This is everything I've always wanted. We certainly had our ups and downs getting here, though." He smiled at me.

"You mean, you certainly enjoyed pushing me away?"

"I'm not going to ever push you away again." He ran his thumb along the palm of my hand.

"I know."

He pulled me into his chest and put his hand on the side of my face. "You're quite sentimental tonight."

I breathed in his heavenly scent. "Sometimes I think about when you said you wanted to go to Vegas and..."

"This is what I want too."

"Are you sure? You said you didn't want a big wedding and I..."

"Penny. The first time I got married, I wasn't in love. I didn't have a say in any of the plans. I wasn't excited to walk down the aisle. And before I met you, I never thought I'd get married again." He ran his fingers through my hair. "No one's ever loved me like you love me. This is what planning a wedding is supposed to be like. I liked looking at venues, picking flowers, being excluded from helping you pick out a dress..."

I laughed.

"I've had fun doing all of it. This is going to be our wedding. And I'm so excited to marry you. I thought I didn't want this back then, but I want it now. I want to see you walk down the aisle toward me. I want our friends and family to clap when we have our first kiss. And I want to have a first dance. I want all of it with you."

"I think we should choose this one then," I said and looked down at the chocolate cake. "I'm still going to try all the others though. This place is amazing."

James laughed and released me from his embrace. "There is one last thing to do here."

"What's that?"

He picked up a piece of cake in his hand and lifted it toward me.

"Don't you dare, James."

Before I had even completed the sentence, he smashed the cake against my face. He laughed as I wiped it off my nose.

"Oh, I'm going to get you." I picked up a piece of cake and chased after him.

***

James opened the door for me. As soon as we were both inside, he put his arm across my shoulders.

"They're over there," I said, nodding toward where Sierra was waving her hand in the air. They were sitting at a table and there were two empty seats. "I'll sit next to her."

James laughed. "You're so cute."

We walked together toward my fellow interns.

"Hey, guys," I said. I was about to sit down next to Sierra, but she tapped on the chair. "You can sit here, Mr. Hunter. It's so great that you could join us."

James squeezed my shoulder. "Thanks." He smiled at me and sat down next to her. "But please, you can all call me James."

Sierra beamed.

I internally rolled my eyes and sat down between James and Zach.

"Hi, Penny," Zach said. He was the only one that seemed to realize I had said anything. "You have some icing in your hair, I think." He pointed to the left side of his head.

I wiped above my right ear.

Zach laughed. "No, not mirrored. It's on your left."

I wiped above my left ear.

"You got it." He took a swig of his beer.

James put his arm back around my shoulders. "How are you guys liking the internship?" he asked.

"It's awesome," Tavon said. "Anderson is letting us go through your current marketing strategies to see if we have any ideas."

"And do you have any?" James asked.

Tavon cleared his throat. "Well, we just got started..."

"I'm just kidding," James said. "We don't have to talk about work. Did any of you grow up in the city?"

"Yeah, I did," Zach said. "I went to NYCU like Penny, but we didn't have any classes together. You went to Harvard, right?"

"Yes."

"Did you get a masters there too?" Tavon asked.

"No, I just went to undergrad. I started laying the ground-work for Blive Tech while I was still in school, so I jumped right into that instead of going for my masters."

"And you were one of the youngest millionaires ever right?" Tavon asked.

"Yeah, I guess so."

"That's freaking awesome. What made you sell Blive Tech when it was going so well?"

"A number of different things. Mainly I just wanted a new challenge."

"And that's why you started teaching?" asked Sierra.

James smiled down at me. "Yes. I taught in New York for a little bit and then transferred to the University of New Castle. I really enjoyed it."

"It's a shame you had to stop."

"Not really. I got everything I wanted from it."

"What, a girlfriend?" Zach asked.

Zach, what the hell?

James laughed. "No. I loved teaching. It was a nice change of pace. But I missed running a business. Well, yeah, and I guess I got an amazing girlfriend out of it."

"Weren't you still married when you moved to Delaware?" Zach asked.

Is he purposely trying to torture me?

James cleared his throat. "I had filed for divorce before mov-ing."

"I was reading about your first wife too," Sierra said. "It's so sad what happened. Were you really childhood sweethearts?"

James looked uncomfortable. "No. It's a long story. Did you guys want refills?"

"That would be great," Tavon said.

"I'll be right back." James squeezed my shoulder and walked toward the bar.

"Oh my God, he's even sexier in normal clothes," Sierra said as soon as James had walked away. "I've never seen him in jeans before."

"What is wrong with you guys?" I said.

Zach laughed. "We're just trying to get to know him."

"No, I agree with Penny," Tavon said. "You guys are being embarrassing. Sierra, stop flirting with him."

"I'm not flirting with him," she said and crossed her arms.

"Penny?" Tavon was looking at me for help.

"You kind of are."

"I'm so sorry. I'll stop." Her face had turned slightly red.

"It's okay," I said.

"And Zach, why are you attacking him?" Tavon asked.

Zach shrugged. "Just trying to figure him out." He was looking at me. "Gauging his reactions to different things."

"Zach, I asked you to drop it..." my voice trailed off when James came back over. He had a beer in his hand and a waiter was following him with a tray of drinks.

"I opened up a tab for the table," James said as he sat down. He immediately draped his arm back around my shoulders.

"Thanks, man," Tavon said. "So what made you get into tech in the first place?"

"Honestly, it was forced on me."

Everyone laughed. I looked up at James. I had never asked him that question and I was curious about the rest of his answer.

"I liked reading in my free time. And my parents hated that. They put a computer in my room and kept giving me games to play on it until I finally got interested."

"You do realize that's the opposite problem all our parents had with us, right?" Sierra asked.

James laughed. "I think they knew there was an opportunity for advancement there. Whereas being an author wasn't something they wanted for me. My older sister was already interested in literature. And they were right. The opportunities in this field are endless."

"So you originally wanted to be an author?" Sierra asked.

James shrugged. "No. I don't know. I was young. I didn't really know what I wanted to be."

I bit my lip. He was never allowed to dream about what he wanted to be. His parents had decided that for him early on.

"Did you play any sports growing up?" Tavon asked.

"Some. Never for very long. I always went back to tech."

"So, were you like a nerd in school?" Sierra asked. "I can't picture that at all."

"I'm still a nerd," James said.

"You are definitely not nerdy looking," replied Sierra.

James laughed awkwardly and turned away from her. "What about you, Tavon? Did you play sports?"

"Soccer. Second team all-conference my last two years in high school."

"My little brother was good at soccer too. I used to love going to his games," James said.

I took a sip of the beer that the waiter had handed me. I knew that Rob had played soccer growing up. He liked to brag about how awesome he was.

"You like beer?" Zach asked me.

I turned toward him. "I'm used to hanging out with the guys."

He smiled. "I pegged you for only drinking girly drinks."

"You pegged me wrong."

"And what about you, Zach?" James asked, cutting our conversation short. "Any sports growing up?"

"I ran track."

"Do you still run a lot?"

"Almost every day through Central Park before or after work."

"I like running through Central Park too. I always try to get Penny to come with me, but I haven't convinced her yet."

Sometimes James ran with Mason. They always made everything a competition. Whenever James came back completely worn out, I knew he had been racing Mason through Central Park. Bee and I always joked that they complained about us on their runs. But I had a feeling that they just talked about real estate. Or mergers and acquisitions or something super boring. Bee and I went to yoga classes together at least once a week and we never complained about James and Mason. We were happy. There wasn't anything to complain about.

"You should try it sometime," Zach said, pulling me out of my own thoughts.

James pulled me a little closer to him.

I laughed. "Running? Oh, no. I do not like running." As far as I was concerned, James gave me plenty of cardio exercise. Althhough, I'd never pass down a walk through Central Park with James' hand in mine. "I'll stick to yoga," I said.

"You do yoga?"

"A few times a week, yeah."

James cleared his throat.

"I played volleyball in high school," Sierra said.

"So did I," I said. "What position did you play?"

"Outside hitter," Sierra said and turned her attention back to James. "James have you ever played before?"

"Just in gym class," he replied. "And I guess some beach volleyball, but that's pretty different."

"Beach volleyball is the best. Where have you played?"

James shrugged. "It's been awhile. The last time I played was probably spring break my senior year of college."

"That's not that long ago," Sierra said.

"For you guys, maybe." James laughed. "I'm turning 30 next month."

"Thirty isn't so bad. Isn't that the new 20 or something like that?" Tavon asked.

"It sure doesn't feel like it."

I smiled up at him. Was he upset about turning 30? He hadn't mentioned it to me. But it was definitely a milestone. Everything that was going on was a lot of change for him too. I needed to plan something really special for his birthday. Meggings weren't going to cut it.

"At least you got the whole hot young wife thing going on," Zach said.

I laughed awkwardly.

James set his beer down on the table. "Penny, do you want to dance?" He stood up before I had even answered.

"That sounds great." I grabbed his hand and let him escort me onto the small dance floor. There were only a few people dancing.

"Zach seems to like you quite a bit," he said and pulled me in close, despite the fact that it wasn't a slow song.

"He doesn't. He's purposely trying to push your buttons."

"Why?"

"I think he's trying to see how you'll react."

"He wants me to knock him out?"

I laughed. "No, I don't think either of you want that."

"He's certainly tempting me."

"I think he's more so trying to see if you'll hit me."

"What?" James pulled back slightly.

"Remember when I told you that one of the interns thought you were abusive because of the bruise on my cheek? That was Zach."

"Oh." James touched the side of my face where my bruise was still slightly visible. "It kills me that anyone would think I did that. I would never hurt you."

I grabbed his hand and moved it back to my waist. "I know, James. Try to ignore him. The last thing you want is to get in a bar fight with one of your employees. That's a lawsuit waiting to happen."

"Then he should probably stop hitting on you."

"He's not. And what about Sierra hitting on you?" I gave him a playful smile.

James laughed. "I think she's had too much to drink."

"I hope that's the reason. I mean, I'm sitting right there. What is her problem?"

He grabbed my hand and spun me around before pulling me back in close.

"I don't think any of them really care to get to know me, " I said. "They just wanted to meet you."

"I'm sure that isn't true."

"The only one talking to me was Zach and he was doing it to piss you off."

James laughed.

"The woes of dating a celebrity."

"Baby, I'm not a celebrity."

"You basically are. And everyone that works for you idolizes you."

"I only care about what you think of me."

I stared into his eyes. "Do you wish you were an author?"

"I'm happy exactly where I am."

"You know, if you wrote a book it would automatically be a best seller. You already have name recognition."

"I'm happy exactly where I am," he repeated. "I wouldn't change a thing."

I stared into his eyes. "What do you and Mason talk about when you run together?"

James smiled. "Guy stuff."

"What does that mean?"

James spun me around again.

"Does that mean you talk about me and Bee?"

"Sometimes."

"Good or bad things?"

"Let's just say I know who's going to win our bet."

"What?! You know when Mason is going to propose to Bee?!"

"I can't say anything else."

"James, you have to tell me."

He laughed. "There's no way I'm telling you. I have inside information. And you're just going to leak it to Bee."

"I won't, I promise."

"Penny, you're a terrible liar. I told Mason I wouldn't tell anyone."

I pursed my lips. "Husbands and wives don't keep secrets from each other."

"Some bro code breaks marriage code."

"It does not."

"No, it doesn't. But we're not married yet. Ask me again next Saturday and I'll tell you."

"Fine." I sighed. "I was thinking about calling off the wedding, but I guess I can't now."

"Very funny."

I stood up on my tiptoes and kissed him. His hands slid down to the top of my ass as he kissed me back. He didn't seem to care at all that his employees could see us. And the way he was kissing me made me not care either.

"Do you want to get out of here?" he asked. His voice was low and seductive.

"Are you caving?"

"No, but I think I'll be able to get you to."

I shook my head back and forth. "If you cave we can leave right now, though. And you can do whatever you want to me."

He lowered his eyebrows.

"If not, your new friends are waiting for you."

James laughed. "You mean your new friends." He leaned in a little closer to me. "I'm not caving, Penny. But I guarantee that this game will be over by the end of the week."

"Is that so?"

He winked at me and grabbed my hand. I reluctantly followed him back to the table.

"We have a game to play," Sierra said.

Hopefully it wasn't who could flirt better with James. "What's the game?" I asked.

"Two truths, one lie. We'll go around and each say two truths and one lie about ourselves, and then everyone else will guess which thing is a lie."

"Okay, let's play." I took a sip of my beer.

"I'll go first," she said. "I haven't been to church in years. I flunked chemistry in high school. And I have never had a one night stand."

"The last one was a lie," Tavon said.

"Nope." Sierra's cheeks blushed.

"What do you mean that's not a lie?" Tavon asked.

Sierra shrugged. "It wasn't my lie."

"We're going to have to fix that."

Sierra laughed.

"Well, you probably didn't flunk chemistry," Zach said. "So I'm gonna say that's the lie."

Sierra shook her head.

"You really flunked chemistry?" I asked. "I hated science too."

She laughed. "Yeah, I had to retake it. I just hated that class so much."

"How on earth did you get this internship?" Tavon asked and lightly touched her shoulder.

I tried not to laugh. Tavon had clearly found his mission for the night. Sierra was in trouble.

"Okay," Tavon said and cracked his knuckles. "I've lost more money in blackjack than I care to admit. I've never broken a bone. And I have a huge penis."

"The huge penis thing is a little subjective, don't you think?" Zach asked.

James laughed. This was the most inappropriate game ever to play with your boss. James smiled at me. But he seemed to be enjoying himself. Now that the inquisition was over, he probably felt a little more comfortable.

"Oh, no. It's huge." He winked at Sierra. Her cheeks got even redder.

"The blackjack thing?" I asked. I couldn't picture Tavon in a casino.

"Yeah. You got me. I don't even know how to play black-jack."

"Okay, my turn," Zach said. "I've been in several bar fights. I was in foster care growing up. And I play the piano."

I pressed my lips together. Was that why he knew what abuse looked like? Because he was in foster care? Was he abused? I felt bad for giving him a hard time. He was just trying to help me.

"Well, there's no way you play piano," Tavon said.

"No, I do play."

"Really?" Sierra asked. "Are you really good?"

Zach shrugged. "I'm okay."

"You're lying about the bar fights," James said.

Zach nodded. "Yeah, when you grow up in foster care, you don't need to go out seeking fights. Your turn Penny."

I didn't know what to say. I felt like I needed to apologize to him for being so defensive when he was just trying to help me. But James wasn't abusive. I'd try to talk to Zach about it again later. Maybe he'd believe me now that he had hung out with James. "Um. Well, I didn't have a date to prom. I was seduced by my college professor. And I've...gone skinny dipping."

"I'm sure you had a date to prom," Zach said. "That's your lie."

I shook my head. "Nope. I never even had a normal date un-til college."

"You're kidding," Tavon said.

"No."

"What's her lie, James?" Tavon asked.

James smiled at me. "The second one. But that's subjective too. She thinks she was the one that seduced me, not the other way around."

"Yeah right," Sierra said. She cleared her throat. "Sorry."

James laughed. "I disagree too. I definitely seduced her."

I rolled my eyes. We loved to disagree about this. But really, we both seduced each other. It had been pretty clear from the start what we both desired. "We agree to disagree."

"Your turn, James," Zach said.

"Okay, let's see. I've lost more money in blackjack than I care to admit," he said.

Tavon laughed.

"I used to hate romantic comedies but now I love them. And teaching was the best decision I ever made."

"Which one is a lie, Penny?" Sierra asked.

James raised his left eyebrow at me.

I had no idea. It was possible that James had been into gambling at one point. He certainly had a lot of money he could lose. James and I didn't watch that much T.V. but we had watched a few romcoms together. It was possible that he liked them now that he was happy. I could imagine that he hated them when he was married to Isabella. James certainly loved teaching. And if he hadn't taught at the University of New Castle, we never would have met. I smiled back at him. "The last one."

James nodded. "It was only the second best decision I ever made."

"What was the first?" Sierra asked.

"Asking Penny to marry me."

It suddenly felt like we were the only two in the room. Next Saturday I would be the luckiest girl in the world.

"Aww," Sierra said, interrupting the trance I was in. "You guys are so cute."

"How much did you lose in blackjack?" Tavon asked.

James laughed. "I don't remember. You'd have to ask my friend Mason. I'm pretty sure I blacked out the last time I went to a casino."

I shook my head. I was glad the two of them talked about real estate now. Blacking out at casinos was probably best to leave in the past.

CHAPTER 19
Friday

James was hanging out with his friends tonight. Normally I'd be watching T.V. with Tyler, but I hadn't heard from him or Melissa since Tuesday. I wasn't going to push them. Fridays were the one night a week that James and I usually didn't spend together. And just because two of my best friends weren't speaking to me, it didn't mean James had to skip his night out.

So instead of going to Tyler's, I had made plans with Bee. When James hung out with his friends, it usually meant Mason was also a part of the shenanigans, which left Bee free to hang out. Most Fridays Bee came over and hung out at Tyler's with me. They had known each other back at the University of New Castle too. And apparently Tyler had never liked Bee's ex fiancé, which made them bond instantly.

But sometimes Bee would hang out with her other friends. So tonight I was crashing her girls' night at a bar near her advertising agency. I had spent time with Marie and Kendra before. And despite the fact that they were both really nice, I always felt a little out of place. Like Bee, they were super successful women and I was just a girl who had been given her first marketing job. Maybe they'd have some advice for me.

I stepped out of the subway and made my way up the stairs. James hated that I used the subway. But he also refused to let me drive any of his cars while we were in the city because he deemed it unsafe. Which didn't bother me at all. I had no desire to drive through the crazy busy streets of New York City. The thought scared me too. However, Ian was our only driver, which usually resulted in me saying James could take the car. I didn't mind the subway. I had gotten used to the smell of urine and the random homeless people sleeping in the corners of the subway cars. Besides, it made me feel like a normal New Yorker.

All week long I had tried to tempt James into seduction. Apparently I wasn't great at being sexy, because he hadn't caved yet. But he had said he'd have me begging by the end of the week and I couldn't wait to see what he had in store. I silently laughed to myself. He had successfully turned it into a competition despite me sincerely thinking it would be good to wait till our wedding night. He had already gotten his way.

Every now and then I found James' behavior frustrating. But for the most part, I liked that he always knew what he wanted and what was best for me. I knew that from the outside looking in, it may look like I was a pushover. That wasn't how it felt though. We both gave and took a lot from our relationship. Just because I wasn't rich and successful didn't mean I didn't have anything to offer him. And even though people judging me bothered me sometimes like James' control issues, for the most part I had learned to ignore it. I didn't care that people didn't understand why James wanted to be with me. The important thing was that I knew he wanted to be.

I opened up the door to the bar and stepped inside. The air conditioning was on full blast and it made me shiver. James and I had never gone this long without having sex and strange things were turning me on. I swallowed hard and reminded myself that the shivers weren't from him but from cold air. Hopefully James was as amped up as I was and tonight he would confess that he couldn't go another day without having me. Especially since tonight I was planning on pulling out all the stops that I was too tired to last night. The thought made me smile as I made my way over to Bee, who was waving her arm in the air to call me over.

"Hey!" I said and sat down in the empty stool.

"Girl, I can't wait till your wedding," Kendra said with a huge smile. "So what's the situation with the single guys that are going to be there?"

I laughed. "You mean like how many will be there?"

"Mhm."

"There's a bunch of James' friends from college that are coming that I've never met. I think most of them didn't say they were bringing a plus one. And a few of his colleagues who I know are single. I can't remember, have you already met Rob and Matt?"

"What, is that like a gay couple or something? I'm talking about straight, single guys here, Penny."

Bee laughed. "She's met them. Matt is Mason's younger brother and Rob is James' younger brother. They were at my birthday party." She paused for a second. "Now that you mention it though, they would make kind of a cute gay couple."

"Oh, those two." She rolled her eyes. "You're right, I have met them. They're too young for me. But the other options sound promising. I am so getting laid."

Marie laughed. "Okay, now that the important question is out of the way...are you getting nervous?"

I took a deep breath. "I'm not, actually." I had thought after Isabella's threat that she would have been horrible all week, but I hadn't heard from her. And James' parents hadn't contacted us at all. Those had been the only two things I was stressed about. The wedding itself didn't make me nervous. It felt like I had been waiting forever to marry James. "I'm just so excited."

Marie smiled. "That's good. God, I was so nervous the week before I got married. I just kept thinking about all the things that could go wrong. Like tripping down the aisle, or..."

Bee lightly pushed Marie's shoulder. "Don't make her worry. It's good that you're excited, Penny. We're all so excited for you."

A waiter came by and dropped off four cosmopolitans. Bee and her friends always ordered them when they went out. It gave the whole night a Sex in the City vibe, although Kendra was the only one that was single.

"How's the new job going?" Bee asked and took a sip of her drink.

Luckily my bruise had faded so I wouldn't have to talk about being called Fight Club. "It was a weird first week. Having to tell the other interns that I was basically just handed the job was embarrassing. You're all so successful. And I..."

"Okay, you can stop right there. Marie and Kendra, absolutely," Bee said. "But you know how I got my job. James only gave you an internship. You still have to work your way up. You still get to prove your worth."

I laughed. "I forgot about that, actually."

"And everyone's going to forget that James gave you your first marketing job. It's not a big deal. Besides, you're marrying him. You're taking his last name. People are going to automatically respect you."

"Do I sense a hint of jealousy?" Marie asked.

Bee laughed. "Mason and I are enjoying the here and now. And we're too busy to get married."

That's how I had felt while I was still in school. Bee and Mason were growing their business together. They worked all the time.

"Mhm," Kendra said. "So when do you think Mason will pop the question?"

Bee shrugged. "Sometime before we have kids? I don't know."

"Are you seriously thinking about having kids soon?" Kendra asked. "Ugh, they're always so sticky."

Marie laughed. "Sticky? Actually, that's a pretty good way to describe the little monsters."

"Not soon soon," Bee said. "Like I just said, I'd want to get married first. So it's a few years out. We have talked about it though."

"I'm thinking pretty soon myself," Marie said with a smile.

"Nooooo!" Kendra yelled. Some people in the bar turned to look at us. "You can't have kids yet. None of you can. I'm not ready."

"You're not ready?" Marie asked. "You're not the one whose body is going to turn into a watermelon."

Kendra laughed. "True. But I'll be an unofficial aunt. Which means I have to agree to the when. And I say not yet. I need these girls' nights. I can't have you guys all fat in here. How will I ever pick up men that way?"

"But you'll look so good in comparison," Bee said.

"No. Pregnant women have that whole glowing skin thing going on. You're all trying to ruin my life." Kendra turned to me. "And you're awfully quiet. Does that mean you're going to start popping babies out right away too, miss soon to be missus?"

"Oh, I...no, I don't know if that's...well, probably not." I took a huge sip of my cosmo. *God is this strong.* I coughed and looked back up. They were all staring at me.

Kendra's face got a little softer and she glanced at Bee.

Bee gave me an encouraging smile. "What, James doesn't want a million little kids running around?"

I looked down at my drink. "We just haven't talked about it much." I knew he was worried about being a bad father. But he was stronger than he realized. He wasn't going to break again. His life was good now. We were good.

"Isn't that kind of something you're supposed to talk about before getting married?" Kendra asked. "Ow!" she yelped. I looked up to see her giving Marie a death stare.

"You're so young," Marie said. "You two have plenty of time to figure it out. Besides, you're just starting your career. You'll probably want to work for several years before starting a family."

"Mhm." I wasn't so sure about that. But I was young. Being with James always made me try to act older than I was. I had plenty of time to convince him that it was a good idea, though. Right now I just wanted to focus on us.

Bee pulled out her phone. "Oh, no." Her face drained of color.

"Are you okay?" I asked.

Bee looked up at me. "I thought you said you'd tell James to not let Mason throw his bachelor party? You said you'd talk to him."

"James said he didn't want one and then he never mentioned it again. I figured it didn't matter. I meant to ask you about that, though. What's wrong with Mason throwing it?"

Bee's face went from pale to bright red. "Ummm...well..."

"I'm really sorry, I kind of thought you were just joking around about it."

"I wasn't joking, Penny. This is a disaster."

"I mean, I can talk to James tonight if it's that big of a deal..."

"It's too late. They already left."

"What?"

"They kidnapped him." She tossed me her phone. It was a text from Mason:

"I hope you had a good day at work, baby. Also...we kidnapped James for the weekend. We'll all be back late Sunday night. And we stole James' phone. So tell Penny so she doesn't worry. I love you! P.S. Don't be mad. I promise to make it up to you Sunday night."

I couldn't help but laugh, but I immediately stopped when I saw Bee's face. "Bee, they'll have fun. Don't worry about it. Plus it sounds like you're going to have a fun Sunday night."

She snatched her phone from me and started texting Mason back.

"Will you just tell me what's bothering you?"

"Mason used to be a man-whore," Kendra offered.

"Kendra! Penny is marrying his best friend. Don't tell her that." Bee looked so embarrassed.

I laughed. "Bee, I already knew that. And I don't see why that matters. He *used to be* is the key there. He's not now."

"Wait, you knew about his side business when we first met and you didn't tell me? A little heads up would have been nice." She laughed and instantly seemed a little more relaxed. But I had no idea what she was talking about.

"What side business?"

"You didn't know? What is wrong with me?" She put her face in her hands.

I looked over at Kendra and Marie but neither of them seemed to want to say anything now. I didn't care what Mason's embarrassing side business was. "If you're worried about him cheating on you or something, you have nothing..."

"Oh, God, no. Mason wouldn't do that. At least, I can't picture him doing that."

"He wouldn't," Marie said. "He's head over heels for you."

"So, it's fine," I said.

"No, I mean, I'm worried about James. Mason isn't good at...pacing himself." She drew her eyebrows together.

I knew Mason knew about James' problems. But I hadn't realized that Bee knew. It made sense though. I knew that Mason was a man-whore because James had told me. And she knew about James because Mason had told her.

"James knows how to pace himself." I didn't want to be having this conversation in front of Marie and Kendra. "It's going to be fine. They're just gonna have fun." Now I was trying to convince myself. I thought about what James had said yesterday when we were playing two truths, one lie. One time he was with Mason he had gotten so drunk that he blacked out and lost a ton of money gambling. That was probably a long time ago, though. James didn't do that kind of stuff now.

Bee nodded. "But I don't know what kind of place Mason's taking him to. It could be really bad. Mason's really good at doing stuff like this. I'm worried he's going to take it too far."

I swallowed hard. I still didn't really understand what she was getting at, but I had an unsettling feeling in my stomach. I hadn't had sex with James all week. He was just as horny as me. And Mason had just taken him God knows where. "I'm just going to call him real quick." I pulled out my phone and pressed on his name, even though I knew Mason had said they had taken his phone. It went straight to voicemail. "Where do you think they went?" I tried to make my voice sound normal as I put my phone back in my purse, but I'm pretty sure I sounded panicky.

"I don't know," Bee said.

"What's Mason's side business?"

"He doesn't do it anymore. He's retired." She gave me a small smile, but it was far from encouraging.

"Bee, please just tell me."

CHAPTER 20
Friday

So Mason had a shady past. Not a big deal. I pulled out my phone and tried James' number again. Nothing.

I was glad the walk home from the bar was long. I needed the time to clear my head. My mind drifted back to the first time I had ever met Mason. I laughed to myself. He had been asking James if he needed his services, but I had been too love blind to notice. But James had told him he wasn't interested. James would never cheat on me. *Would he?*

I didn't understand his issues and I wasn't sure I ever would. I took for granted the idea that he was addicted to me. Not because I wanted him to be sick, but because that was how he acted, like he couldn't get enough of me. But what if he was just addicted to sex? I had been withholding sex from him. What if he needed that? That was ridiculous. If he needed it, he would have caved days ago.

James wasn't an addict. I knew that he thought he was, but he wasn't. He was depressed in college and he was depressed when he was married to Isabella. He needed an outlet for his anger. He needed something more from his life. That didn't mean he was an addict.

"Penny, I couldn't stop."

His words seemed to echo in my head. Maybe he couldn't stop, but he hadn't had a reason to. Because he was depressed. But now he had me. I was enough. I had to be enough.

I grabbed the door handle of my apartment building and made my way over to the elevators.

"Mrs. Hunter?"

I turned my head. Sometimes people called me that by mistake. The man at the reception desk was smiling at me and held up a manila envelope.

"Miss Taylor. Our wedding isn't until next week," I said and walked over to him.

"Congratulations." He seemed sincere and gave me another warm smile. "These came for you today." There was also a small envelope on top of the large one. "I was just about to run them up to you, but here you are."

"Thank you so much." I grabbed the papers from him and looked down at his name tag. "Cliff. And please just call me, Penny."

He nodded. "Have a good evening, Penny."

"You too." I walked back over to the elevator and quickly got on. I opened up the top envelope and pulled out a handwritten note:

Stop calling him, Penny. He's fine. Don't you trust me?
-Rob

I laughed out loud and the other woman in the elevator gave me a weird look. I looked back down at the note. Despite the fact that he knew me so well, I didn't trust Rob at all. But I wasn't worried about his influence this time. I was worried about Mason's. And who knew who else was even with them?

The other woman got off and I was alone again. Rob knew me so well. He knew I'd be worried. I'd just have to believe that James' friends had his best interests in mind. I had spent so much time with Mason. He was a good guy. All the weird things about him suddenly made sense though. At first his gaze had always made me feel uncomfortable. He had probably been grading me or something. I laughed at the thought. Mason was certainly a man-whore before he met Bee. But he was completely different now.

Besides, I trusted James. That was what truly mattered.

I got off the elevator and unlocked our door. I kicked the door closed with my foot as I opened up the other envelope. The apartment was dark. Ellen would have left hours ago. I pulled out the papers from the envelope as I switched on the lights. When I looked down, my body froze.

It was a picture of James with his arms wrapped around another woman. They were standing outside a nice house, probably in some suburban neighborhood. There were at least a dozen pictures of the two of them. The first few were of them hugging. The woman looked so surprised to see him. She had stepped back and looked up at him with a huge smile on her face. And then it looked like she hugged him again. Her head was pressed against his chest. James' chin rested on top of her head. His eyes were closed. He looked content. He looked happy. The last image was of her pulling him inside her house.

My whole body felt cold. I wouldn't have known who it was if I hadn't seen a picture of her just the other day. *Rachel.* She looked older, but it was definitely her. She was more sophisticated looking. She was even prettier than she had been in high school.

I felt my chest tighten. I turned over the images. They were dated from this Tuesday. Rachel had been his errand. That's why he didn't have any bags or anything when he had come home that night. That's why he had wanted to watch T.V. He didn't want to talk to me about what he had been doing. What had he been doing exactly? Clearly something that he wanted to hide from me. We had promised each other no more secrets.

I looked back inside the envelope. There was a post-it note stuck to the bottom. I quickly pulled it out and looked at the note scrawled across it:

I told you that you didn't know him. He'll never love you the way he loved her. Can you live with that?

Of course Isabella had sent these. She was just messing with my head. I'm sure James had a reason for visiting Rachel. Maybe they were still friends. But wouldn't he have told me that? I looked back down at the picture of James resting his chin on the top of her head. *Why did you lie?* Withholding information was the same as lying. James and I knew that better than anyone. Was there still something going on between them? Was this why he didn't cave in our game? Because he was sleeping with someone else?

"He'll never love you the way he loved her."

I picked up my phone and called Rob. He had to let me talk to James. I just needed to hear his voice. I needed to hear him say he loved me. The phone rang a few times and then Rob picked up.

"We're kind of busy, Penny. Didn't you get my message?"

"Yes, but I just need to talk to him for a second."

"No can do, babe."

"Rob, seriously, it'll just take a second."

"Geez, Penny, you keep him on a tight leash. You have to let him live a little. We're just having fun, he's fine."

I pressed my lips together. "I know he's fine. Please, Rob, it's important."

"Then why don't you tell me about it? I'm a good listener."

"It's not..." I sighed. There was no way I was going to talk to James' brother about this. "Can you at least tell me where you are?" Maybe I could call the hotel they were staying at and get in contact with James that way.

"I forget what it's called. Mason booked it."

"Are you still in New York?"

Rob laughed. "We're not even in the country."

Fuck. "So what country are you in?"

Rob laughed again. "What is this really about? Are you trying to get phone sex?"

I wanted to kill him. "Robert Hunter, put your brother on the phone this instant."

"I like when you act all kinky."

"Rob!"

"Penny!" There were some muffled voices after Rob's voice.

"Is that him?"

"No!" Rob yelled. "Stop it!" He started laughing really loudly. "No! Mason, help!" Rob's laughter completely filled the phone and then the line went dead.

I wanted to laugh at how ridiculous Rob was. Instead, I started crying. It suddenly felt like everything was slipping away from me. I had gotten so used to James being there to comfort me that the thought of him not being there made me cry even harder. I lay down on the couch and covered my face with my arms.

"He'll never love you the way he loved her."

I needed someone to calm me down and tell me everything was going to be okay. I needed my best friend back.

CHAPTER 21
Saturday

It was a good thing that Ellen didn't work on the weekends. It would give me time to clean up the mess I had made. I had somehow ended up in bed with all the pictures spread out, a bottle of wine, and a pint of Ben and Jerry's Chunky Monkey ice cream. And lots of tears. I had tried to find out Rachel's last name, but I didn't have much information to go on. I wanted to walk up to her house and tell her to stay away from James. But that was ridiculous anyway. He had gone to see her, not the other way around.

I stepped off the elevator.

"Penny!" The man at the front desk called as soon as he saw me.

I knew my eyes were still slightly red from crying all night. I walked over to Cliff, trying to avoid direct eye contact. "Good morning, Cliff."

"Good morning. You've got more mail this morning." He handed me a few envelopes, which included another manila envelope. This one didn't have an address. It just said Penny Taylor on the front.

I glanced up at him. "Did someone drop this off?"

"I'm not sure. It was just in your box when I got here this morning. I can call the guy who was on duty earlier if you'd like?"

"No, that's okay. Thanks," I mumbled. I turned away from him and walked out of the building and into the bright sunshine. Ian was already waiting there with the car. I climbed in and stared down at the envelope. It was a bad idea to open it. Isabella was just trying to mess with my head.

I bit my lip and tapped on the glass that separated Ian and me.

He lowered the partition. "Where to, Penny?"

"Where did you take James on Tuesday after work?" I asked.

"He had some errands to run."

"I know. But where specifically?"

Ian disconnected our gaze in the rearview mirror and turned around to look at me. "If you're trying to figure out what James got you for your wedding present, I have no idea." He gave me a small smile. It wasn't guilty looking necessarily. But I knew he knew. He wasn't my employee. There was no reason why he should divulge to me where James was. He had probably signed some confidentiality agreement.

I laughed. "You got me. Sorry, never mind. Can you just take me to Kleinfeld's?"

"Of course. Are we picking up anyone on the way?"

"No. My friends are meeting me there." I wasn't sure why I lied. I didn't want Ian to pity me more than he already seemed to. No one was coming with me to my dress fitting. I had asked Bee to come last night, but she already had plans this morning. Jen had gone back to California after the engagement party. My mom was coming up Thursday for the wedding, and I didn't want to bother her with a day trip. And Melissa still wasn't talking to me. I could feel Ian's gaze on me in the rearview mirror. I felt like I was going to cry again. "I need to make a quick phone call," I said and closed the partition so he couldn't see me anymore.

Maybe I should try Melissa one more time. I called but it went straight to voicemail. I hung up without leaving a message. There was nothing to say. "I'm sorry I slept with your boyfriend two and a half years ago, but can you please come help me make sure my wedding dress looks good?" didn't seem quite good enough. She had to get past it in her own way.

I looked down at the manila envelope. Isabella had moved on from James while they were still together. And now they had been separated for over three years. I had been with him most of that time. Why did she suddenly care again? She just wanted what she couldn't have. And now she wanted me to open this envelope. I didn't want to give her what she wanted. But it was like it was staring at me. I needed to know what was inside.

I unclipped the top before I could change my mind and pulled out another photo, just one this time. There was a post-it note in the middle of it:

He's been pretty busy this week. He can't control himself, remember? It's a sickness. I tried to warn you.

My heart starting beating really fast. I slowly removed the post-it note and looked down at the photo. Isabella had James' suit jacket collar gripped tightly in her hands and she was kissing him. James' hands were wrapped around her back. Like he wanted it. I shut my eyes tight. No. *No.* It was photoshopped. That's what it was. James wouldn't kiss her. He wouldn't do that to me. *He loves me.* I opened my eyes and stared down at the picture. It was in James' office. It must have been taken on Monday when she had shown up. So James told her he'd get a restraining order against her after making out with her? This is why he actually stood me up for lunch? So he could shove his tongue down his ex wife's throat? I felt like I was going to throw up.

"He can't control himself, remember?"

I needed to talk to him. I needed to hear his voice. I put my face in my hands. I was letting Isabella win. She was successfully manipulating me. But what else was I supposed to think when I saw that picture? What other explanation was there?

If I couldn't talk to James, I needed to talk to Melissa. She was always the best at calming me down from stuff. Maybe Tyler could convince her to talk to me. I picked my phone back up and called him. He answered right away. "Hey, Penny. I missed you last night."

I didn't know what I was supposed to say to that. I missed him too, but I wasn't really allowed to miss him right now. "Yeah, I went out with Bee and her friends. I hope you had a good night with Melissa. Actually, that's why I'm calling. Is she there? She hasn't answered any of my calls, and I..."

"She's been working a lot. She had to go in early this morning too, so she's not here."

"Oh. Okay." I was having a hard time controlling my voice.

"Penny, are you okay?"

"I'm fine. But I have to go."

"Penny, where are you?"

I took a deep breath. "I'm on my way to Kleinfeld's."

"Was Melissa supposed to go with you?"

"Yeah. It's not a big deal though. I've already picked the dress. It's just a fitting. I can do it myself."

"I can come."

"You don't have to do that."

"I want to."

I bit the inside of my lip. "It'll just make Melissa mad. Thanks for offering, but I have to go, Tyler."

"Penny..."

"I'm sorry." I hung up the phone. Now I just seemed to be pushing away the people I was closest to. But if everything was slipping away, I might as well slide down the slope even faster. I might as well end up at the bottom alone if I was losing the only person in the world I loved. I ran my fingers across the picture. I loved him. Why would he do this to me? Was it something I did?

Of course it was. I had been stressed out for weeks. I hadn't had sex with him in days. I was a mess. And it was more than that. It was my biggest fear coming true. I wasn't good enough for him. I had always known that. Maybe he was finally realizing it too.

The car came to a stop and the partition started to lower. I quickly wiped away the tears from under my eyes and slipped the picture into my purse so Ian wouldn't see it.

"We're here...are you okay?"

"I'm fine."

Ian handed me a tissue.

"Thank you." I grabbed it and blotted my eyes.

"Call me when you're done, okay?"

"I'm just going to walk home. Thank you, though."

"James wouldn't want you to do that."

Well James was certainly doing a bunch of stuff earlier this week that I didn't want him to do. "I'm not sure he really cares about what I do." I opened up the door and climbed out before Ian could respond. I walked into the building and gave the receptionist my name. In a minute I was being escorted to a room in the back of the store.

I wasn't sure why I was here. I wasn't sad now, I was just angry. Did he even want to marry me? Was he going to sneak around behind my back all the time?

"Are you waiting for anyone?" The woman said and gestured for me to sit in a chair.

I put a smile on my face. "Nope, just me." No one came to dress fittings alone.

"Okay, dear. Let me go get your dress, I'll be right back."

I nodded and took a deep breath. *James loves me.* He had probably gone to go see Rachel for closure or something. He'd be able to tell me on Sunday night. And Isabella had probably attacked him with that kiss. She was a psychopath. He could explain it all tomorrow night. Everything was fine. *I'm fine.* I was here trying on a wedding dress because I was going to marry the man of my dreams in one week. Next Saturday James and I would be married and it would be the best day of my life. Isabella couldn't sabotage us. I took another deep breath.

It felt like my heart was beating in my throat. I trusted James. Everything was going to be fine. I leaned my head against the wall behind me. Last night I had been worried about what he might do during his bachelor party. I had no idea what he had already done.

"Okay, let's see how it fits."

I shook my thoughts away and stood up. I plastered my fake smile back on my face. "Okay." I walked into the dressing room with her, took off my clothes, and stepped into the dress. She pulled it up past my waist and zipped it in place.

It fit even better than the sample had. It was perfect. James would love it.

I immediately burst into tears. "I'm sorry." I tried to clear my throat. "I don't know what's wrong with me."

"Everyone always gets emotional when they try their dress on." The woman smiled and handed me a tissue box. "You look absolutely beautiful."

I quickly grabbed a tissue and blew my nose. I wasn't crying because I was happy and excited. I was crying because I wasn't sure if James even wanted to see me in this dress anymore. *I'm fine.* It didn't matter how many times I had said it, it didn't make it true.

"We'll have to take it in a little under the arms," the woman said. "And shorten it another inch. Can you come back in a few days?"

I wiped my eyes with another tissue. "The wedding is next Saturday. Will there only be one more fitting?"

"That should do it. How does Thursday sound?"

"That sounds good. Do you have something for that night?" My mom was coming up Thursday after work. It would be so much better once she was with me.

"The latest appointment we have is at 4 o'clock. Does that work?"

James could deal with me skipping out on work a little early. And my mom had already been toying with the idea of taking a half day on Thursday. She wouldn't want to miss my final fitting. "Yeah, that works."

The woman wrote the date and time down on her business card and handed it to me. "Is there anything you want to change?"

I stared at my reflection in the mirror. "No. It's perfect."

"Have you already tried on veils?"

"A couple. I think I'll wait till Thursday to choose one if that's alright."

She nodded. "Okay. Let me help you out of the dress."

***

I walked out of the store a few minutes later.

"Penny?"

I turned around to see Tyler leaning against the wall outside of Kleinfeld's. It was so nice to see a familiar face.

"I would have come in, but it didn't seem like you wanted me to." He scratched the back of his neck. "But I could tell you were upset."

My bottom lip started quivering again. I couldn't seem to control my emotions ever since I had gotten those first pictures from Isabella. I walked over to Tyler and gave him a big hug. For the first time since James had left, I felt a little calmer. "I missed you too," I mumbled into his chest. I was making his shirt wet from my tears, but he didn't move away.

"Do you want to tell me what's going on?"

"No."

He laughed and pulled back. "Well, are you hungry?"

"I'm starving." I had skipped breakfast because I felt nauseous after eating tons of ice cream and drinking wine last night. But being paranoid all morning had made my appetite come back.

"Let's get lunch."

I wasn't sure if I should protest. Having lunch with him might make Melissa take even longer to get over this whole mess. My train of thought was waylaid when Tyler grabbed my arm.

"Come on. There's a diner down the street from here that has a really good grilled cheese."

I smiled. He knew I couldn't resist a grilled cheese sandwich and fries. We walked toward the diner in silence. He was probably wondering the same thing I was about Melissa's reaction to this. I didn't want him to be in the doghouse because of me.

As if sensing what I was thinking, he opened up the door for me, and said, "I'm not leaving one of my best friends alone when they just burst into tears in the middle of the sidewalk. Food. Now."

"When did you get so bossy?"

He shrugged. "I don't know. Apparently girls dig it, though."

I laughed and walked into the diner. It smelled like hot grease and all things wonderful in the world. We got seated in one of the booths by the windows. I slid in across from him and picked up a menu.

"You're really not going to tell me what's wrong?" Tyler asked.

I bit my lip. "It's just been a really bad week."

"Because of your new job? Or the last minute wedding stuff?"

I shrugged. "Everything. I've been so stressed out ever since graduation."

"I remember that feeling. Moving here was probably the scariest thing I ever did. Sometimes the real world sucks." He looked down at his menu and then set it aside.

"Especially when two of your best friends aren't speaking to you."

"I never agreed to that," said Tyler. "I'm here, aren't I?"

The waiter came over and Tyler ordered each of us a Cherry Coke, grilled cheese, and French fries.

"And what is Melissa going to say about that?" I asked. "She won't even speak to me."

"James came around. She will too."

I sighed. "Not fast enough. I need her right now."

"I know. I'm sorry about the timing of all this." He scratched the back of his neck.

"It's not your fault."

"Well, it kind of is. Apparently I talk about you too much." He smiled at me. "But we always have the best stories. Remember the fall cricket fiasco? How can I not talk about that?"

I started laughing. "That was the best. I mean, horrible, but hilarious." His neighbor had kept blasting music at all hours of the night. So we had gone to the pet store and bought tons of crickets. For some reason Tyler knew how to pick locks. He said it was a fraternity thing. The plan was to release them in his neighbor's apartment. But the bag had a hole in it and the crickets escaped all over Tyler's apartment instead. It took him weeks to catch them all. And for the longest time afterward we'd still hear chirping noises and go on cricket searching missions on Friday nights.

"It's like my go to party story."

"It's a great story."

He shrugged. "Melissa hates it."

I shifted in my seat. "Do you think you could try to get her to freak out about this after the wedding?"

"I've tried talking to her. I can't believe she didn't come with you to this. She's your freaking maid of honor."

At least he understood.

"Not that I minded stepping up." He gave me a small smile. "And I think you should tell me what's really bothering you. On top of your two best friends banging."

I laughed and pulled the picture out of my purse. I needed to talk this through with someone. Tyler was my friend. If Melissa wasn't around, I was allowed to go to him for help. "Isabella's been sending me pictures, trying to freak me out or something."

"She's so insane."

"I know. And I know that's all this is. But I can't help but think it's something more." I put the picture down on the table.

"What the fuck?" Tyler picked it up. He looked really mad.

"She came by the office the other day. He told me she wanted to be friends or something. But he said he told her to leave us alone. This has to be from that day. Do you think it looks like she surprised him? Like, does it look like he's kissing her back?"

Tyler's jaw clenched. He didn't say anything.

I laughed, but that didn't seem to make Tyler look any less pissed. "You're supposed to be calming me down, Tyler."

He put the picture back down on the table.

"I mean, I know his hands are on her back. But maybe they were hugging goodbye. Isabella loves making scenes. He has to act a certain way around her so she won't freak out."

"He had to kiss her?" he asked.

"No. But I mean, maybe she just kissed him?"

Tyler lowered his eyebrows. "Yeah, maybe. Have you asked him about it?"

"He's away for his bachelor party all weekend. And the guys took his phone." I wasn't going to get into that whole fiasco. Those were all the details Tyler needed to know about that.

Tyler shook his head. "You said pictures? Are there more?"

"There were some of him with this girl he dated in high school. She was hugging him and he was going into her house. But I know it was kind of a rocky breakup. Maybe he just needed closure, you know? Before we tie the knot? I mean, that's definitely a thing people do, right?" I sounded pathetic.

Tyler sighed. "I...I don't know what you want me to say."

"Tell me it's going to be okay. Tell me Isabella is just messing with my head. There's an explanation for all of this. He's just not here to tell me. And I feel like she knows that. She could have sent me this picture earlier this week. She chose now to do it. She's manipulative and crazy."

"She's definitely crazy. And it's going to be okay." He sounded so sincere, but I didn't really believe him. His eyes gave him away. He looked mad.

"You think he cheated on me, don't you?"

Tyler shook his head and grabbed my hand. "No, he wouldn't do that. You're getting married in one week. James loves you. Everything is going to be fine." He squeezed my hand. "It's going to be okay."

I took a deep breath. His voice was soothing. I wasn't sure if he believed what he was saying, but it was nice to hear.

Tyler let go of my hand when the waitress came back over with our food. "Do you know where Isabella lives?" he asked as soon as the waitress left.

"No. Why, do you want to unleash hundreds of crickets into her apartment?"

"It's not a terrible idea." He took a bite of his sandwich. "Do you have her number?"

I shook my head. "This is really good," I said after I took my first bite.

"Mhm. What's Rachel's last name?"

"I don't know. And Tyler, I don't want you to do anything about it. I just needed someone to talk to."

"But maybe we should..."

"Nope."

"Or we could..."

"No."

He laughed. "Okay. I guess I'm not a great girlfriend. I'm used to trying to fix things, not just listen."

"You're such a boy. But don't worry, you're a fantastic girl-friend too."

He laughed again. "Well, actually, I could use some advice too. I think I'm going to ask Melissa to be my girlfriend. It could help smooth things out between you guys too."

"I don't want you to do that just so she's ready to be my maid of honor again."

"No, that's not it. I really like her. And I think mainly she's just upset because I won't commit, you know? But I think I'm ready for that. I'm ready to grow up."

"Ugh, growing up is so overrated."

He smiled. I could see it in his eyes. He did like her. It was so nice seeing him happy. But I still felt compelled to ask.

"So, you do really like her?"

"Yeah. She's so easy to hang out with. When she's not mad at me that is. We became really good friends after you moved here. Our relationship progressed so naturally. And she's beautiful. And so smart. And she's incredibly passionate." He immediately looked down at his food. His face looked a little red. "Yeah, it's still weird talking about this with you."

"A little." I laughed. I wasn't sure I wanted to hear about my two best friends' passionate lovemaking.

"Okay, let's just agree to be friends that talk about everything except for our sex lives." He put his hand out for me to shake.

"Deal."

"Um, so, I was thinking I'd surprise her after work. With some flowers or something. And ask her officially. Hopefully she won't want to move out either. I've gotten used to waking up next to her." He looked a little embarrassed again.

"I think she'll love that."

"Yeah?"

I nodded. I knew this would mean my relationship with Tyler would change. It would be different with Melissa too. But if it meant they were both happy, then I was happy too. I could adjust. The past few weeks I had handled so much change. I could handle one more thing.

"Well, she gets off in about half an hour. I should probably get going. If you're okay?"

"I'm good."

"You sure?"

"Go ask my best friend to be your girlfriend."

He stood up and pulled out his wallet.

"It's my turn." I shooed him.

He smiled. "See you later, Penny."

"Bye, Tyler." I watched him leave the restaurant. It was probably the last time I'd hang out with him one on one. He probably knew it too.

I sighed and looked down at my half eaten sandwich. Maybe I should go try to confront Isabella. I didn't want her to think she could intimidate me. Even if she had. I didn't want to give her the satisfaction. She was just messing with me.

Ian probably knew where she lived. It was just a question of whether or not he would take me there. I grabbed my phone and texted Ian to pick me up at the diner.

In a few minutes I saw the car pull up outside. I quickly paid the bill and walked out of the restaurant. Ian opened up the car door for me. Before he could ask me where I wanted to go, I climbed into the car. I couldn't make eye contact with him when he asked.

When he got into the car, he lowered the partition. "Where to, Penny?"

I looked out the window. "Can you take me to Isabella's?" I kept my eyes glued on the window, despite the awkward silence that greeted my ears.

"Sorry. What's her last name?"

"Hunter." I turned toward the front of the car. Luckily I only had to look at him through the rearview mirror because I was starting to feel sweaty.

"I don't..." He cleared his throat. "I don't think I'm supposed to take you there."

He wasn't supposed to take me there? *God, James.* Had he seriously told Ian where he could and could not take me? I didn't want to lie to Ian, and I certainly didn't want to get him in trouble. But I needed him to take me to Isabella's. "I have lunch plans with her. I don't want to be late."

Ian glanced out the window at the diner that I had just come out of.

Crap. Why am I such a terrible liar? I was even worse when I was angry. I tended to speak before I thought it out.

"Penny, I'm going to take you home."

"Ian, please. I need to talk to her."

"James doesn't want you to be in contact with her."

Why? Because he doesn't want me to catch them making out? I swallowed hard. That wasn't fair. It was just a picture. There was so much behind a captured image. I looked down at my hands. "What, did he give you a list of places where I'm not allowed to go or something?"

"I'm not at liberty to discuss that with you."

I spent a lot of time with Ian. Whenever I was in the car with him, I usually lowered the partition and chatted with him. I considered him to be a friend. But he wasn't. He was polite and courteous to me because James paid him to be. Ian wasn't my friend. He wasn't even my employee, he was James'.

"Okay," I said and looked back out the window. I felt like a petulant child. James had a way of making me feel like that. But he was right. I shouldn't be going to see Isabella. There would never be a reason for me to go see her. Ever.

***

I got out of the car without saying anything and walked toward the front of the apartment building.

"Penny, I'm sorry."

I turned around and looked at Ian.

I shrugged. "If you're not allowed to take me there, then you're not allowed to take me. It's fine."

"Look, I'll take you if you really want to go. James doesn't have to know." He stared at me, wanting to know if I'd keep the secret. He was putting his neck out for me. Maybe he thought of me as more of a friend than I realized.

"No, that's okay. James knows best, right?" I gave him a small smile.

"You really don't want to see her anyway. Trust me. She's not...nice."

He knows her? I hadn't even thought about it before. "Did you work for James when they were still married?"

Ian nodded. "Yeah, he even kept me on the payroll when he went to teach at the University of New Castle for a year. So that I wouldn't have to keep my job with Isabella. We didn't get along very well. He probably did it because he knew Isabella would fire me." He laughed.

"He knew he was only staying there for a year?" I asked as nonchalantly as possible.

"Well, I mean, he came back before a year so I had to start back up again a few months early. With you." He smiled. "But, yeah, he said he'd be back in a year when he left."

James had told me he was taking a break by teaching. He had never put a date on it though. He had never told me that his plan was always to come back to New York. I thought we had decided to make our fresh start here together. I had that same eerie feeling that I had when we had just met. That he was the hunter and I was the prey. I folded my arms across my chest, suddenly cold. Why did it feel like I still didn't know him?

"Are you okay?" he asked.

I had gotten lost in my thoughts. I nodded my head and smiled. "Yeah. I'm just feeling a bit tired. I'm going to go take a nap."

He nodded.

I walked into the building. The wave of air conditioning made me shiver. It was freezing. It felt like I was in the middle of a New York winter.

"Penny!" Cliff called as I made me way to the elevator. "I have a package for you."

Oh God. But when I turned around, it was a box sitting on the counter, not another manila envelope. I let a sigh escape from my lips as I walked over to Cliff and lifted up the box. "Thanks, Cliff."

As I stepped onto the elevator, I looked down at the box. My momentary relief completely evaporated. It was addressed like the last envelope had been, with just my name and no address. The elevator dinged. I absentmindedly walked into our apartment. My heart was racing. I set the box down on the counter. I had this weird, all consuming fear that there was going to be a bloody limb in the box. Part of me wanted to laugh it off, but the other half of me was wondering just how crazy Isabella really was. She followed James to Rachel's. She had gotten someone to take pictures of her in James' office in order to capture her kissing him.

I shouldn't look in the box. But it was like I had no control over my body. I tore off the brown paper and looked down at the shoebox. There was a post-it note on top of the lid:

He's not good at forever. His words are as empty as the promises he can't possibly keep because his love is as fleeting as his addictions.

James talked about a forever with me before he had even officially divorced Isabella. He jumped into a life with me head first. But it was because he had never experienced something so real before. It didn't matter what Isabella said about Rachel. He loved me more than he ever loved her. And he definitely loved me more than he loved Isabella. James kept his promises to me. Always. He was good at forever because he was my forever.

But I still opened the lid of the shoebox. I wasn't scared of Isabella. Whatever was inside couldn't take away the fact that I knew he was the love of my life. And that he meant every word he ever said to me.

Inside there were dozens of handwritten letters and short notes. On top of the jumbled up letters was another post-it note:

Love is something to hold on to when your past is dark. When you need an escape from your reality. When you're an addict.

Fuck you, Isabella. She didn't know him. She never did. James was in control of his own fate. He wasn't addicted to me. And he was certainly never addicted to her. I picked up the first letter that was underneath her note:

My beautiful Isabella,

Today we start our lives together. There's nothing I want more than to fall asleep with you in my arms and to wake up to your smile for the rest of my life. I've been dreaming of this day my whole life, the day you'll finally be mine, the day we finally become one. Marriage, starting a family, growing old together, I want everything with you and only you. You are the love of my life. You are my heart and soul. You are my happily ever after.

I'll love you always and forever,

-James

I could picture him writing this to me on our wedding day. He had even said some of these things to me before. Almost word for word. This was how he had felt the day they had gotten married. His words were so full of hope. They were so full of love. I felt a tear fall down my cheek.

He had made it seem like he never loved her. Like he was forced into it. But he had said he tried to make it work. He had wanted it to work. That letter didn't make it seem like he was trying to love her. It made it seem like he did. I sat down on one of the stools at the kitchen counter and reread the letter.

Maybe I was wrong. His words were so heartfelt. Had he actually been in love with her when they got married? That wasn't what he told me, though. I pulled out the picture from my purse and stared at the two of them kissing. He wasn't pushing her away. Maybe he still loved her.

I grabbed another note from the box.

My love,

You love me despite my flaws. You understand me better than anyone else ever has or ever could. The best decision I ever made was marrying you.

Yours,

-James

I could feel my heart beating in my throat. I picked up another note and read one after another.

Isabella,

Your eyes sparkle in the sun. I get lost in them every time we're together.

Love,

-James

To the sexiest woman I know,

When we're not together I dream of you. My lips against your soft skin. My fingers in your silky hair. The taste of you drives me crazy, baby. I'll never get enough of you. I can't wait for this business trip to be over. Not having you every night is torture. I feel like a teenager again.

Thinking of you,

-James

My beautiful wife,

I can't wait to have children with you. I can't wait to start our family. You're going to be a wonderful mother. You're so loving and caring. I'm ready to try. A bunch of little yous running around would make me the happiest man in the world.

Love always,

-James

I couldn't read anymore. All the words were blurry because of my tears. He loved her. He loved her so much. These were sweet notes written to a woman he was head over heels for. He wanted to start a family with her.

And he didn't want one with me. I put the notes back in the box and closed the lid. He was ready to have children four years ago, but he wasn't ready now. It didn't seem like he ever wanted kids with me.

James meant everything to me. He was my whole world. And now it felt like my whole world was crumbling in front of me.

The pictures could be explained. He went for closure with Rachel. Isabella kissed him, not the other way around. Those could all be logically excused. But these notes? He lied to me. James had loved Isabella. He didn't have to lie to me about that. He could have said he loved her. And that she cheated on him and it broke his heart. The only reason you lied about a divorce was for one reason: if you were still in love with the person. And you wanted to convince yourself you weren't.

I wanted to grab a box of notes James had written for me, get lost in them, and forget about everything he had ever said to Isabella. But I didn't have a box of notes from James. I mostly had emails and texts. And the few handwritten notes I did have weren't anything like this. They were telling me he had gone for a run. Or to remind me about a dinner we had to go to.

James was my first love. He was my only love. But I wasn't his. He had made it seem like I was. At least his first love like this. A great love. The kind you see in movies and read about in books. But it didn't seem like I was.

I didn't know him at all.

CHAPTER 22
Saturday

I wasn't sure how long I stood there, staring out the window. The sun had set over Central Park and the lights were coming on, lighting up the walking paths. It was so beautiful that it didn't even seem real. That was the same conclusion I had come to about my relationship with James too. It was too good and too perfect to be real.

I knew he was out of my league. But I thought he loved me. I knelt down in front of the window and pressed my forehead against the glass. I closed my eyes and savored the feeling of the cool glass on my forehead. There weren't any tears left inside of me. I had tried to call James a few times, but it always went straight to voicemail. It wasn't his fault, but each time he didn't pick up it just validated all my fears.

This was how Isabella wanted me to feel. She had won. It hadn't been a fair fight at all. I touched my cheek where she had slapped me. She had even warned me. I shook my head. *No.* Isabella had said she had two weeks to win James back. If she was sending me this stuff, I didn't even want to know what she was doing to him. I already knew she had kissed him. Maybe that wasn't the end of it.

My phone started buzzing in my pocket. I pulled it out. *Mason.* I quickly answered it. "Mason!"

He laughed. "Hey, Penny. Having a good weekend?"

"Can I talk to him?"

Mason laughed again. "Jumping right into things, then? So, about that...you need to stop calling. You're distracting him from having fun."

"I'm sure he's having quite enough fun."

My comment was greeted by silence.

"Where are you guys?"

"Costa Rica."

What the hell were they doing in Costa Rica? "What hotel?"

"Nice try, Penny. I'm not telling you where we are. You're not allowed to infiltrate his bachelor party."

"Mason, I really, really need to talk to him."

"Umm...I would hand the phone over, but he's currently in-disposed."

"Indisposed? What have you been doing?"

He laughed. "I'm just kidding. He's taking a shower."

I breathed a sigh of relief. It didn't matter how upset I was, I would always worry about him. "Has he been getting packages? Or any mail there?"

"No?"

"Has he been acting weird?"

Mason laughed. "He's not getting cold feet, if that's what you're worried about."

"Okay." *Well, that's good.* Isabella probably didn't know where they were.

"I promise I'm taking good care of your fiancé. You don't need to worry. I'm not going to let him fuck up the best thing that's ever happened to him."

That was sweet. It was also apparently untrue. "That's not what I'm worried about."

"Are you okay, Penny? You can talk to me you know."

Talk to James' best friend about this? No, I can't. "I need to talk to him, Mason."

"I'll give him a message for you."

"That's okay. I'll just...see him tomorrow night. Right?"

"I'll have him back before midnight. I promise."

"Okay. Bye, Mason"

"Wait. There was a reason I was calling."

I didn't say anything.

"I think Bee's phone died. I haven't heard from her all day. Could you go over there and see if she's okay? And tell her to call me?"

"So you want me to tell Bee to call you, but you won't let me talk to James?"

"Yeah."

"You're a terrible person." I couldn't help but laugh at the irony.

"And that's why you love me."

There was some noise in the background.

"Rob's back," Mason said. "I have to go. Please check on her, Penny." The line went dead.

***

Even though I wasn't allowed to talk to James, at least I knew he was safe. That was the only reason I had walked over to Trump International. And because Bee's phone had gone straight to voicemail when I called her.

I paused in the lobby, remembering the day that James had brought me here when he was still my professor. It had been perfect in every way. I laughed to myself. This was also the first place I had ever met Mason. I remembered how his stare had made me uncomfortable. It was almost like he could see me. Really see me. But he was probably just sizing me up for his side business.

Bee worked hard. She had probably just fallen asleep early in front of the T.V. or something. I got onto the elevator and listened to the fancy elevator music playing. It was strange that Bee and Mason lived in a hotel. But they had made their apartment very homey. I always felt comfortable there. Besides, living like you were in a hotel was kind of fun. Even though their apartment was technically classified as a condo in the hotel, they could still order room service whenever they wanted.

I stepped off the elevator and made my way down the hallway. The sound of music blaring got louder and louder as I got closer to Bee's apartment. I stopped outside her door and knocked. The door flew open.

"Welcome to your bachelorette party!" Bee screamed. "It's about time you got here." She grabbed my arm and pulled me into her apartment. "I was starting to think Mason forgot to call you."

Bee, Kendra, Marie, and Melissa were all decked out in sparkly dresses and looked super excited. And maybe a little intoxicated. Melissa was even smiling at me, which was a good sign.

"You're two shots behind," Kendra said.

"This is really nice of you guys, but I don't really want a bachelorette party," I said and stood in the doorway. "Can't we just stay in and watch a movie or something?"

"Don't be ridiculous," Kendra said and brought two shot glasses over to me. "Besides, it's too late. We've already planned the whole thing."

I looked down at the two shot glasses she had shoved into my hands.

"Come on," Marie said. "With everything we have planned, you're going to need that."

Oh God.

"Don't be such a party pooper," Melissa said and gave me another smile. She used to say stuff like that to me all the time in college. It was nice that she was finally talking to me again. I didn't want to fight with her. All I really wanted was to be curled up in my bed back home, though. I sighed and downed one shot and then the next.

"First things first," Bee said. "Put this on." She grabbed the shot glasses from me and handed me a sparkly dress.

James didn't like when I wore stuff like this. At least, in public.

"Melissa picked it out for you. So you know it's going to fit perfectly. Go change."

"Can't I just wear what I have on?" I was wearing jean shorts and a baggy t-shirt.

Kendra laughed. "Absolutely not. Get to it. We have a huge list. It's going to take us all night to get through all this stuff."

Maybe this was exactly what I needed. I wanted to have fun tonight and forget about everything that had been going on. That probably wasn't possible though. I walked down the hallway and into the bathroom. The dress was tight and ended right below my ass. My boobs weren't big, but this dress made them look huge. I looked like a total slut. Luckily I was wearing flip flops. Heels would have tipped the scales to making me look more like a hooker. I didn't dwell on the fact that my eyes were still red from going in and out of hysterical crying fits all day.

"There's a pair of shoes out here for you to wear too!" one of the girls yelled from the other room.

Shit. I walked back out into the kitchen and looked down at the stilettos they wanted me to wear. "What are we doing exactly? Are we going to be walking a lot? I think I'll just stick with these shoes."

"You can't wear a dress like that with flip flops," Melissa said.

"And everyone's going to be looking at you, because you're the girl of the hour." Bee pulled a pink sash over me and added a sparkly tiara to the top of my head.

I looked down at the sash. It had 'bachelorette' written across it in a fancy font. I could feel my face turning red.

Marie clapped her hands. "You look perfectly embarrassed. Penis cookie?"

"What now?"

Marie held a plate of cookies shaped like penises in front of my face.

I started laughing. "No, I'm good right now. Thanks, though. They're very anatomically correct, huh?"

"Thanks, I made them myself," Marie said. "I'll bring a few with us. Let's get going."

"Really, no movie?"

Bee laughed and hooked her arm through mine. "Trust me, this is going to be so much better. We can watch a movie tomorrow while we're working through these hangovers."

***

"So, you need to ask a random guy to buy you a drink," Marie said as she looked down at a list she had.

"Can I see that?" I tried to snatch it from her, but she moved it away too quickly.

"How about him?" Kendra said and pointed to a guy at the bar. He was wearing jeans and a t-shirt. His hair was shaggy. It looked like he belonged at the beach instead of in a bar in New York. He was probably a tourist. Which meant he wouldn't want to pay for a drink that was way too expensive for a girl he didn't know.

"He looks like a tourist."

Melissa laughed. "So? That means he's here to get laid. He'll definitely buy you a drink."

"I don't want to lead him on."

"You aren't. You're wearing a freaking sash that says you're getting married any day. You're fine. Go ask him."

Bee gave my shoulder a little nudge. "You aren't going home until you do everything on that list. You might as well get it over with."

This was going to be mortifying. I slid off my bar stool and walked over to him. I leaned on the counter next to him. "Hey," I said. My voice sounded nervous and not flirtatious at all.

He turned away from the guy he was talking to. "Hey." He looked down at my sash and smiled at me. "One more crazy night, huh?"

"Not exactly. Look, so my friends over there..."

He looked over my shoulder.

"No, don't look." I grabbed his arm.

He laughed. "Okay, not looking."

"Well, they have this list of things I have to do, and one of them is to ask a stranger to buy me a drink. But I know you don't want to do that. So, you can tell me when they aren't looking and I'll slip you ten dollars. And could you just order me a drink with that?" Then I can go back there and pretend you bought me a drink?"

The more I spoke, the bigger his smile got. "I don't know, their eyes are glued on you. You might not get an opportunity."

"Crap. They're looking right now?"

"Mhm. So maybe it's easier if I just buy you a drink." He lifted up his arm to call over the bartender.

"You don't have to do that."

"Isn't that why you came over?"

"Kind of. But I was just going to pretend..."

He laughed again, drowning out my words. "You know, you could have just asked me to buy you a drink. I didn't need the whole story. All a beautiful woman like you needed to do was say you were thirsty. The whole bar would be buying you drinks all night long."

"Thanks. I'm sorry. I don't know what I'm doing. I've never flirted with a guy at a bar before."

"You're flirting with me? I thought you were getting married?"

"No." I could feel my face turning red. Two shots was enough for me. I didn't need anything else. "I mean, yes I'm getting married. And no, I'm not flirting with you. I just meant, I don't usually talk to strangers in bars."

"You're even sexier when you blush. What's your poison?"

"Something not very strong."

"Whiskey it is then." He ordered before I could correct him. Whiskey was super strong. Where the hell was he from? He handed the glass to me.

"Whiskey? Really?"

"I was thinking that if you haven't flirted with a guy in a bar, then you haven't really lived yet. Maybe a strong drink will help you decide to change that tonight."

I shook my head. "Let me pay you for this."

"That's okay. You can repay me at the end of the night." He winked at me. "Let me know if you need to cross off anything else on that bachelorette party list of yours. I'm happy to help."

"Okay, thanks." My voice had gotten weirdly high pitched. I quickly walked away from him.

"See, that wasn't so bad," Kendra said. "What did he get you?"

"Whiskey." I slid it toward her.

"Oh, no. Number two is drinking whatever he buys you." She slid the glass back to me.

I looked to Bee for help.

She shrugged. "I actually came up with that one. So, how did it go?"

"It was awkward. I'm pretty sure he thinks I'm going to sleep with him at the end of the night because he bought me this." I drank a sip of the whiskey. *Ew.*

"Yeah, it's a total bucket list thing for guys," Marie said. "To have sex with a girl who's destined to be married. It's the ultimate one night stand."

"The unicorn of one night stands," Kendra corrected.

"Can I take this sash off now?" I asked.

"Finish your drink."

I drank the whisky as fast as I could. "It's so gross."

Kendra laughed. "I love whiskey."

"Then why didn't you drink it?"

Kendra grabbed the list and waived it in the air. "Okay, number three." She smiled. "Ask a guy if you can see his six pack."

"Nope." I clapped my hands together. "Let's go to the movies. There's this new one out that I really want to see..."

"There," Melissa said. "He definitely has abs of steel. Let's see 'em!"

She was pointing to a guy who was wearing a tight t-shirt. He was clearly ripped. And he liked showing off that fact or else he would have worn a shirt that was a little looser.

"And don't forget number four," Marie said. "You have to touch them."

"I'm not going to do that."

"You only get to veto one thing. Do you really want to waste it already? This list gets raunchier and raunchier."

"I can't get Marie back because she's already married. But the rest of you? Your bachelorette parties are going to be the absolute worst."

"Sounds good to me," Kendra said. "The sexier the better, I always say."

"Ugh."

"Just think about what James is doing right now."

I did not want to think about what James was doing right now. At all. Bee gave me a sympathetic smile. I sighed and walked over to the guy they had pointed to. The whiskey had made me a little more confident. The compliments from the guy who had bought me a drink didn't hurt either.

"Hey, you."

He smiled at me. "What are you drinking?"

"All sorts of stuff. Whiskey most recently."

"I wouldn't have pegged you as a whiskey kind of girl. But I like it. Let me get you another."

"Oh, no. I didn't like it. Actually, I came over here because I'm on a mission."

"Is that so? What's your mission, sugar?"

"Well, it's my bachelorette party."

"I can see that." He nodded toward my friends.

"Mhm. Well, I noticed that you look very strong."

He smiled. "Well, I can certainly pick you up."

That was the worst pick up line ever. I laughed awkwardly. "I bet. So, I'm supposed to see if you'll let me see your abs."

He raised his eyebrow. "Do you want to see my abs?"

No. I shrugged. "Are they worth seeing?"

"How about you tell me." He lifted up his shirt to reveal his perfectly sculpted torso. "What's the verdict?"

"I don't know if I can tell without touching them."

He laughed. "I don't bite. Well, sometimes I bite."

I internally rolled my eyes. Before I could chicken out, I put my hand out and brushed my fingers against his abs.

He grabbed my hand and pressed my palm firmly against his torso, moving my hand down to the waistline of his jeans.

I quickly pulled my hand away.

"How about we get out of here? I can make your last night as a single woman a night to remember."

"Thanks for the offer. But I really just had to touch your abs." I walked away without saying anything else. This was entirely inappropriate. I didn't want to be doing this. The thought of James running his hand along some random girl's stomach made me feel nauseous.

"You got really into that one," Marie said. "And I don't blame you. God, those abs are amazing."

"They weren't as nice as James'. Can we get going? I'm not feeling very well."

"That's because you need another drink." Melissa slid me a shot glass. There were at least a dozen on the table. I had a feeling they were playing a drinking game at my expense.

"Drink, drink, drink," Kendra said and slammed her fists on the table.

I quickly downed the shot and tried to ignore the burn down my throat. I was already tipsy. This was going to probably put me over the edge. I shook my head back and forth.

"Here," Marie said and slid a napkin with a penis cookie on it toward me.

I laughed. "I'm really not hungry."

"Okay, then that triggers number five. If Penny passes on the cookie, she needs to convince a guy at the bar to eat said cookie."

"I'll just eat it." I lifted up the cookie.

"No way, missy," Melissa said and grabbed my hand. "Number five has already been triggered. Who at the bar looks hungry for a penis?"

"How about that guy," Bee said. She was pointing to a guy in the corner with a plaid shirt and hipster glasses.

"Hipsters probably don't think it's cool to eat penis cookies."

Bee laughed. "I'm giving you an easy one. Hipsters will do anything to fit in. Just tell him eating normal shaped cookies is so cliché."

"Fine." I sighed and slid off my stool. God this was humiliating. I walked over to the hipster and took a seat next to him on the couch.

"Hey," he said as soon as I sat down. "Having a fun night?"

"Actually, it's been mortifying."

He laughed.

"Could you eat this cookie?"

He lowered his eyebrows. "Are you trying to drug me?"

"No, no. It's just a normal cookie shaped like a penis."

He laughed again.

I held it up for him to see.

"Oh, wait. You're serious?"

"My friends have this weird list of stuff I have to do. One is getting a guy to eat this cookie. I promise there's nothing wrong with it. Besides, normal shaped cookies are so mainstream, don't you think?"

The hipster stared at me skeptically.

"I'll do it." Someone had flopped down on the couch on the other side of me. His arm was behind me on the couch, but he wasn't touching me. He was dressed similarly to the hipster. Maybe they were friends.

"That would be amazing, thanks."

"Take a bite first so I know it's not poisoned. Anton made a good point." He nodded toward the hipster.

"Fair enough." I took a bite. "It's actually really good." I handed him the cookie.

"So can I just eat it, or do I have to suck on it weirdly or something?"

Anton laughed.

"You can just eat it," I said.

The guy shrugged and bit the balls off.

Anton started laughing again, egging his friend on.

"Mmm mmm good," he said and put the rest of the penis in his mouth.

I couldn't help but start laughing too. He had just devoured that penis cookie.

He was having a hard time swallowing while he was laughing. His arm had fallen off the back of the couch and landed around my shoulders.

Awkward. I immediately stood up. "Thanks for that, guys." I quickly walked away before they said anything else to me. I was a little out of breath when I made it back to the table. I didn't want random guys putting their hands on me.

"Nicely done," Bee said. "The hipster's friend seemed to really enjoy that penis. You probably should have asked him if he liked it."

"I wasn't going to ask him that."

"Well, you need to. Number six is verifying whether or not he liked that dick," Kendra said.

"What is wrong with you guys?"

Kendra laughed and slid another shot toward me.

"You're really going to make me go back over there?"

"Do the shot and you'll be fine."

"So I just need to ask if he liked it?"

"You have to ask if he liked that dick."

I shook my head. "Can I pass on that one?"

"Trust me, you need to save your veto," Bee said.

God. I grabbed the shot and downed it. I took a deep breath and walked back over to the guys on the couch. "Hey," I said very unseductively. I was totally channeling the scene from The House Bunny where the manly girl told a guy she was dropping off some timber.

The guy who had eaten the cookie looked up at me. "You ran away pretty fast."

"Yeah, sorry about that." I sat down on the arm of the couch. "I came back over to see if you liked that cookie."

"I liked making you laugh." He gave me a charming smile.

I laughed awkwardly. "But did you like...that dick?" *Geez.*

He laughed. "I'm not gay if that's what you're asking. Trust me." His eyes had landed on my legs.

"Oh, no, I didn't think you were." I quickly stood up. "Have a good night, guys." I made my way back to my table despite him calling after me. My heart was beating fast. "This is so awkward," I said and sat down in my chair. "Please can we just go home?"

"We'll give you an easy one next," Marie said. "Let's skip to number nine. All you have to do is make googly eyes at someone until they send us a round of drinks."

"You still have a million shots on the table."

Kendra laughed. "Honey child, we're only just getting started."

I sighed.

"How about him," she said and pointed to a guy at the bar. "He's been staring at you all night."

I turned to see who she was pointing to, but immediately looked away when I made eye contact with him. "Some random guy isn't going to send us all drinks. Don't be ridiculous."

"You have years of being single at a bar to fit into one night. So put your hand through your hair and casually look back over at him."

"Ugh." I tucked my bangs behind my ear and looked back over at him as discreetly as possible.

He smiled at me and I immediately turned away.

"He really can't keep his eyes off you," Kendra said. "And he's handsome. I bet he's great in the sack."

I laughed. "Is that the thing I have to veto? Done. I'm not hooking up with a stranger."

"We would never put that on the list," Bee said. "Well, Kendra wanted to but I told her no."

"Thank you." I shook my head.

"You know what really make guys possessive?" Kendra asked. "Seeing a girl they want with another guy. If we really want that sexy man to buy us drinks, we should make Penny do number ten."

"Perfect," Melissa said. "You have to dance with that first guy who bought you the drink."

"He already thinks I'm going to sleep with him at the end of the night. Please don't make me talk to him again."

"You won't be talking. You'll be dancing," Melissa said. "And make sure you walk by the guy who's going to be buying us drinks later."

"Should I shove a penis cookie in his mouth while I'm at it?"

"That's not a terrible idea. I can add that to the list," Marie said and lifted up her purse. "Just let me find a pen."

"Don't you dare." I got up before any of them could add another stupid thing I had to do.

"A whole song, Penny!" one of them yelled after me.

I walked toward the guy who had bought me a whiskey, making sure to pass the one they wanted to buy us a round of drinks. I smiled shyly at the guy. It looked like he thought I was going to stop and talk to him. I noticed him frown as I leaned against the counter near my future dance partner.

"Back already?" he said with a smile. "How'd you like the whiskey?"

I laughed. "It was awful."

"I'm sure it wasn't that bad."

"Oh, it was. Thanks for that."

"Anytime." He seemed pleased with himself.

"You said you'd be willing to help with..."

"Do you have something else fun on your list you want me to do for you?" he said, cutting me off.

"Yes actually. Will you dance with me?"

He smiled. "I'd love to." He downed his drink and whispered something to his friends before walking with me toward where the DJ was set up in the back of the bar.

Unfortunately it was a slow song. He grabbed my hand and pulled me in close. I could smell the whiskey on his breath and it made me ridiculously uncomfortable. I tilted my head to the side so I was staring over his shoulder. *Just one song.*

"Whoever you're marrying is a very lucky guy," he whispered in my ear.

"Thanks." Did James think he was lucky? I had thought so before yesterday. But I wasn't sure anymore. *Does he even love me?* The alcohol and my friends' laughter had momentarily distracted me from the notes he had written to Isabella. He loved her so much. I didn't want to be here right now. I just wanted to go home.

"You're beautiful, you know."

For some reason his words made me want to cry. I didn't say anything. I just turned my head away from him even more. The song would be over any second.

"What are you thinking about?" he asked.

I suddenly felt even more uncomfortable. "I miss him." All I wanted was to be in James' arms. I needed to hear him say that everything was okay. And that he loved me.

"You don't have to go home alone tonight." His hands slid down to my ass.

I pushed on his chest and stepped back. "I'm sorry, I'm not...I'm not looking to go home with anyone."

"Let me buy you another drink."

"No, I've already had too much to drink. I'm sorry." I quickly walked away from him and ran directly into the guy I was supposed to be making googly eyes with.

"You okay?" he asked.

I looked over my shoulder. "Yeah, I'm fine. I just..." I shook my head.

"Bad night?"

"Honestly, I miss my fiancé. His friends kidnapped him for his bachelor party this weekend. So my friends decided to throw me a bachelorette party. All I really wanted to do tonight was watch a movie."

"Honestly, I'd rather be watching a movie too."

I smiled. "I'm not interested in going home with anyone tonight. I'm just going to go back over to my table."

"I'm not trying to sleep with you. I mean, you're gorgeous. But I'm not an asshole."

I looked up at him.

"You're engaged."

"I am."

"I was merely going to try to get your number in case things went south."

"Things aren't going to go south." I wasn't able to admit that they had already started to. James and I were still fine. We had to be.

He shrugged. "I was engaged once. I didn't think that would end either."

It was like he knew what I was going through. "What happened?"

"I don't think commitment really means the same thing today as it used to."

I thought about the pictures of James with Rachel and Isabella. I thought about all the love notes. "You're probably right. It still means something to me, though."

"So how about I just buy you a drink and casually slip you my number?"

I laughed. "Actually, I could use your help."

"And what do you need help with?"

"My friends have this list of stupid stuff they want me to do. Including getting someone to buy us a round of drinks."

"Let's go see what they're drinking then." He touched the small of my back for just a second to direct me back to the table. When we got there, he put his elbows down on the table and smiled. "Ladies."

They all giggled.

"Can I offer you some refills?"

"That would be fantastic," Kendra said.

"What were you drinking?" he asked and smiled down at me.

"If I could just get some water, that would be great."

He nodded. "Probably a good choice. You seem a little drunk."

I couldn't even argue with him. My friends had been shoving drinks in my face since I had arrived at Bee's. "Maybe you should just get a round of waters for the table."

"Are you sure you don't need more shots?" He smiled and looked down at the table covered with shot glasses. Half of them hadn't been touched.

"I think we're good there. Just water."

"If that's what the lady wants." He winked at me and leaned in close. "Hopefully free drinks count," he whispered into my ear. "If not, I'll be by the bar. And here's my number just in case your fiancé takes commitment as loosely as my fiancée did." He slid his business card into my hand.

I looked down at the card and then back up at him, knowing perfectly well that I would never call that number. "Thanks."

"Really, water?" Melissa asked as soon as he walked away.

I laughed. "He was nice. I didn't want to make him pay for a whole round of drinks. Plus, you guys are getting me wasted. I can barely walk in a straight line." At this point, I probably couldn't.

"That's okay, it still counts," Bee said. "Plus," she grabbed the business card out of my hand. "Penny just scratched off number seven too."

"You got his number?" Kendra clapped her hands together. "Oh my God, he's like a walking sex ad."

I laughed. "Did you want it?"

"Yes please." She snatched the business card out of Bee's hand. "I bet he's amazing in bed."

Marie rolled her eyes.

"Speaking about sex," Kendra said. "On a scale of one to ten, how good is James in bed?"

"An eleven."

They all laughed.

"I haven't met an eleven in years," Kendra said. "I think all the elevens are in relationships. And why wouldn't they be? Their dicks are like fucking Gods."

Marie laughed. "You put too much emphasis on sex. There is so much more to a relationship than that."

"I thought Carter was good in bed?" Kendra asked.

"He is. I'm just saying..."

"Mhm," Kendra said, cutting her off. "All about that dick."

Melissa laughed.

"And what about you?" Kendra asked Melissa.

"What about me?"

"Are you seeing anyone right now?"

Melissa glanced at me. "Yeah. Actually, I just started dating Tyler."

Kendra squealed. "The cute one that Bee and Penny always hang out with?"

Melissa took another shot from the table. "Yup, that's the one."

"And how is he in bed?"

"Well...I personally think he's an eleven."

This is so awkward.

Kendra smiled. "Usually younger guys have no idea what they're doing. But every now and then you find one that's super eager to please. I think I might just be in the mood for a younger guy tonight." She looked around the bar.

Melissa grabbed the paper from Kendra. "Okay, what's next?" She looked down at the paper and then handed it back to Kendra. "Do you want to skip around again? How about we do number 12?"

"No, let's just do what's next. Oh, perfect. List everyone you had sex with in order from best to worst, Penny."

"I'm going to veto that one," I said.

"Seriously? We have you making out with a stranger near the bottom of the list."

"What? I'm not doing that."

"I know. That's why you have to do this one. We all knew you'd veto that one."

"I..."

"Just tell us. Or is the list too long?"

I laughed nervously. "Um, no. Just, James at the top obviously. And then Austin. That's it."

"You've only slept with two guys? What is wrong with you?!"

"I've only slept with two guys," Bee said.

"Yeah, but I already knew you were lame," Kendra said. "Penny, you're getting married. And you're telling me you only slept with two guys?!"

"Well, that's not true," Melissa said. "She's slept with three guys." Melissa was staring at me. She looked like she was about to cry. "Right?"

Fuck. "Oh, I mean, yeah, I guess. It's three. I don't know what I was thinking." I was thinking I didn't want to talk about this. *Shit.*

The tray of waters had just arrived at our table. I grabbed one and took a huge sip. My head was too fuzzy to think straight.

"How mysterious," Bee said. "It must be someone she wishes she hadn't slept with. Who was it, Penny? You have to tell us now. I'm sure Melissa will if you don't."

I kept my mouth shut.

"She slept with Tyler during one of the many times she broke it off with James," Melissa said. "Or he broke it off with her. I don't remember which. They were so toxic at first. All they did was fight. Isn't that right, Penny?"

I fidgeted with the bachelorette sash.

Bee's eyes had gotten a little bigger. Kendra and Marie were looking back and forth between Melissa and I.

"So, you really thought Tyler was that bad in bed?" Melissa asked. "You didn't even remember you slept with him? I certainly remember."

"No, it wasn't that. I just thought..."

"That talking about it is awkward?" Melissa took another shot of vodka. "The fact that you slept with my boyfriend isn't awkward at all. The fact that the two of you hang out all the time is super normal. Right?" she said and looked at everyone else at the table.

Kendra cleared her throat. "Next up on the list..."

"Where is Tyler on your scale, Penny? Now I'm just super curious." Melissa's face was bright red. I had been trying to avoid this. I didn't want to fight with her again. Tonight had been going so well.

"I don't know. It was so long ago..."

"God, just tell me."

"Below James." What was she expecting me to say?

"So, he's not as good as James? You're such a bitch."

"No, Tyler's really good in bed. I just...I'm in love with James."

"So, you think Tyler's great in bed? What, do you still fantasize about him or something? You're the worst friend ever."

"Melissa." An exasperated laugh escaped my lips. "What do you want me to say? I had sex with Tyler once almost three years ago. He wasn't your boyfriend then. You didn't even like him. You were dating Josh. And I can't take it back. There isn't anything I can do about it."

"You can stop hanging out with him."

"Fine. Okay. I won't hang out with him anymore. Tyler and I are officially no longer friends. Happy? Is that really what you want me to say?"

"Yeah, that would make me happy."

"Melissa! He's one of my best friends. Why can't you just get over this? It shouldn't be that big of a deal. Tyler and I are past it. Come on."

"Yes, he's one of your friends. But I'm your best friend. Your friendship with me should matter more than it does with him. Why are you holding on to him? Girls and boys can't just be friends."

"Yes they can. I'm friends with Rob and Matt. And I'm friends with Mason." I pointed to Bee. "I was friends with him before he even met Bee, and she doesn't hate that I hang out with him."

"That's because you didn't sleep with him. You can't be friends with Tyler if you want to remain friends with me. You can't. I can't handle it."

Everyone at the table was silent for a minute. I was blinking fast, trying to hold back the tears.

Marie cleared her throat.

"I need to use the restroom," I said quietly. "I'll be right back." I stumbled out of the bar stool and made my way to the bathroom.

"Hey, Penny," said a familiar voice behind me.

The little hairs on the back of my neck seemed to rise. I turned around and looked up at Austin. I hadn't seen him since I moved to New York. He looked the same as he had in college. Except his hair was shorter and he had a five o'clock shadow. I hated that the sight of him made my blood boil. The only person I hated more than him was Isabella. And maybe James' parents. I took a deep breath. "I'm sorry, do I know you?"

He laughed. "I know you haven't forgotten me, baby. You look upset. Are you okay?"

I just stared at him.

"So, you're getting married? James is an unlucky guy."

"Go to hell, Austin."

"That's not very nice to say to the first love of your life. I'm sure you dreamed of marrying me once."

"I never loved you."

He shrugged. "I guess we remember that differently."

"Great. Let's agree to disagree. Have a good night, Austin." I turned around but he grabbed my wrist.

"You know, you're the only girl that ever dumped me."

I pulled my arm away from him. "I didn't dump you. We never even dated."

"Well, you were a constant booty call then. You were so easy. Always ready to please me. Fuck, college was fun, huh?"

I shook my head. *What a dick.*

"Aren't you curious about why I know that you're marrying your professor?"

"You can read tabloids? Congratulations. I didn't know you were literate."

"You're feistier than I remember. I like it. But no, I didn't read about it. Isabella told me."

Despite the alcohol and the anger I felt toward him, my body suddenly felt cold. "What?"

"I ran into her the other day. She's smokin' hot by the way. James made a mistake letting her go."

I noticed the manila envelope in his hand for the first time. *Oh God.* Isabella really was a lunatic. She must have known about my history with Austin. And now she had him wrapped around her finger. *How the hell did she even know I was here?* I looked back up at Austin's face. He was wearing a smug smile. Like the thought of him sleeping with her would upset me. It didn't. They belonged together.

"And she's amazing in bed. Fucking fantastic actually. So much better than you. She's very talented with..."

"Stop. Please stop talking." I didn't care if Austin was fucking Isabella. But I didn't want to hear about how great she was. I didn't want to have to think about James and her together. About how much James had loved her. Or how he might still love her.

Austin smiled. "Touchy subject? Does James compare you to her often? It's really not much of a comparison." He looked so happy with himself.

"James loves me." My words didn't even convince myself.

"Really?" Austin tossed the envelope at me. "I'm not so sure about that."

"You know nothing about him. And you know nothing about me."

"Baby, I know you."

"You don't, Austin. You never did."

"Well, I know you're going to be upset about what's in that envelope."

I looked down at the envelope in my hands.

"I guess I'll read about you calling off the wedding in the tabloids." I felt his hand slap my ass.

I shoved his chest hard, but he didn't even take a step back. Instead, he grabbed the back of my head hard and pressed his lips against mine.

I hit his chest with my fist, but his hand just gripped my hair tighter. His tongue slid against my closed lips. I hit his chest with my fist again and then shoved him as hard as I could. "Get the fuck off me!" I wiped my lips with the back of my hand. "What is wrong with you?"

He smiled. "Call me, Penny. I think your self confidence is just about where I need it to be to pick up right where we left off in college. You know, with you wishing I loved you, and me banging every girl I meet. It'll be like old times. Enjoy the pictures." He winked at me and walked away.

As soon as he disappeared, I let my tears start to fall. I ran to the bathroom and into a stall, locking the door behind me. My heart was beating fast as I opened up the envelope. I pulled out a small stack of photos. There was a post-it note covering the first photo:

A picture speaks a thousand words isn't exactly true for this. All of these pictures really only mean one thing.

I lifted off the note and stared down at an image of James kissing another woman. This time, it was one I didn't recognize. He was wearing a baseball cap and it looked like he hadn't shaved since he left New York, but it was definitely him. I felt even colder than I had when I was talking to Austin. *This isn't real. This can't be real.*

In the next photo, her legs were wrapped around his waist and her back was pressed against a wall. My chest hurt as I stared at the image. There was no explanation for this. It wasn't Isabella attacking him, or him getting closure from his ex. This was passion. This was real. It wasn't photoshopped or fake. James was at his bachelor party hooking up with another woman. But that's what guys did during their bachelor parties. Wasn't it?

In the next photo, his hand was up her shirt. He was clearly grabbing her breasts.

My back slid down the bathroom stall door.

In the next photo, his hand had moved. It was lost under her skirt. Her face had tilted away from his. Pure bliss was written all over it. I knew that feeling. I knew exactly the way he could make me feel. How he could make anyone feel apparently.

I put my face on my knees and let myself cry even harder.

"Penny?"

I tried to stop crying when I heard Melissa's voice.

"Penny? I'm so sorry. I'm sorry about everything. I don't want you to not be friends with Tyler. And I definitely don't want you to not be friends with me over this whole stupid thing. I'll get over it. I will. I'm so sorry. I don't want to fight about this anymore."

Her words just made me cry even more.

"Penny?"

I sniffed from inside the stall.

"Are you okay?"

"No." I knew how my voice sounded. It was desperate. I felt so lost. "I'm sorry too. I'm so sorry." My voice cracked.

"Penny." Melissa knocked on the door. "Penny, let me in." Her voice was a little more demanding the second time.

I reached up and unlocked the stall door.

When she looked down at me, the only thing on her face was concern. She knelt down on the gross bathroom floor and threw her arms around me. "What's wrong?"

Instead of saying anything, I sobbed into her shoulder.

She rubbed my back and kept her arms around me. "It's okay," she said in a soothing voice. "Everything's going to be okay."

I had my best friend back. But I had lost the love of my life. Nothing was ever going to be okay again.

PART 3

CHAPTER 23
Sunday

"God I miss you," James said and then there was long sigh. "I'm calling you from the hotel lobby because Rob won't let me have my phone. We're staying at some place called the Blue Parrot Resort. You can call me back at this number, but I'll be back tonight. I can't wait to see you. Oh, and you'll need the pa...hey, Rob! No, I wasn't calling Penny. Fuck, get off of me!" The recording beeped, signaling the end of the message.

I played the message for the hundredth time. My intense hangover had made me sleep till well past two o'clock. And I had woken up to this message. James' voice was soothing even though his words weren't. He missed me? He didn't fucking miss me. It seemed like he was plenty entertained.

I had called the number back, but I couldn't get through to James. The person on the other end asked for a password. When I didn't know what to say, they immediately hung up on me. I had tried to call back a few more times, but no one had even answered my call. They must have blacklisted my number or something.

There wasn't much information about the Blue Parrot Resort on Google. It was clearly some super private hotel if they required a password to even talk to the concierge. And it was probably as sleazy as it was secretive. I sighed and pressed the replay button. It was so good to hear his voice. The recording beeped, signaling the end of the message.

I knew Isabella was just trying to get in my head. Guys did crazy stuff during their bachelor parties. That was just a fact. And I had touched some random man's six pack last night. If there was a picture of me doing that, it would look bad. The pictures that Isabella had sent me were probably out of context.

I shook my head. What horrible context would have made James hook up with some random whore? The only thing that made sense was that he was being threatened at gun point. The Blue Parrot Resort seemed secretive, but it didn't seem mobstery.

This wasn't what was supposed to be happening before our wedding. We weren't in the movie The Hangover. This kind of stuff didn't happen in real life. I leaned back and folded my arms across my face. I wasn't sure I could go through with the wedding in just a few days, but I still wanted to. I really, really wanted to. If I closed my eyes and pictured him smiling at me, I felt like I could forgive anything. But I couldn't live with him sneaking around. Maybe at first I could, but it would eat away at me. It would slowly kill me. If the man I loved didn't love me back, the best thing I could do was let him go. I wanted him to be happy. I cared about him so much.

But it didn't matter how rational it was. I'd never be able to let him go. I needed him. Even if he cheated on me? Even if he'd do it again? *God.* I sat up and rubbed the tears away before they could start to fall again. James was my rock. He was always there for me. I had let him become my whole world. I needed to let this go. It was just a bachelor party. He had one last hookup as a single man. That was it. The thought of him hanging out with Rachel and kissing Isabella popped back up in my head. I pinched the skin above my nose. *Stop.* None of this was helping.

I put the rest of the pictures into the shoebox full of love notes to Isabella and slid it under the bed. James would be back soon. I didn't want to fight with him. And I certainly didn't want to confront him about cheating on me. I couldn't have that conversation. He had to bring it up. He had to confess what he had done to me. I didn't have the strength to do it. Maybe he was going to come home and break up with me immediately. If that's really what he wanted, would I be able to let him go? Would I even have a choice?

The past few weeks I had been so stressed out. I had lost my perspective. There wasn't anything to be upset about, though. I was lucky. I was madly in love, I had been given a great job, a beautiful new home, and I was getting married. Those were great things. And I was too blind to realize it. Now that I wasn't going to have those things, I realized what they truly meant. But I didn't care about the job or the house or the money. All I cared about was losing him. I felt empty just thinking about it.

I wanted to delay our conversation. I couldn't do it tonight. I lay down in bed and pulled the covers up to my chin. There was never going to be a good time, but it had to be before the wedding. I couldn't walk down the aisle if I didn't know if I could trust him. I needed one more night, though. One more night of his arms around me. I shut my eyes as tight as possible, as if it would make my wish for more time a reality.

***

My eyes opened when I heard the front door close. I must have drifted to sleep waiting for James to come home. I glanced at the alarm clock. It was right before midnight. Mason had kept his word.

I closed my eyes again. *One more night. Please let me have one more night with him.*

His footsteps echoed across the marble in the foyer and treaded lightly on the stairs. But they paused when they reached the bedroom door. He let out a deep sigh.

I closed my eyes even tighter. I could picture him leaning against the door jam. He was probably running his hand through his hair in that sexy way he always did. I took a deep breath. There was a mixture of scotch and his amazing cologne in the air.

He entered the room and I could hear him getting undressed. Then it was silent again. He didn't get into the bed. I could feel his eyes on me. He must have just been standing there, staring at me.

I wasn't sure what I had been thinking earlier. There was no way I could ever let him go. If he was cheating on me, we could work through it. We had to. I couldn't live without him. And I couldn't let him end it with me. We were getting married on Saturday. It was too late for him to change his mind. You had to call off a wedding at least a month in advance unless you were a horrible human being. That was just a rule. And James wasn't horrible. *If he cheated on you he is.* I felt like I was going crazy. One day alone and I had completely lost my mind.

"Are you awake?" he asked softly.

I bit my lip. My tears had started dampening my pillow. If he thought I was asleep, we couldn't have whatever conversation we needed to have.

The bed squeaked as he slid in beside me. "I missed you, baby," he whispered as he wrapped his arms around me.

Was that his excuse for cheating on me? I didn't have sex with him for a few days so he slept with someone else? I thought we were stronger than that. I thought he loved me. It took every ounce of control in my body to stay completely still when it felt like my whole world was collapsing. I wanted to cry loud, ugly tears, but I didn't want him to know I was awake. If this was the last chance I'd have for him to hold me, I wasn't going to ruin it. I wanted to go to sleep and wake up and forget about this weekend.

I took another deep breath, trying to calm myself down. His arms wrapped tighter around me. It seemed like he knew I was awake. I closed my eyes even tighter. I could forgive him. I could forget about all of this. For some reason a memory popped into my head of me telling my mom that I was in love with James. Her response to me had been that maybe it would be love one day.

"I cave," James whispered so quietly that if I had been sleeping, I definitely wouldn't have heard him.

I pressed my lips together and tried to breathe slowly so that he couldn't hear me crying.

"You win," he said and placed a soft kiss against the back of my neck.

Now that he was back he suddenly wanted me again? I felt cheap. Maybe my mom was right. Even though she had said it over two years ago, maybe what we had wasn't love. Because a key part of love in my eyes was being enough for one another. It was about being faithful. I wasn't enough for James. I wasn't sure why I ever thought I could be.

CHAPTER 24
Monday

When I woke up, James' arms were wrapped tightly around me. I tried to take a deep breath, but it felt like I was suffocating. I slowly unwound myself from his arms and slid off the bed. He sighed in his sleep, but didn't wake up.

I pulled on my robe and stared down at him. He was so handsome. I had never taken that for granted. Whenever I woke up before he did, I'd stare at his beautiful face. Someone else had woken up to that face this weekend. Was that why he had finally called me back Sunday morning? Did he feel guilty for what he had done?

I went into the closet and quickly got dressed. We needed to talk, but I couldn't do it right now. I needed to calm down. Because right now, I hated him. I hated how content he looked sleeping. Was he thinking of that slut from this weekend? Or Rachel or Isabella?

The lump in my throat wouldn't seem to go away. My heartbeat wouldn't seem to slow down. And I hated that the only place I could escape to was work. He had imprinted himself on every part of my life. I couldn't get away from him, and I felt pathetic for not even really wanting to escape. He wasn't the addict, I was. And I couldn't breathe without him.

***

It was easier to believe that I could forgive him when I wasn't looking directly at him. The idea of moving past it together and making us a stronger couple seemed logical when I was sitting at my desk.

"I'm usually the first one to get here," Zach said and sat down at his desk.

I jumped when I heard his voice. The office had been completely empty when I had come in an hour ago. "Oh, hey, Zach. Did you have a good weekend?"

"Better than yours, I'm assuming."

"Why would you say that?"

"Your eyes are so red that it looks like you've been here crying all morning. And ice cream for breakfast is usually a sign of depression."

I laughed awkwardly. "This was almost empty." I picked up the pint of Ben and Jerry's that had been completely full earlier and tossed it in the trash. "And I have seasonal allergies."

"Right." He opened up a drawer in his desk and tossed me a small bottle of eye drops.

"Thanks." I tilted my head back and put in the eye drops. My eyes stung for a second, but I assumed they'd be less red in a few minutes. "So, why do you have these?"

"I'd make up a lame excuse about how my eyes get dry because of my contacts. But, honesty is a better policy right?"

"I guess so?"

"I smoke weed in the bathroom with the tech guys sometimes."

I laughed. "Seriously?"

He shrugged. "Yeah, I'm pretty sure those guys are always high. Don't tell Hunter that, though."

Telling James that his tech department was a bunch of drug-gies wasn't on the top of my list of conversational topics at the moment. "It's a stressful job. They probably need a release." I turned my attention back to my computer screen.

"Is that your reasoning with Hunter too?"

"What?"

"The way he treats you. You excuse him because it's a re-lease?"

"You don't know what you're talking about."

"If he's..."

"Zach, I can't have this conversation with you right now. James isn't abusive. He's a good guy. He'd never hurt me." I seemed to choke on my own words.

"Emotional abuse is just as bad as physical..."

"He's not. It's not like that, Zach." Other people were starting to come into the office. I needed to get my shit together and not wear my emotions on my sleeve.

"He was really possessive with you when we got drinks the other night."

"That's because you were pretending to flirt with me."

"Does he always act like that? If you talk to other guys?"

"If you don't drop this, I'm going to tell James you smoke weed in the bathroom every day."

He frowned. "I said sometimes. It's not every day."

"Sometimes is still bad."

"You're such a tattletale." He gave me a small smile.

"Does that mean you'll drop it?"

"Whatever you want, Fight Club. I'm just trying to help."

My phone started vibrating. I pulled it out of my purse to see that James was calling. I was about to put it back in my purse, but I noticed Zach shaking his head. It was pretty clear that he didn't believe me. James may have made a mistake this weekend, but he was a good guy. I didn't want his employees to think he wasn't.

"Hey, James," I said and turned slightly away from Zach.

"Where are you?" He sounded concerned. "I woke up and..."

"I'm at work. I'm being a super great employee." Not really. I was never even sure what I was supposed to be doing. And I had only come here early so I'd have a place to cry alone.

He laughed. "I'd rather you be a bad employee and come home."

"We're only working four days this week. I don't think you can afford to take today off too." I could feel Zach staring at me.

"Fair enough, boss. Did you eat breakfast?" He sounded so cheery. It was disconcerting.

I looked down at the pint of Ben and Jerry's in the trashcan. "Yup."

"Okay. Well, you can hang out with me while I eat mine. I'll be there in a few minutes. See you soon, baby."

The line went dead before I could make up something about having too much work to do. I sighed and looked at my computer screen. *I can forgive him.*

"You good?" Zach asked.

"Mhm. Everything's great."

"You're an awful liar. Just so you know."

"Hey, man," Tavon said and did some weird handshake with Zach. "What were you guys talking about?" He flopped down in his desk chair and put his feet up on the desk.

"Nothing," Zach said. "How was your weekend?"

"Awesome. I freaking love New York. It's basically like still being in college."

I laughed.

"You don't think so, Fight Club?"

"No, not really. College was a lot simpler." At least it had been at NYCU. The University of New Castle had kind of ended in disaster. But now that I had graduated from NYCU, things seemed complicated and shitty. I'd do anything to go back in time. Back before this weekend.

"Well, yeah, but I mean the vibe, you know? It's like a huge college town. There's always something to do."

"There certainly is." At least, always someone to do, if you were James and you were an asshole. *Damn it.*

"You okay?" Tavon asked.

"I'm great. I just don't think New York is all that great. And you know what? Costa Rica is a crappy place too. It's the freaking worst."

"Okay?" Tavon looked at Zach and raised both his eyebrows.

"I'm not crazy."

Tavon laughed. "I didn't say you were. Are you sure you're okay? You're kind of hostile this morning. I mean, I hate Monday's just as much as the next guy. But you're like on a whole other level."

"Yeah, I'm just...PMSing." *God, why did I just say that?!* It wasn't even true.

"Gross. Too much information, Fight Club."

"You asked."

"I did not ask that."

I shrugged my shoulders.

"Anyway, I needed to ask you. What's Sierra's deal?" Tavon asked.

"What do you mean?" I asked.

"You know...like is she single? Is she looking for something casual? Or is she a commitment type of girl?"

"Tavon, you've spent more time with her than I have."

"But what have you found out?" he asked.

"Nothing. Although, I'm going to take a guess and say she's not interested in you."

"Harsh. I guess you are PMSing."

"Sorry, I didn't mean that. But even if she was interested, and I have no idea if she is, you shouldn't get involved. Because dating is complicated. It's exhausting. And terrifying. Just...don't do it. It's not worth this feeling." I was about to burst into tears again.

Zach was staring at me with the most sympathetic expression on his face, which just made me feel even worse.

"Yeah...I was thinking more about a one night stand kind of situation anyway," Tavon said. "To break that streak she has going on."

"All men are disgusting." I stood up and walked toward the break room. It felt like I couldn't breathe. I was glad when Zach didn't follow me to try to squeeze out information from me. I leaned against the counter and poured myself a cup of coffee.

"Hey, Penny," Nita said as she walked into the break room. "I was just getting James his coffee. He's looking for you." She filled up a mug. "Do you want to just give it to him? I need to use the restroom real quick."

Would it be rude of me to say no? Probably. "Yeah, sure."

"Thanks, Penny." She handed me the cup and quickly walked out of the room.

I looked down at the two cups of coffee in my hands. Maybe it was better to get it out of the way sooner than later. I needed to just confront him. And then he'd apologize. Then we'd be good. Simple.

I felt like I wanted to throw up. I tried to tell myself it was from eating a pint of ice cream instead of how worried I was about losing him. Before I could think anymore, I walked out of the break room and toward James' office.

The blinds were open and he saw me before I even attempted to knock. Which was good because my hands were full. He opened up the door, grabbed both cups from me, and placed a swift kiss on my cheek. "Good morning, beautiful." He had a huge smile on his face. His hair was still wet from his shower and it was starting to curl in that way I loved so much. And he was wearing his glasses, which had always been a weakness for me. I hadn't noticed how tan he had gotten earlier when I had stared at him sleeping. It just made him look even sexier, which for some reason made me angrier.

Why does he look so happy? The guilt should be eating away at him. I closed the door behind me and followed him toward his desk.

He placed the mugs down on his desk and then grabbed my arm, pulling me against his chest. "God, I missed you." He pressed his lips against mine before I could protest. I could have easily gotten lost in that kiss. But I couldn't stop picturing him kissing Isabella. I pulled away from him.

"James, the blinds are open."

He winked. "Gotcha. I was thinking the same thing." He let go of me, walked over to the windows, and began to close the blinds. "It's about time we bent those rules. All I've been thinking about since you started working here is having you on this desk."

I swallowed hard. "No, that's not...I don't think we should bend the rules." I sat down in one of the chairs and grabbed my cup of coffee, using it as almost a shield.

He walked up behind me and ran his hand down the side of my neck.

I still got chills whenever he touched me. Even though I was mad at him, that feeling hadn't just disappeared overnight. I still wanted him just as much as I always did. Probably even more since I hadn't been able to have him in so long.

"Rules are meant to be broken." His breath was hot against my neck as he began to massage my shoulders.

Fuck that feels good.

"And I know breaking rules turns you on. You're probably dripping wet right now, just thinking about it aren't you?"

"Stop." I shifted forward on the chair, letting his hands fall from my shoulders. "You're going to make me spill my coffee."

"Penny, I'm caving." He walked around me and leaned against the front of his desk. "I need you. I can't even function anymore. I'm horny as hell."

"Sure you are." He had sex this weekend with some hooker. And he had probably screwed Isabella and Rachel too. *Asshole.*

He lowered his eyebrows. "What, do you want me to beg you? I'll beg if you want, baby." He kneeled in front of me and ran his hands up my thighs. "I need you. Now."

I took a huge sip of coffee instead of answering him. Why was he trying to have sex with me right now? He should have been apologizing. And groveling. He was acting like nothing had happened.

"How was your weekend, James?"

"I missed you."

I pressed my thighs together to stop his hands from traveling any farther. "Tell me about your bachelor party."

He sighed and sat down in the chair beside mine. "It was okay."

"Just okay?"

He ran his hand through his hair. "I think Rob and Matt probably enjoyed it the most. I really just hung out with Mason by the pool."

"Nothing super eventful that you want to tell me about?"

"No, it was just relaxing."

Fuck you. "Nothing you want to talk to me about?"

"Um...no? How was your weekend? Did you have fun without me?"

"Not really, no."

He lowered his eyebrows. "Is everything okay, baby?"

I was getting exasperated. I didn't want to run around in circles. "No, it's not. I had a really shitty weekend actually. I tried to call you a million times, James."

"I didn't have my phone. What did you expect me to do?" He gave me a playful smile.

"To figure out a way to call me back."

"I did. And you didn't pick up."

"Yeah, because I was sleeping. I tried to call you back and they asked for a password. When I didn't know it, they hung up and then none of my other calls went through. Where the hell were you?"

"I told you. It was called the Blue Parrot Resort. It's in Costa Rica. I heard you had a bachelorette party. How'd that go?"

I tried to swallow down the lump in my throat. Is that why he did what he did? Because he thought I was doing the same? I didn't fuck a random stranger. What the hell was wrong with him? Before I could answer him, his phone started ringing.

"Sorry, I need to take this. I missed all my calls this weekend and I don't want to get any further behind. Hold on a sec." He put his hand on my knee, leaned over his desk, and grabbed his work phone. "Hunter."

He kept his hand on my knee as if he was worried I would flee. He was probably right. I didn't think this was how our conversation would go. I thought he'd tell me what happened right away and say how sorry he was. Instead, he was acting like nothing had happened.

"I asked you not to..." his voice trailed off and he shoved his free hand into his pocket. "Really?" He looked down at me. "I mean...I doubt it will change their minds, but it would be great if you tried." A smile had spread across his face. "Thanks a lot, Isabella. Let me know how it goes. Bye."

Isabella? My stomach seemed to churn. "I thought you asked her not to contact us?" I already knew she wasn't listening to his request because she had been contacting me via terrible pictures. But I didn't know she had been contacting him too. I set my coffee down. My hands had started shaking and I didn't want to spill the coffee all over myself.

James hung up the phone. "Actually, she called me Friday night before I was kidnapped." He laughed. "And she apologized again...about how the engagement party went. She said that my parents had invited her and that it wasn't her idea to ambush me. She really seemed sorry. She wants me to be happy."

Bullshit. I had noticed his pause after claiming she had apologized. Was she apologizing for the kiss they shared last week instead? I took a deep breath. "Okay, but why are you talking to her now?"

"She just told me that she's going to try to talk to my parents. She wants them to come around."

"And you believe her?"

He shrugged. "I don't know. I want to. My mom loves her. If anyone can convince my parents to come to the wedding, it's Isabella."

"Is that it?"

"What do you mean?"

"Is that the only reason you're talking to her? Because she's claiming she's going to help you?"

"Of course."

"Do you still have feelings for her?"

He laughed. "No. Penny," he grabbed my hand and sat down next to me again. "If you're worried about me getting cold feet...it's not going to happen. I love you and only you. You have nothing to worry about."

Stop lying. "I don't want you to talk to her anymore."

"Isabella?"

"Yes, your ex wife. She's...toxic."

"She's actually been really nice recently."

To you maybe. Was that her plan? To torture me and weasel her way back into James' heart? She was an evil genius, because I was falling apart and he was calling her nice. "Did you always plan on moving back here?"

"What?"

"Ian said that you paid him a year's salary so he wouldn't have to work for Isabella when you moved to Delaware. He said you were coming back in a year. You never told me that."

"I thought I'd come back, yeah. I just needed a break from this lifestyle. When I left New York, I never imagined I'd meet someone like you."

"But you did meet me. And you never told me about your master plan."

"It wasn't a master plan. The date wasn't set in stone. It was tentative. My life was a mess. I couldn't plan that far ahead. I was still figuring out what I wanted."

"Because of Isabella. And now what? You want to be friends with her?"

"It wasn't because of Isabella. Our marriage had never been good. I knew she had been cheating on me for months before I caught her in the act. I was a mess because I had my own issues to work out. I needed to find a purpose, something to live for."

"But you loved her. It must have torn you apart when you found out she was cheating. Right? Because it hurts to find out that someone you trust is fooling around behind your back. Especially when you have to find out instead of them telling you."

"I never trusted her. And our relationship wasn't built on love. You know that."

Liar. All those notes he had written to her flashed through my mind. Just thinking about them made my chest hurt. *Can't you see that you're killing me?*

His eyes softened slightly as he watched me slowly fall apart in front of him. "Penny, what's going on? Are you having second thoughts?"

"I don't know." I immediately saw the flash of doubt on his face. It was the same way he had looked at me back when he was a professor. Like he didn't believe I could possibly love him. He wasn't supposed to be the one feeling hurt right now. He was the one that cheated on me. If he was scared of losing me, all he needed to do was apologize.

"Hey." He put his hands on either side of my face. "Whatever doubts you're having, please just tell me. Whatever you're worried about, I know we can work it out. I love you with everything that I am."

He still wanted to be with me? Maybe I was blowing everything out of proportion. Men did stupid stuff during their bachelor parties all the time. I had seen movies where guys did

way worse than bang a random girl before committing to someone for the rest of their lives. James wouldn't fool around on me
behind my back when we were married. It was just because it was
his last night as a single man. And he had Rob and Mason egging
him on, and who knows who else. James had told me he never
cheated on Isabella. He wouldn't cheat on me either. He loved
me. The way he was looking at me couldn't be faked. I had to
trust him. "You promise?"

"I promise. What's bothering you?"

"I...it's nothing. If you still love me..."

"Penny." He leaned forward and placed a soft kiss against my
lips. "I'll never stop loving you. You are the only thing I'm ever
sure about. It's you and me. It'll always be you and me."

I put my arms around his neck and breathed in his familiar
scent. *You and me.* I needed to let this go. If he wasn't talking
about it, it was a mistake. It was a one time thing. I bit my lip.
That's what he had said to me when we had crossed the line of
being a student and her professor. But it was never a one time
thing and it was never going to be. *Don't cry, don't cry.*

"So, about me caving..."

"I should probably get back to work." I pulled away from him
and stood up, grabbing my cup of coffee. I wanted to forgive
him, but I needed more time. Right now the coffee in my hands
was the only thing keeping me from being bent over his desk. I
gripped the cup even tighter.

"Are we okay?" He look dejected.

"I don't want the other interns to think I don't do any work."

He nodded, but he still looked upset. "Let's go to Totonno's
Pizzeria for lunch."

"Not today. I wanna bond more with Sierra. She just moved to New York and I wanted to see how she's adjusting. I was in her place not too long ago."

It looked like he wanted to say something, but instead he pressed his lips together. *Just say it, James. Tell me what you did. Tell me that you're sorry.* It would be so much easier for me to move past this if he owned up to his mistakes.

I turned away from him. "I'll see you after work." He still didn't say anything. I quickly walked out of his office and closed the door behind me.

CHAPTER 25
Monday

"Hey, Rob," I said as soon as he picked up the phone. I had eaten lunch as quickly as possible with the other marketing interns. Now I was standing outside the office, hoping I could get some answers.

"Hey, sexy, what's up?"

I rolled my eyes, even though he couldn't see me through the phone. "I was just calling to see if you had fun during James' bachelor party."

Rob laughed. "That's a ridiculous question. It was fucking awesome."

"So, what did you guys do?"

"Well, I won over the hottest girl there and Matt acted like a little bitch about it."

I laughed. "Congrats on your conquest. What about James and Mason?"

"They were super lame. They sat by the pool all day."

"And what about at night?"

"Are you trying to find out if we hired strippers, got him wasted, and then he engaged in tons of unprotected sex with strangers and now has a baby momma?"

Jesus. "Did you? Did he?"

Rob laughed. "You'll never know. But you know how he gets when he's off the rocker..."

"Rob." My voice sounded strangled. "Seriously, did James cheat on me?"

"If he did, it was with Mason."

I sighed.

Rob laughed. "No, he didn't cheat on you, Penny."

"You're sure?"

"I mean, I didn't watch him every second. But he barely participated in everything we had planned. The only sex he had was probably with his hand while he stared at a picture of your beautiful face."

I shook my head. This conversation hadn't made me feel any better. "Okay, thanks, Rob. I'll see you on Friday."

"Wait. Penny, are you really worried about this?"

"Yes. And I'm pretty sure you wouldn't tell me even if you did know. So I'm sorry that I called. Please don't tell James. I'm just freaking out over nothing."

"That's not true. I like you way more than I like James. I'd tell you anything. I really don't think he did anything stupid this weekend. Despite all of our best attempts."

I laughed and looked across the street at Central Park. There was more bothering me than just what did or didn't happen this weekend. "Do you know if he still has feelings for Rachel?"

"Rachel?"

"The girl he dated in high school?"

"Oh. That Rachel."

How many Rachels has he dated?

"No, I don't think so. He was pretty torn up when they called it off, but he was just a kid. Everyone romanticizes their first love. No one holds on to it, though."

James was my first love. I was holding on to that. This conversation wasn't calming me down.

"Are you getting cold feet or something?"

I looked down at my feet. "No. I'm worried that he is."

"He's not. If there's one thing I'm sure about, it's James' addiction to you. I mean, like, obsession." Rob cleared his throat. "Sorry, those weren't the best words. What I mean is that he loves you."

"So, you think that's true too?" Isabella had said that to me. It was different hearing it from Rob. I believed Rob.

"That he loves you? Yes, he's crazy about you."

"No, that he's addicted to me."

Rob paused. "You know it's different. You're actually good for him. Perfect, really. The two of you together just makes sense. He's good now. He's happy. You did that."

For some reason, hearing that made me feel like I could breathe again.

"Trust me, James isn't having cold feet. All he did all weekend was try to get his phone back so he could call you. By the way, were you okay? You called him like a million times. You're awful at being alone."

I am awful at being alone. "Yeah...I just...it doesn't matter. I really have nothing to worry about?"

"Nothing. Except for me trying to be your last hurrah before you get married on Saturday. But really you should just be looking forward to that."

"Rob, I'm not sleeping with you."

"Can't blame a guy for trying."

I laughed. "Thanks for calming me down."

"You know what else is good for calming nerves..."

"I have to get back to work. Thanks, Rob." I hung up before he could tease me anymore. I felt a million times better after talking to him than I did after talking to James. But maybe it was because James really hadn't done anything. Isabella was just fucking with me.

CHAPTER 26
Monday

I walked past Nita's desk and straight toward James' office. The blinds were still closed from earlier, which usually signified he was in some kind of meeting, but I didn't care. I knocked on the door and opened it before James had time to respond. He looked up from his desk. He still looked as upset as he had when I had left him this morning.

I quickly closed the door and went straight toward him. "I cave too." I sat down on the edge of his desk.

"Penny, if there's something bothering you, I think we should talk about it. Please just talk to me. Tell me what's wrong." He put his hand on my knee.

"The only thing bothering me right now is that you're not fucking me." I pulled off my blouse and tossed it at him.

"If you would just tell me what it is..." His words stopped when I unhooked my bra. I let it slowly slide down my shoulders.

"Is this what you want, Mr. Hunter? To fuck your new intern?"

His Adam's apple rose and fell.

"Because that's what I want. I have a huge crush on my boss." I put my high heel on the edge of his chair, right between his thighs. "I know it's wrong, but I can't stop thinking about you." I knew he was horny. And I knew he'd love this scenario. Him sitting at his desk with his glasses on reminded me of being in his class. He had stared at me like this during his lectures. That thrilling, terrifying feeling that someone might catch us made me feel alive. This put us right back where we had been at the University of New Castle. It felt so right.

He stood up and put his hands on either side of me on the desk. "Everyone's going to know that you're fucking your boss. Everyone's going to know that you're mine."

"If that's what you want, you better make me scream." I grabbed his tie and pulled his face to mine.

His tongue invaded my mouth, claiming what was already his. I began unbuttoning his shirt, trailing my fingers down his pecs and six pack. God I missed him. And I missed bending the rules, or breaking them completely. It made me want him even more. This dynamic never felt wrong. I was never not enough for him like this. I was his escape and he was mine.

I pulled back. "Just this once, Mr. Hunter." I was panting. I couldn't even remember the last time I had been this turned on. It was the same reaction that I had when he said it was going to be a one time thing when he was my professor. It just made me want him even more.

"Just this once?" He raised his left eyebrow. "I better make it memorable, Miss Taylor." He pulled my ass to the edge of his desk and ran his fingers up the insides of my thighs. "You'll never be able to forget me. You'll never be able to scream another man's name."

I whimpered at his words. My whimpers quickly turned into moans as he pushed my thong to the side and slid a finger inside of me.

"Fuck you're so wet." His voice was deep and alluring. I could hear how much he missed me in his words. I was the one he needed. Not Isabella or Rachel or some random girl. He wanted me.

I bit his lower lip and grabbed his belt. "We can skip the foreplay." I unhinged his belt and undid his pants. "I need you. Now. Before we get caught."

He bunched my skirt up around my waist and quickly pulled my thong down my legs. His hands moved back to my ass and he thrust himself deep inside of me.

Oh God.

The groan that escaped his throat sounded more like a growl than anything.

I grabbed his tie again so that his mouth would be back on mine. His fingers dug into my skin as his length moved in and out of me.

It felt like forever since I had felt like this. I had missed this feeling, being so full and so loved at the same time. And all I needed was more. "Harder, James."

"Baby, you have no idea how much I missed you." He thrust forwards, and pushed my back flat against his desk. I heard something crash to the floor and the sound of glass shattering.

"What was... "

He put his lips around one of my nipples and sucked hard.

"Oh God, James."

He sucked on my nipple even harder and hooked his arm under one of my thighs. The position allowed him to thrust even deeper inside of me.

Yes!

He moved his hips faster and faster, building that warm feeling deep in my stomach. Making love to James was sometimes all I wanted. But this raw intensity was what I really needed. I craved this more than anything else. I loved how rough he was. And how he knew how to manipulate my body into putty in his hands. I was always at his mercy. He tilted his hips, hitting the spot that always pushed me over the edge.

My fingers dug into his shoulders.

Him groaning against my nipple sent shivers through my whole body. I couldn't hold on much longer. The reminder of how I could make him feel was almost even better than the friction of him inside of me.

"Come for me, Penny."

"Not yet." I clenched my teeth together. I didn't want this to end yet. "Don't stop. Please, not yet."

"Don't worry, we're only just getting started. Come, baby." He lightly bit down on my nipple and tugged.

The sensation seemed to have a direct line to my groin. I felt myself starting to clench around him.

His grip on my thigh tightened as he continued to move his length in and out of me, faster and faster. "Now, Penny."

My back arched and all my worries began to float away, replaced by pure bliss. "James!" *Yes!* I reached out for him. He grabbed my arm and pulled me back to a seated position as his lips smashed against mine. There was an urgency to the way he kissed me, a hunger. And I wanted to satiate that need. He continued to thrust in and out of me, riding out my orgasm.

I fisted my fingers in his hair to pull his lips away from mine. "Do whatever you want to me."

His dick swelled inside of me.

"Whatever you were dreaming about when we were apart. I want it too."

His desk phone started ringing. James pulled out of me, picked up the phone and yanked hard, ripping the cord out along with the phone. It immediately stopped ringing. "Give me your hands."

I put my hands out in front of me and watched him wrap the phone cord around my wrists, tightening it so that it only just dug into my skin. I looked up at him. "You dreamed of tying me up?"

"I dreamed of having you in every way possible." He grabbed my ass and lifted my legs around his waist. "But my fiancée is incredibly horny. And I know you. You're in the mood for more than just making love." He walked us around to the other side of the desk, set me down on the edge, and put his lips to my ear. His warm breath made my skin tingle. "You want it rough and dirty, and I'm going to give you exactly what you want. Close your eyes, baby."

His words immediately heated me up again. I closed my eyes and felt something silky drape across my eyes. It must have been his tie, even though I hadn't seen him take it off. He tied it behind my head and he cupped my chin in his hand. His thumb ran across my bottom lip. "Do you want to play a game?"

I felt empty without him inside of me and vulnerable without my sight. My thighs instinctively moved together, but he was standing between them. I felt his warm skin against mine, which sent goose bumps down my legs. I had said whatever he wanted, and now my heart was beating out of my chest. But it was more from anticipation than fear. "Anything you want."

He placed a soft kiss against my lips and put his hand between my breasts. "Lie down," he said and lightly pushed between my breasts until my back was pressed against his desk again. I felt his hands on my hips, slowly removing my skirt, leaving me completely naked. I heard him walk around to the other side of his desk. He grabbed my hands and pulled them above my head. When he released me a moment later, I couldn't move my arms.

He leaned down and kissed the crook of my neck. "Stay there." I heard his footsteps leave the desk.

"Where are you going?"

"I'll be right back. Stay still."

I tried to move my arms again, but couldn't. "Don't you dare leave me like this, James." But the door had already closed.

Shit. This was why people didn't have office sex. I still couldn't move my arms. What was I attached to? I put my heels on the edge of the desk and pushed back until I could move my arms slightly. I ran my fingers along the phone cord until I felt the knob to his desk drawer. The knot was insanely tight. My fingers fumbled as I tried to untie it.

A knock on the door made me jump. *Fuck!*

"Now that's a sight to see," James said.

"James, what the hell?" I pulled on the phone cord and made the drawer open and slam shut. "Anyone could have walked in."

"The door is locked. I never even left." His voice was getting closer. "I just wanted to see what you did when you thought I wasn't watching." I felt the tip of his cock press against my lips. "And you're terrible at following directions." He put his erect cock into my mouth. "I asked you to stay still."

I couldn't say anything with his dick pressed to the back of my throat.

"Here's how this is going to work." He slowly moved his length in and out of my mouth. He tasted like sex and that unique taste that was all his own.

I tightened my lips around him.

"Fuck." He pulled out of me. "Now, you're going to stay still." He ran his finger down the center of my stomach. "This sexy line right here that runs right into your belly button is one of my favorite parts about you."

I felt something hot spread onto my stomach. I immediately tried to sit up.

"Stop." He grabbed my thighs to prevent me from moving. His warm tongue danced along my stomach and down, stopping right above my clit. "The thing is, I love foreplay. I love seeing you squirm. I love when you beg me."

He poured more of the hot liquid onto my stomach. This time, I stayed still. It wasn't burning me; it was warm, almost pleasant.

"Each time you move, I'm going to have to stop whatever I'm doing to lap up the coffee before it spills on my desk."

Coffee? This was going to make such a mess. I didn't want to picture Nita's face when James asked her to clean this up. "What are you going to be doing to me?"

"Teasing you until you follow the rules."

"James, don't you have a lot of work to catch up on? And someone might stop by to talk to..."

He pressed a finger down hard on my clit.

God. My back immediately arched.

His finger moved away as quickly as it had come and I felt his tongue slide down my stomach. "You're so bad at this."

"James."

"Penny." He poured more coffee on my stomach. I felt it flow downward and pool in my belly button. "How about you tell me why you were upset earlier." He kissed the side of my neck.

I kept my mouth shut.

He ran his fingers up the insides of my thighs and lightly nipped the top of my thigh, right beneath where I wanted him most.

I moaned softly.

"Tell me." He kissed the same spot and his hot breath lingered between my thighs.

I needed him. "You kissed Isabella."

His hands fell from my thighs. "What?" The seduction from his voice was gone.

I didn't want to tell him about how Isabella had tricked me. Not when I couldn't see his reaction. Not when I was tied to his desk with no clothes on. "I saw you," I lied. "Last week when she came here to talk to you and you ditched me for lunch." I pulled on the phone cord and made the drawer slam shut again. "I saw you kiss her."

"Jesus, Penny, why didn't you say something sooner? I didn't fucking kiss Isabella."

He was awfully defensive. The anger in his voice was palpable. "I saw you." I bit my lip. It wasn't really a lie. I had a photograph proving it. I tried to move again, but the phone cord dug into my wrists.

"Stop." He grabbed my arms to make me stop moving. With his other hand, he ran his thumb along my bottom lip again to keep me from biting it. "Then you only saw it for less than a second. Because she tried to kiss me, but I shoved her off immediately. I thought she was hugging me goodbye."

"Why didn't you tell me?"

"Because there was nothing to tell. Isabella means nothing to me. I wasn't going to upset you for no reason."

"For no reason? Your ex wife kissed you and now you've been exchanging phone calls. You said she was being nice. What was I supposed to think?" *And she's been harassing me.*

"That I would never cheat on you."

I pressed my lips together. I immediately felt more liquid being poured onto my stomach. "James, I don't want to play this game anymore. Untie me."

"You don't trust me." He didn't ask it, he said it as a statement.

I wasn't sure if I did or didn't. I wanted to. Rob had made it seem like he hadn't cheated on me during his bachelor party. And James had just proved my suspicion that the kiss with Isabella wasn't what it seemed. Everything that Isabella had sent me was complete bullshit. "I do trust you."

"You don't. How do you not know how I feel about you after all this time? After everything we've been through?"

"I'm sorry. I do trust you."

"You trust me with your body." He ran his hand down the side of my waist and over my hip. "You're so beautiful." His voice sounded sad.

"James, I trust you."

"Not entirely."

"I do."

"Then prove it."

"What?"

He sunk his finger deep inside of me.

Fuck. I was just about to arch my back, but he grabbed my breast hard and held me down against the desk.

"Stop moving." His voice was forceful. He slid another finger inside of me, stretching me wide, and squeezing my breast even harder.

My body squirmed and his fingers immediately slid out of me. His tongue lapped up the coffee. He left a trail of kisses down my stomach and poured more coffee.

I felt his breath between my thighs again.

"If I wanted to be with someone else, I wouldn't have proposed to you." He thrust his tongue deep inside of me.

Oh my God. I could feel his anger with each ferocious stroke. He was devouring me. I knew he was punishing me, but it felt so amazing. His tongue was even warmer than usual because of the hot coffee. It felt unbelievable. I moved my heels to the edge of the desk so that I could get some leverage to match his strokes, but his tongue stopped and the warmth was gone. "James." I wanted to grab the back of his head and hold him in place. I pulled against my restraints again.

"Stop moving." He lapped up the coffee, his tongue somehow even arousing me when it wasn't deep inside my pussy.

"James, this isn't proving..."

He grabbed my hips and flipped my body so that my stomach was pressed against his desk. My feet barely touched the ground. I could feel papers sticking to my stomach. He slapped my ass hard. "Why aren't you listening to me?"

I liked the sting of his palm. And he knew it.

He slapped me again. "Why don't you trust me?"

"You proposed when we were still in Delaware. You could have changed your mind. It's been two and a half years."

He slapped my ass again.

Fuck.

He slapped me again in the same spot and then gently massaged my ass cheek. "And all I've done is love you."

He was right. Each and every day, he always told me and showed me just how much he cared. I didn't doubt his love. I was an idiot for thinking those pictures were real. "James..."

He slapped my ass again and slid his fingers back inside of my wetness. Not slow and loving, but fast and rough. He was fucking me hard with his fingers and I couldn't focus on what he had just said like this. I gripped the edge of the desk with my hands as he picked up his rhythm. I needed more. As if answering my unspoken thoughts, he ran his thumb against my clit. I moved my hips back into him.

His response was a hard slap against my ass. "You're getting cold feet."

I clenched around his fingers, feeling them even more intensely. "I'm not."

His fingers moved even faster. "Don't you dare come."

"James..."

He slapped me again. "Not until I tell you to." His thumb began to massage my clit in rhythm with his fingers fucking me relentlessly.

"I can't." I gripped his desk even tighter.

He slapped my ass again. "Why don't you trust me?!"

"Because you're too good for me!" I was surprised by my own honesty. But that was it. All of it stemmed from my own insecurities. Why on earth was he marrying me?

"You have no idea how you make me feel." He removed his fingers and slammed his cock deep inside of me.

I moaned way louder than I meant to. He felt so good inside of me.

"You have no idea how much I need you." He thrust faster, pressing my hips against the edge of his desk. "How much I crave you when we aren't together." He pulled my hair so that I was arching my back.

The phone cord dug into my wrists, but I barely noticed. It was like he was fucking me back in his office at the University of New Castle, savoring how he felt inside of me, enjoying it more than he knew he would. Each thrust made me climb higher and higher as his hips slammed into my sore ass cheeks.

"How much I love you." His pace was relentless.

"I love you too." Tears starting biting at my eyes. It was too intense.

He tilted his hips ever so slightly, hitting that spot of my anatomy that made me lose control. "Then come for me."

As soon as I clenched around him, he exploded inside of me. The familiar warmth spread up into my stomach, more forcefully than it ever had. I came hard as he continued to thrust in and out of me.

His groan of satisfaction made me feel more secure than I had in days. And he was suddenly being slow and gentle with his strokes. As if he needed me to know that it was more than just fucking to him. But I knew that. I had just gotten in my own head. He loved me just as much as I loved him.

He groaned again before pulling out of me.

I sighed and let my body relax against his desk. I had missed this feeling.

His fingertips trailed up over my ass, back, and neck until they slowly began to untie the silky tie from around my eyes.

"You're the one that's too good for me. I know you don't be-lieve me, because you're too stubborn to listen to my reasons."

I couldn't help the smile that spread over my face. This wasn't the first time I had told him he was out of my league. No matter what he said, I didn't understand. Because he was James Hunter. It would never make sense to me. He had chosen me for some reason. I was the luckiest girl in the world. I was always just wor-ried the luck would eventually wear off.

"We were never going to be just a one time thing, baby." He kissed the side of my jaw. "We never could be. I can't even role play that scenario anymore...Miss Taylor."

The tie fell from my face and I opened my eyes. James was kneeling in front of me smiling. He was staring at me intently.

"Soon to be Mrs. Hunter, I hope?"

"Yes. I'm sorry. I just missed you and..."

He silenced me with a gentle kiss. "It's okay. But don't be afraid to talk to me about how you're feeling. You need to trust me." He ran the tip of his nose down the length of mine. "I would never cheat on you. You mean the world to me. All I need is you."

"I do trust you." I felt so foolish. I looked down at my hands and then back up at him. "Are you going to untie me?"

"I think I'd rather work like this." He sat down in his chair with a smirk on his face.

I laughed.

He buttoned up his shirt and put his tie back around his neck.

"Really, I need to get back to work." I lifted my wrists as much as I could.

He looked down at his watch. "You probably should get back. I actually have a lot of work I need to get through." He rolled his chair forward and slowly untied the phone cord from my wrists. As soon as my hands were free he kissed the inside of each of my wrists. They were red from me pulling on the cord so much. He glanced back up at me.

"It's okay. I liked it."

He ran his thumbs along the insides of my wrists. "You're definitely everything I need."

I pushed myself up and leaned forward to kiss him. He grabbed my ass and pulled me against him, kissing me hard before setting me back down on my feet. When he pulled back he had that boyish grin that I loved so much. I took a deep breath. We were good.

"Let's find your clothes," he said with a wink. His hands fell from me as he leaned down to grab my bra.

There was a paper stuck to my sticky stomach. I peeled it off, but before I could look at it, James grabbed it. He crumpled it up and threw it in the trash.

"What was that?" I asked as I put my bra back on.

"I got distracted this morning. I keep rewriting my vows to you."

My eyes darted back to his face. "James, I thought we agreed to just repeat the words that the minister says. You know I hate public speaking."

He smiled and handed me my shirt. "Baby, you're great at public speaking. You would have gotten an A in my class if you hadn't started sleeping with me. Or if we hadn't gotten caught."

I laughed and pulled my shirt on over my head. It stuck awkwardly to my stomach even when I tried to smooth it into place. I needed to go to the bathroom to wipe some of the stickiness from the coffee off of me. "We didn't really get caught."

"I know." He grabbed my waist and pulled me back against his chest. "My horrible ex wife, who I have absolutely no feelings for whatsoever, who I definitely don't want to kiss, gave us away."

I straightened his tie for him. "Who I want you to stop talking to."

"Okay. Done."

"Yeah?"

"All my friends say I'm whipped anyway. Might as well prove them right."

I lightly pushed his shoulder. "I'm not trying to boss you around."

"I know." He ran his fingers through my hair. "I just want you to be happy. I think Isabella was serious about getting my parents to come around or I would have hung up on her. I know you still want that."

I shook my head back and forth.

"You really don't want them to come?"

"No. I was the one that uninvited them, remember?"

He raised his left eyebrow.

"Fine. I'd still like them to accept me," I said. "Even though they're horrible. Maybe. But I don't want them to be forced into it by Isabella. I don't want her help with anything."

"Fair enough. No more Isabella. She is officially out of our lives."

I breathed a sigh of relief. "Thank you."

"And that's why you talk to me when you're upset. So I can fix it. Now where did your underwear go?"

I laughed and grabbed my thong off the ground.

James' eyes wandered up my legs as I pulled my thong and skirt back on.

"So much for waiting until our wedding night," I said.

"Insatiable as ever."

"You turned it into a game. You know how competitive I am."

He laughed. "That's not why you caved, though. You caved because you needed me. Just as much as I always need you. That's why we're getting married. There was no reason to hold off on having sex until our wedding night. We already know where we both stand." He tossed the phone at me. "Tell Nita to get me a new phone."

"No way. I'm not doing that." I threw it back at him. "I'm not her boss. And I don't want to have to explain what happened to it."

"So you want me to explain what happened?"

"Don't you dare. Just tell her it fell off your desk. And please don't make her clean up this mess." I walked to the other side of the desk and picked up a frame that had fallen. The glass was shattered. It was a picture of James and I at the beach. He had this habit of staring at me instead of the camera whenever some-one was taking a picture of us. This one wasn't any different. I was smiling and he was looking at me with the most loving ex-pression on his face. Like I was the only thing he saw. "I love this picture."

"We'll have a better one soon." He grabbed the broken frame from me and pulled out the picture. "Of when we share our first kiss as husband and wife. That's the one I'll want on my desk." He handed me the photo and tossed the frame in the trash. "Now that the other marketing interns know we're together you can have a picture of me. I'll get you a new frame."

I smiled back up at him. I had no idea why I had ever doubt-ed him.

"And don't worry about what Nita thinks. She is very aware of the fact that your afternoon lunch visits the past few years sometimes resulted in sex because I always asked her not to dis-turb us and winked at her."

"No you didn't..." I stopped when I saw the playful expres-sion on his face. "James! You didn't really, did you?"

"You'll never know. And besides, everyone who walked by my office recently knows we just had sex. You were pretty loud."

"I was not."

He shrugged his shoulders. "I guess we'll see."

My face turned red. "I wasn't loud."

"You should probably get back to work, Miss Taylor. I have a ton of work I need to get done this week so I can marry you." He sat back down at his desk.

"I love you."

He smiled at me. "I love you so much."

I walked out of his office with a huge smile on my face. It felt like a weight had been lifted off my shoulders.

Sierra cleared her throat when I sat down at my desk and leaned toward me. "Your hair is a little messed up," she whispered and touched the side of her head.

"Oh, thanks." I ran my fingers through my hair.

"Was it super windy outside or something?" she asked.

I had told them all that I was going to make a quick phone call after lunch.

"Yeah, the wind has really picked up." *Please stop talking about this.*

"Weird. I always check the weather forecast, and I didn't think there was a storm coming. I should have worn a jacket."

"Sometimes they just sneak up on you." My eyes were glued to my computer screen.

"You just had sex, didn't you?" Tavon asked.

"What? Psh. No."

Tavon laughed. "You just fucked James in his office."

"I did not." I ran my fingers through my hair again. I could feel Zach staring at me. He was clearly judging my relationship.

"Then why are you blushing?" Tavon asked.

"I'm not. It's just hot in here."

"And the sex hair?"

"The wind."

Zach laughed.

I looked up, surprised that he was laughing.

"Make up sex is always the best," he said. "Just makes you want to keep coming back for more."

I rolled my eyes.

"Did you really just have sex in his office?" Sierra asked.

I sighed. They had caught me red handed. "Fine, you caught me."

"You two don't have much self control," Tavon said.

"It's not like we do it in his office all the time or anything."

"Office sex seems like so much fun." Sierra immediately blushed after saying it.

"Maybe I can help you make that fantasy come true?" Tavon said.

"I don't think so," she said. "I just meant in theory."

"It's fun in reality too."

Sierra looked back down at her computer screen. "We work at an open desk pod. We can't have sex here."

"But you want to have sex with me?"

She laughed. "I didn't say that."

"We could do it in the copy room. Or the mail room. The possibilities are endless really."

Sierra's face turned more and more red each time Tavon spoke.

"So, everything's good in paradise then?" Zach asked me.

"Really good, yeah."

"Good. You know guys, the bathroom always works too," he said, joining in Sierra and Tavon's conversation.

I shook my head. I really didn't think there was much of a chance that Sierra was going to hook up with Tavon. But I never thought that I'd hook up with my professor. And I never thought

Tyler and Melissa would get together. Sometimes you found love in the most unexpected place.

Tavon stretched. "I could use a bathroom break right now, actually. If you wait a minute to follow me, no one will suspect you." He winked at Sierra.

Sierra shook her head back and forth, but I watched her stare at Tavon as he walked away. I couldn't help but think she was in way over her head with him.

CHAPTER 27
Thursday

I woke up to the sun streaming in through the window. James was still sleeping peacefully. We had gone to bed after a shared shower, and his hair was slightly curly in that way I loved. It reminded me of being in the rain with him.

The past few days had been amazing. I was finally able to focus on how excited I was about the wedding. I bit my lip. I was incredibly nervous about the vows. We hadn't talked about it again, but I was pretty sure he was going to say his own. I needed to come up with something. But no matter what I wrote down, I felt like it wasn't good enough. Like he was going to be grading me on my response. I shook the thought away. He wasn't my professor anymore.

I wanted to run my fingers down his abs, but I stayed still. *I'm marrying James Hunter.* I suddenly felt incredibly giddy. *This is really happening.*

My mom was coming tonight for my final fitting. James was putting my parents up in a hotel near our new apartment. I wasn't sure why he always insisted on paying. Probably because I made him feel guilty for not inviting them to stay with us. I guess it was a little weird that my parents knew we were sleeping together. James still felt a little uncomfortable with the dynamic. But now that I was out of school, the age difference mattered even less. When we became husband and wife everything would be even less awkward. And my parents both loved James. He just wasn't used to having that in his life.

He slowly opened his eyes and smiled. "Were you watching me sleep again?" He grabbed my waist and pulled me closer to him.

I laughed and rested my head against his chest, breathing in his heavenly scent. "I can't help it. It's hard not to stare at you."

He tucked a loose strand of hair behind my ear. "Two more days."

Two more days!

***

Today was my last day of work before the wedding. And I was excited to get it over with. I just wanted to be able to focus on the wedding. Melissa had called me last night and said she'd come to my dress fitting too. She finally seemed excited about being my maid of honor. Maybe she was just happy that I was tying the knot so I wouldn't run off with Tyler. I laughed to myself. I really hoped that Tyler and her made each other happy. I rested my back against the side of the elevator.

"What are you thinking about?" James asked and squeezed my hand.

I leaned closer toward him and whispered, "That I'm excited this is the last time I'll walk into your office as Penny Taylor."

He smiled down at me. "Do you want to go out to dinner with your parents tonight? I can get us a reservation at that new Thai restaurant near Kleinfeld's."

"Actually, we're going to be around so many people the next few days. Could we maybe stay in tonight, just us? Maybe we can rent a movie or something? I just wanna relax."

He looked even happier than he had a second ago. "That sounds perfect. I'll let Ellen know we'll be there for dinner."

The elevator doors opened. James kept his fingers intertwined with mine as we walked off the elevator. He stopped right in front of his office door. "I have a lunch meeting today that I couldn't get out of. And I'm slammed with last minute things that need to be finished before I take all of next week off. But I'll see you back home for dinner." He leaned down and kissed me.

I didn't care that he was kissing me at work. I was never going to take another moment with him for granted. When he pulled back, my face was flushed.

"Have a good last work day as Miss Taylor." He ran his thumb over one of my rosy cheeks.

"Have a good last work day as a single man."

He laughed. "Don't worry, my friends aren't going to kidnap me again. I'll see you tonight, baby." He kissed me once more and then disappeared into his office.

I felt even giddier than I had back at the apartment. I made my way through the maze of cubicles toward the marketing interns' desk pod. As soon as I saw my desk, my smile disappeared. There was a manila envelope underneath the picture of James and I at the beach. Why couldn't Isabella just leave us in peace? I lifted up the new frame and grabbed the envelope.

"Did you see who dropped this off?" I asked Zach. He was the only one there. I wanted to know who Isabella's minion was. Maybe it was just Austin. They deserved each other.

"No, no one's been over here. Maybe someone dropped it off last night?"

"Yeah, maybe." I sat down and looked over my shoulder to make sure no one was around to see whatever was inside. I pulled out a new stack of photos. There was a post-it note covering up the first picture:

The truth doesn't seem to bother you. It's your life. I can't stop you from marrying him. But I can get you to give me what I need.

I lifted off the sticky note and swallowed hard. They weren't pictures of James. This time, they were pictures of me. *Fuck*. The first one was of me hugging Tyler outside of Kleinfeld's. Then of him holding my hand inside that diner. The rest were from my bachelorette party. Me talking to guys at the bar, touching some random guy's abs, and dancing. There was another post-it note on top of the last picture:

Wire 20 million dollars to my account number below. I'll go away forever. I'll stop calling James. I'll stop interfering with his parents. I'll be out of your life forever. And if that isn't enough motivation, I also won't show the pictures to James. You can finally have the happily ever after that is your immature vision of reality. You have until the bank closes at 4 o'clock.

There were some numbers at the bottom that must have been the bank account number. I lifted up the last sticky note. The last picture was of Austin kissing me, right before I shoved him off. I bit my lip. *That bitch*. I took a deep breath. All these photos were taken out of context. I could explain them to James. And it just made me realize even more that the pictures she had given me of James were only half the truth.

She was like an evil villain, but she was a bad one. And I wasn't going to fall for her games anymore. She would never get another dime of James' money. I pushed the pictures and notes back inside the envelope and tossed it into the trash.

I turned around again. It felt like someone was watching me. I guess someone was. Or else these pictures wouldn't exist. Neither would the ones of James. I had been so happy a second ago, and now I felt like I was on edge.

"So, are you going through with it?" Zach asked.

"What?"

"Marrying your abusive boyfriend?"

"He's not. And you're awfully judgmental. You don't know me or him."

"We're all trying to get to know you."

"Fine. You want to know what I'm going through? His ex wife hit me. That's why I had a bruise on my face. And she's been harassing me. And threatening me. She's doing everything she can to make me call off the wedding. So I don't appreciate you hounding me on this. I don't need anyone else against me. It's exhausting."

"I just meant like, where did you grow up?"

I laughed. *God, I'm such a mess.* I took a deep breath and turned my computer on. "I grew up in Wilmington."

"Isn't that where Fight Club was filmed? What an interesting coincidence. So, did you at least hit her back?"

I looked up at him. "No."

"You should fight back, Fight Club."

"I have no intention of joining the dark side."

"I'm just saying...it's easier to fight fire with fire."

I shrugged my shoulders. "I just want her to disappear."

"I never said to kill her."

I laughed again. "That's not what I meant."

"I don't know. Rich people make people disappear all the time."

"I'm not rich," I said.

"You're about to be."

I shook my head. "You're ridiculous. Don't you need to go catch up with the tech department in the bathroom?"

"Maybe you should join us. You need to relax. So what if Hunter has a psycho ex? You won. He's marrying you."

"Thanks. But I'm going to pass on your enticing offer."

"I want in on whatever you two are talking about," Tavon said and plopped into his seat.

"We were just talking about how Zach gets high in the bathroom," I said.

"Shit, you told her about that? What the hell is wrong with you? She's sleeping with the boss, man."

I laughed.

"What, did you already tell him?" Tavon asked.

"I guess you'll never know." I hadn't yet, but I would eventually. I was pretty sure that James started his first tech company as a way to distract himself from his drug problem. And he spent most of his twenties getting over that time in his life. He wouldn't be happy to know that his employees were lighting up in the bathroom. It wasn't a conversation I wanted to have with him two days before our wedding.

"You deserve to be fired, Tavon," Sierra said and sat down at her desk. "I'll tell Mr. Hunter myself."

"Oh, come on," Tavon said. "You knew what saying yes to a date with me would mean."

Sierra's face turned red. "I did not know. Where I'm from, people don't sleep with each other on the first date. You're disgusting. Tell him, Penny."

"I..." my voice trailed off. I had slept with James before we had even officially had a date. And he was my professor. I wasn't the one to lecture Tavon for being forward. "I mean, you have to read the situation."

Zach laughed.

"Oh my God," Sierra said. "Did you sleep with James on your first date?"

"Um, kind of?"

"Okay," Tavon said. "Tell us the whole story.

***

The rest of the morning I spent laughing and bonding with the other marketing interns. They were all really nice. Extremely nosey, but nice. And I didn't blame them. I kind of did have the inside scoop on their boss.

Before lunch, Andy stopped by with an ad idea he wanted us to go over. They were teaming up with Mason and Bee's advertising agency for it, and it was fun going through the idea knowing that we'd be handing it over to Bee afterwards. Although, I'd be on my honeymoon when it was passed on to them. The afternoon flew by as well.

I was just about to shut down my computer so that I'd be in time for my dress fitting, when I got an email alert. I clicked on the box that had popped up:

You only have half an hour until I give James the pictures.

I deleted the email and shut off the computer. My heart was racing even though I knew the threat was empty. The pictures didn't matter. I didn't even talk to James about the pictures Isabella had sent me of him, and we were fine. It was just creepy that she knew my email.

"See you in a few weeks, guys." I stood up and grabbed my purse.

"I still can't believe you didn't invite us to your wedding," Tavon said and put his hands behind his head.

"I didn't know you when I sent out the invites. And we already gave them a headcount. I'm really sorry."

Tavon sighed. "It's fine. Want to go out with me on Saturday?" he asked Sierra.

"I don't think so." She turned to Zach. "Would you like to hang out Saturday night?"

Zach smiled. "I'd love to."

"Asshole," Tavon said. "I called dibs."

Zach shrugged. "Our bromance isn't strong enough to honor your dibs. Besides, Sierra clearly doesn't like you."

"She's just playing hard to get."

Sierra laughed. "No, I'm not. Congrats, Penny. And I hope your dress fitting goes well."

"Good luck," Zach said with a smile. I was glad that he had finally let go of his theory that James was abusive.

"Break a leg." Tavon laughed. "Just kidding. I don't know what to say. You're too young to get married?"

"Thanks for the support, Tavon."

"Don't listen to him. He's just jealous that you found your person. And he can't even get a date," Sierra said.

"Bye, guys," I said with a laugh. "Take care of James' company while we're gone." I felt a little guilty walking away from them. If I hadn't been such a mess when I first started the internship, I would have bonded with them sooner and could have given our wedding planner an updated headcount. I tried not to think about it as I made my way toward James' office. I wanted to say hi before I went to my fitting.

Right before I grabbed the handle my phone buzzed. I pulled it out of my purse and looked down at the text I had just received:

"If you go to James I'll leak all the photos."

Jesus. How did she have my phone number? This was crazy. I needed to tell James right now. He'd know how to handle her. I didn't want to deal with this alone anymore.

I reached for the handle again as another text came through. This one was a picture. But it wasn't one of the ones she had sent me this morning. It was of James and I having sex. On his desk in his office. *Holy shit.* Another one came through. And then another. And another.

I put my face in my hand. What was wrong with me? Obviously she had planted a camera in there if she had gotten that picture of her kissing James last week. I was such an idiot. I didn't think at all. My phone buzzed again, but this time there was a message:

"You thought I was talking about the other photos from this morning? Aw, Penny. You underestimate me. These photos will be leaked to every sleazy tabloid if I don't see the money in my account in 20 minutes. And don't you dare run to James. If you do, I'll leak the photos. If you call the cops, I'll leak the photos. We're ending this right here, right now. And there's more pictures where that came from. You're quite flexible."

You sick fuck. This wasn't just some petty game. She'd ruin James' reputation. My hands were shaking. James was the C.E.O. of a huge company, he was well respected, he was a freaking philanthropist. He was a good person. These pictures would make it seem like he didn't have control. I stepped away from

James' office and looked back toward the cubicles. I had tossed out the envelope that had Isabella's account information in it, but I could dig it out of the trash. Would she really leak the photos if I went to James? I had already tarnished his reputation once. I didn't want that to be on my hands again.

My phone buzzed again.

"Step away from his office. Here's my account number again. You're running out of time." The account number was written at the bottom of the text.

I turned around. How is she watching me? I could feel tears begin to well in my eyes. I couldn't risk it. James could lose everything. 20 million dollars wasn't that much to him. And maybe we could get it back later. She didn't say I couldn't tell him afterwards. I didn't have time to think right now. I was running out of time.

I ran toward the elevator and called Ian.

He picked up on the second ring. "Hey, Penny. I'm waiting outside to take you to Kleinfeld's."

I stepped onto the elevator and pressed the button to close the doors. "No, Ian. I need you to drive me to the bank."

"Okay, which bank?"

Shit. I knew James had set me up with my own account when we moved to New York despite my protests. I had never accessed it before. Every now and then I used the credit card he gave me to buy expensive dresses for functions I went to with him. But I had no idea how much was in the account. Hopefully it would be enough. *What bank was it?* "Just the normal one."

"United Bank? The one that James uses?"

"Yes." I tried to hide my sigh of relief. "Yup, the normal one."

Ian laughed. "You got it."

I hung up the phone when he came into view. He was parked right outside the office building and the door was already open for me. "How long will it take to get there?"

"It's just down the street."

"Thank God."

He gave me a funny look, but closed the door.

As soon as the car was moving, I felt even more nervous. Was I doing the right thing? James wouldn't want those photos all over the internet. I didn't have a choice. We pulled up outside of a building that said United Bank. "Thanks, Ian," I said and got out the second the car stopped. I ran up the steps and into the bank. It was insanely fancy inside. It looked more like a hotel than a bank. There was no line, so I walked directly up to the teller. "Hi, I need to transfer some money."

She stared at me for a second. "Yes, Miss..."

"Taylor. Penny Taylor. I have an account here, but I don't know the account number off the top of my head." *Or at all. I hope this is the right bank.* I had a couple thousand dollars in my own bank account. That wasn't going to appease Isabella.

"Okay, hold on one second. Penny Taylor..." She stared at her computer screen as she spoke. "And you're looking to transfer money?"

"Yes, just to a different account."

"How much are you looking to transfer?"

"20 million." I had lowered my voice slightly. She was going to think I was crazy.

The woman's fingers stopped and she looked up at me. "Let me just get a manager for you to sit down with. Excuse me."

"I'm in a bit of a hurry."

"Okay, Miss Taylor. Just let me go get him." She disappeared through a door.

I pulled out my phone. I only had twelve minutes. It felt like I was having a heart attack. I put my hand on my chest.

"The manager will be right out," the teller said as she came back up to the counter. "If you don't mind taking a seat." She gestured toward a group of plush chairs. This was taking too long. I sat down and tapped my foot nervously. A few minutes later a man emerged from the back.

"Hello, Miss Taylor. You must be James' fiancée." He put his hand out toward me. "I'm Ed and I'll be helping you out today."

I immediately stood up and shook his hand. "Yes, hi, it's nice to meet you. I'm kind of in a rush. I need to get this done before the wedding."

"Of course. Right this way." He took me to his office and sat down behind his desk. "So, James added you to several of his bank accounts when he updated his will a couple of years ago, in addition to the one that is just under your name."

"Mhm." I sat down across from him. I had no idea that James had done that. He trusted me with his money. And I was here giving it away to Isabella. My stomach seemed to flip over. Was I doing the right thing?

"And you understand that all of your joint assets are not liquid. You don't have 20 million dollars sitting in the bank. A lot of your money is currently tied up in investments. Properties, stocks..."

"Yes, of course." I hadn't even thought about that. No one had 20 million dollars just sitting in the bank. That wasn't financially responsible. "Is there any way to liquidate some of those assets?"

Ed scratched the back of his neck. He was starting to look uncomfortable. "Are you sure you want to do that?"

No. "Yes."

"James' portfolio is very diverse, but if you're looking for liquid assets immediately, the best way is probably through stocks. I'd advise you to call James' broker to get his take on what stocks are best to sell at the moment. How about you come back tomorrow? The stock market closes in several minutes as well as this bank and..."

"Could you just do it for me? Just take your best guess on which to sell?"

"Miss Taylor, I'm not a financial advisor. I'm just the manager of the bank. And I don't have access to your stocks."

My phone buzzed and I looked down at the text that had just come through:

"James' broker's name is Bill O'Neill. I'm sure you have been added to that account as well. You have ten minutes, Penny."

My hands started shaking again. I looked over my shoulder. How did she know everything I was doing?

"Miss Taylor, if you'd like to call James to discuss..."

"No, that's okay. Do you have Bill O'Neill's phone number so I can call him real quick?"

"Of course." Ed stared at his computer for a second and then typed a number into his desk phone and handed it to me.

"Hey, Ed!" Bill O'Neill said when he picked up the phone. "Did you catch the game..."

"Hi, Bill. This is actually Penny Taylor, James Hunter's fiancée."

"Oh, hi, Miss Taylor. I've heard so much about you. Did you catch the Mets game last night?"

"No. Actually, I'm kind of in a rush, Bill. I need to liquidate some of my stocks."

Bill cleared his throat. "Let me get James on the other line."

"No! I mean, he wanted me to handle it." I dropped my voice slightly. "I need to transfer 20 million dollars for an investment opportunity that he doesn't want to miss out on."

"Great, great. What company is James investing in now?"

Um... "Uber." It was the first thing that popped into my head.

"I thought he already invested in that?"

"Well, just, more, you know. When he sees a good investment he likes to go hard." *Go hard?* I was so bad at lying. I could feel Ed staring at me. I had told him I needed to do this before the wedding. Investing in Uber had nothing to do with that. My stories were already losing substance. "So, if I sell some stocks, will we be able to get enough money in my bank account?"

"Sure. But the trading floor closes in just a few minutes..."

"Then we better hurry this along."

Bill cleared his throat. "What were you interested in selling?"

"Apple." Again, I just said the first thing that popped into my head.

"Are you sure? It's on an up and..."

"I'm sure."

"I'd really feel more comfortable if I got James in on this call. I know that he likes Apple and..."

"I'm marrying him on Saturday. If you don't assist me with this, the first thing I'll do as his wife is convince him to get a new stock broker."

"Right. Very well. Sorry, Miss Taylor." There was a pause on his end. "What else would you like to sell? That was only two million."

Two million in one stock? "How about GM?" I said. I didn't know enough about stocks to be having this conversation.

"He doesn't have any investments in GM."

Crap. "Right, I forgot. How about Google then?"

"Okay. That's another 10 million."

"Great. What are some of the highest yielding stocks?"

"He's made a ton of money in oil."

Oil? James was very environmentally conscious. Why did he have oil stocks? "Sell all of those." Maybe he'd thank me later for that one.

"I only need to sell a few of them to get you the money you need. Do you have a preference?"

"No, just do it." I looked down at my phone. I only had 3 minutes left. Ed was already packing up his briefcase for the day. *Shit!*

"Okay, it'll take a few minutes for the funds to appear in your account."

I wasn't sure if that would cut it, but there was nothing else I could do. "Thank you for all your help, Bill. I'll make sure to let James know how accommodating you were."

"Very well. And congratulation on your upcoming nuptials."

"Thanks." I hung up the phone before I said anything else stupid. "Ed, can we set up the transfer now?"

He looked down at his watch. "The bank closes in a few minutes and it usually takes some time for the funds to appear..."

"Bill said it would just be a few minutes. I have the account number I need the money in right here." I pulled out my phone.

Ed looked even more uncomfortable than he had a minute ago as he sat down. "That's not the account number for Uber."

I laughed nervously. "No, it's not. I just needed Bill to sell the stocks for me. He was more likely to do it if he thought we were investing in something else profitable."

"I see." Ed tapped a few keys on his computer. "So, whose account is this?" He wasn't making eye contact with me.

"A last minute wedding venue expense."

"For 20 million dollars?"

"You know James. He's extravagant. Has the money trans-ferred yet?"

"It'll be another minute. Just let me fill in the information for the transfer."

I looked down at my phone again. *One minute.*

"Here we are," Ed said. "Would you like me to print out a copy of your transaction or send an email copy to you?"

"A print out please." I didn't want him to accidentally send a copy to James. I needed to tell him about this without him find-ing out first. I knew how bad it looked.

A printer hummed to life in the corner. Ed stood up and grabbed the small slip that had printed out. "20 million to the account number you had listed." He handed me the slip of paper.

Hopefully we had gotten it done just in time. "Thank you so much, Ed." I stood up and grabbed the sheet of paper. My moth-er and Melissa were probably wondering where I was. But something made me stop before I walked out of the office. James added me to all his accounts and to his will a few years ago. But he had never told me. Why hadn't he told me? I turned around. "Who else is in the will?"

"Excuse me?" Ed had shut off his computer and snapped his briefcase closed.

"In James' will. Who else is a beneficiary?"

"Just you, Miss Taylor."

Just me? I swallowed hard. He couldn't leave me with all his money. "But if something happened to both of us..."

"There is a contingency where all the money goes to a dozen or so charities in the case of an untimely death to both parties. And the businesses would be left to his brother and sister."

I didn't know what to say. James had left all his money to me even before we got married. He was even leaving me responsible for running his businesses. He trusted me. More than anyone else in the world. What had I just done?

CHAPTER 28
Thursday

I stared at my reflection in the mirror as the woman clipped another veil into my hair.

"Penny..." my mom said. "Sweetie, you look so beautiful."

I immediately burst into tears. *Oh God.* I had made a mistake. I needed to call James. My dress felt tight and uncomfortable. I didn't want any of this. I never wanted a fancy wedding. James had told me he didn't either. He said he had already done all that. He wanted to get married in Vegas. But I had said no. I had told him I wanted my family and friends to be there. Why were we doing this? Why was I making him do something he didn't want to do? I didn't need any of this.

Melissa grabbed a tissue and handed it to me. "Penny, that one's perfect. The diamonds match the straps on the dress. It's absolutely gorgeous."

I nodded. They thought I was crying because I liked the veil. I blotted my eyes. "Let's get this one," I said and pulled it out of my hair.

My hands wouldn't stop shaking. I pushed the veil into the sales associate's hands so that no one would notice. Isabella still hadn't contacted me. I didn't know whether or not she had gotten the money in time. The pictures could be all over the internet already.

"Can you help me get out of this?" I asked the woman who was helping me.

She nodded and we went back into the changing room. As soon as I was back in my normal clothes, I grabbed my cell phone. Still nothing.

"Do you girls want to go get some dinner?" my mom asked. "My treat."

"I can't, Mom. I told James I'd have dinner with just him tonight."

"Of course." My mom gave me a smile. "Melissa, do you and Tyler want to join Peter and me for dinner?"

"We'd love to, Mrs. Taylor."

The sales associate handed me my dress in a bag. "You're all set."

"Thank you," I said and took the dress from her.

"Penny, your hands are shaking." My mom stood up and took the dress from me. "Are you feeling okay?"

"I'm just nervous."

"Sweetie." My mom embraced me with a huge hug. "I was nervous before my wedding too. But you have nothing to worry about. You and James have such a strong connection. And you've already been through so much together. The two of you can face anything. Everyone can see the love that you share. I'm so happy for you." She squeezed me once more and then released me from her embrace.

"You two were made for each other," Melissa said with a smile. "There is no other way to describe what you guys have."

"How are you and Tyler doing?"

Melissa's smile got even bigger. "So good. And I think I owe you a thank you for that. He told me that he talked to you about it."

"I'm so happy that it all worked out."

Melissa threw her arms around me. "I'm so sorry about every-thing, Penny. I don't know why..."

"It's okay." She had already apologized a dozen times.

"I just...I love you so much and I'm so happy for you. I'm sorry if my attitude ruined anything leading up to your wedding."

"It didn't." At least, it didn't matter now. I was just happy that we were friends again. She was back just in time to be my maid of honor.

She unwrapped her arms from around me and squeezed my shoulders. "And you're going to be the most beautiful bride. Why are you crying again?"

"I'm sorry." I laughed and quickly wiped my tears away before they could stream down my cheeks. "I don't know what's wrong with me." But I did. I had this awful feeling in my stomach that this wedding wasn't going to happen. I had just stolen money from James. My reasoning didn't matter. I had probably just lost his trust. Isabella was a better villain than I had given her credit for this morning. She had played this whole thing just right.

"You're just nervous," my mom said. "Try to get some sleep tonight. You'll just be excited tomorrow when the celebrations start. And I can't wait to meet James' parents at the rehearsal din-ner."

I hadn't told my parents about the disaster at the engagement party. I wasn't sure why. They would probably never meet James' parents. But I didn't want them to think that reflected poorly on James. He'd be better at explaining it to them than I would. I still had so many unanswered questions about his childhood.

Melissa was staring at me with a funny look on her face.

When my mom turned away to grab her purse, I shook my head at Melissa.

She just shrugged and pretended to zip her mouth shut.

"Thank you," I mouthed silently.

We all made our way outside. It was still hot out. I gave my mom and Melissa both a hug goodbye. "Have fun at dinner."

"Thanks again, Penny. I really owe you one," Melissa said. "We'll see you tomorrow night."

"Mhm. Bye, Mom."

"Don't be nervous, Penny. James is one of the good ones."

I tried not to start crying again as I nodded my head. He was. But I didn't feel like I was. "See you tomorrow!" I turned away from them and walked toward the car where Ian was waiting.

Ian smiled at me. "Are you excited for the wedding?" he asked as he took the dress out of my hands.

"Yes." My voice sounded small as I hurried into the car. I just needed to get home and tell James. Everything would be fine. I'd tell him about all the pictures Isabella had sent me, and the texts. Maybe he could figure out how she seemed to know my every move. We could figure this out together.

"What kind of dress did you get?" Ian asked as he pulled away from the curb.

I laughed. "I don't really know the style. It's pretty though."

I could see Ian's smile in the rearview mirror. "I'm sure you'll look beautiful."

"Thanks, Ian."

"Do you know when Jen is coming in?"

My phone buzzed and I pulled it out of my purse. There was a new text:

"Thank you for your assistance, Penny. There is one more thing, though. You can never tell James that you transferred the money to me. Or that I was the one that asked you to do it. If I find out that you told him I was involved in this in any way, the photos will be leaked. So keep my name out of it. I'm officially out of your life. Good luck getting to know the man you're marrying. You're going to need it."

I swallowed hard. I wasn't allowed to tell him? My chest started hurting again. I pressed my hand against it and tried to take a deep breath. What if James found out on his own? What was I supposed to say? I couldn't lie to him. He'd be able to tell. Not that Ed and Bill didn't realize I was lying. But James knew me better than anyone. He always knew if something was bothering me.

"Penny?" Ian said.

"What?"

"Do you know when Jen is coming in?"

I tried to focus on what he was saying. "Um, she's coming in tomorrow morning."

"Would you like me to pick her up from the airport and take her to the hotel?"

"That would be great, Ian. Thanks."

I couldn't even get joy out of how excited he looked. Ian had a crush on Jen for as long as I knew him. Maybe he'd finally tell her that he liked her this weekend. Weddings were romantic.

Ian turned into the parking garage beneath our apartment building. I grabbed my dress off the hook in the back seat.

"Thanks for the ride, Ian."

"Would you like me to carry that up for you?" he asked.

"No, that's okay. Thanks." I got out of the car and walked slowly toward the elevator. *Please don't know. Please don't know. Please don't know.*

I leaned against the side of the elevator and closed my eyes. Even if he did know, I could just tell him I couldn't tell him what had really happened. He had to believe me. He trusted me.

I unlocked the door and walked into our apartment. James wasn't in the living room or in the kitchen. "James?" I called as I walked upstairs and into our bedroom. There was no answer as I hung up the dress. Maybe he was picking up dinner somewhere. I walked over to our bed and grabbed the box full of notes and pictures that Isabella had sent me. I didn't want to talk about any of this. It was time to let all of this go. I walked out of our bedroom and back down the stairs, with the box under my arm. If I could believe James hadn't cheated on me after seeing these pictures, then he could believe me when I told him whatever ended up coming out of my mouth about his missing 20 million dollars.

God. I was so screwed. Maybe I could tell him I made an investment. Or that the dress cost a lot of money. *Or just tell him the truth.* But I couldn't risk it. Isabella was watching me somehow. She knew what I was doing. I didn't know how, but she did. She had eyes and ears everywhere.

"How did it go?"

I almost jumped when I heard James' voice. I put the box on the kitchen counter and turned around, shielding it from his view. "Good. I think you're going to like the dress."

James had a glass of scotch in his hand. He sat down on the couch and took a sip. He looked tired. "You look beautiful in everything, Penny." He said it without looking up at me.

I glanced down at the box and then back at him. I'd throw it away in a minute. I walked over to the couch and sat down next to James. "Are you okay?" He must already know. I could tell something was bothering him. He never drank alone unless he was upset.

"I got a few interesting phone calls tonight."

"Yeah?"

He took another sip of scotch and set it down on the coffee table. He wanted me to say something, but when I stayed silent, he said, "My parents called."

"They did?" I couldn't help the excitement in my voice.

"Apparently Isabella actually talked to them. They want to come to the wedding. They want...well, I don't know what they want. Another chance, I guess? They said they were sorry."

"James, that's great."

He shrugged. "I guess. Isabella really came through." He shook his head. "She's changed. She's actually changed."

No. She hadn't changed at all. I bit my tongue. Maybe she was being nice to him to his face but she had just stolen his money. I needed to tell him. Were the photos leaking worse than him thinking I stole money from him? My hands were shaking so badly that I had to tuck them under my thighs so he wouldn't notice. "What did you tell your parents?"

"That I needed to talk to you first."

"James, I think they should come."

"I knew you'd say that. That's not what we need to talk about. What were you doing tonight?"

"Getting my dress." My throat felt dry.

He looked back down at his half empty glass of scotch. It didn't seem like it was his first glass. He seemed distant and spaced out. "I got an email from my stock broker, Bill O'Neill, today. A memo for the stocks I sold after work today. You can jump in any time, Penny."

Shit. I had forgotten to tell Bill to not send any emails. I bit my lip. I didn't know how much James knew. Offering any information would just make it worse.

James downed the rest of his scotch. "So, I called him. Apparently I'm investing in Uber? Again?" The more he talked the angrier he looked.

I still stayed silent.

"So I called my bank to see what account the money had been transferred to. But it was gone. Once the money came through, it was transferred to an account that wasn't mine. Why aren't you saying anything?" He looked so mad.

"You don't understand."

"I know I don't understand. That's why I'm trying to talk to you. Why did you liquidate 20 million dollars worth of stocks?"

"I'm sorry. I can't tell you." *Please believe me.*

He laughed. "Penny." He stood up. "When you turned my parents down for money, I was so sure. I was so sure that what we had was real. That you weren't after me for my money."

"I'm not. And the fact that you weren't sure about me until I turned down your parents' money..." I tried to swallow my tears. "How could you not be sure? When I gave up everything to be with you? When I said yes to your proposal? James..."

"Then why the hell did you just steal 20 million dollars from me?!"

"I didn't steal it. My name was on your accounts."

"Jesus, Penny. And when did you realize I added you to all my accounts?"

"Today."

"Don't lie to me. You promised you wouldn't lie."

"Today, James. I didn't know until today."

He nodded. He seemed to believe me. Which was good, because it was the truth. "How long have you been planning this?"

"I haven't been planning anything, James. I had to transfer the money. I didn't have a choice. I was..."

"Stop lying! You promised you wouldn't lie to me," he repeated. He ran his hands through his hair. "Isabella tried to warn me. She said that you didn't love me. She always said you were after my money."

"Why would you believe her? Have the past two and a half years meant nothing to you?"

He shook his head. "Because she was right. You just wanted me for my money."

"I fell in love with you when you were my professor. You could have been broke. I still would have loved you, James."

"You don't love me. Stop lying to me. What's the point now? You got what you wanted. Just go."

"That's not true. I love you. All I want is to marry you. I'm not going anywhere."

He pulled out something from his pocket and tossed it at me. "You don't love me."

I unfolded the pictures. They were the ones of Tyler hugging me and holding my hand in the diner. Isabella was a fucking liar.

"You still love him." He sounded more hurt by this than the fact that he was missing 20 million dollars.

"I never loved Tyler. James, you know that. I love you. I've only ever loved you." I stood up, but he took a step back from me.

"Then why did you do it?!"

"I..." I didn't know what to say. I didn't have an answer. "Those pictures aren't what you think. I was upset when you were at your bachelor party. Melissa wasn't speaking to me. Tyler was just being a good friend. He went and asked Melissa to be his girlfriend right after this," I said and waved the pictures in the air. "Isabella took these and she's..."

"I know. I know that Isabella took these. She gave them to me a few days ago. And she told me I couldn't trust you. But I didn't listen. Because I trusted you. With everything. I was wrong." It looked like he was about to cry. I had never seen him like this.

I wanted to comfort him. I took another step toward him, but he took a step back. "You weren't wrong, James. You can trust me. Please just believe me. We're being blackmailed. I had to transfer the money so there wouldn't be pictures of us having sex leaked all over the internet."

He laughed and shook his head back and forth. "God, all you do is lie. You're leaving me, right? That's what this is?"

"No."

"And you needed money before you left me?" he said like he hadn't even heard what I had just said. "So you could run away with him?"

"What? No." I wanted to laugh. This whole thing was ridiculous. "I don't love Tyler. I don't want to be with Tyler. And we're certainly not running away together. James..."

"Then why did you transfer 20 million dollars into Tyler's bank account?"

"I didn't." I transferred it to Isabella's account. *Fuck.* That bitch set me up. "I didn't." My voice sounded so small. *Oh God, no.* My whole body felt cold.

"Yes you did. At 4 o'clock you transferred 20 million dollars of my money to Tyler Stevens' bank account."

"No. James." I could hear the desperation in my voice. "This isn't what you think."

"Stop it." He ran his hands through his hair again. "Isabella knew. That's why you didn't want me to talk to her. She knew you didn't love me. She knew you just wanted my money."

"I do love you. I love you so much."

"But not as much as you love him? Penny, I trusted you."

"Then trust me now. We're being blackmailed."

"Just stop!" His voice was so loud. "Who the fuck would blackmail you into giving my money to Tyler?"

"I can't tell you."

"Because the answer is no one! Your lie doesn't even make any sense."

He didn't believe me. "We are being blackmailed. I just can't tell you by who or they'll leak..."

"Photos of us having sex? Yeah, I heard you the first time. I need some air." He walked past me. He stumbled slightly and caught himself on one of the stools in the kitchen.

I had only ever seen him this drunk once before after hanging out with Rob back in Newark. "You can't leave. You're drunk. Please just sit down."

"Like you care."

"I do care."

"What because you love me?" he scoffed. "No one loves me. Keep the money. Just get the fuck out of my house."

"James." I put my hand on his arm.

He recoiled from me, like my touch caused him pain. "Leave." His voice was firm.

"I'm not leaving until you listen to me."

"Go be with Tyler. Go be happy. That's all I ever wanted. For you to be happy."

"You make me happy."

"Please just go." He wiped his hand underneath his eyes. I had never seen James cry. It killed me. He was crying because he thought I didn't love him. It felt like my heart was breaking.

"Those pictures aren't what they seem. I don't love Tyler. I love you. I love everything about you. This whole thing is just a misunderstanding."

He pulled out a few more pictures from his pocket. "Like this?" He slammed the picture down on the counter. It was of me touching that random guy's abs at the bar. "Or this?" He slammed down the picture of Austin kissing me.

"They're like the ones of Tyler. They were taken out of context. It was my bachelorette party. There was this list of stupid stuff my friends made me do. And Austin kissed me. I shoved him off right away. Isabella made him..."

"Just save it. I don't care, Penny. You're not my problem anymore."

"Problem? Is that what I've always been? Just something you had to take care of?"

He shook his head. "You certainly can't take care of yourself. You're immature. And selfish. And ungrateful."

"Ungrateful for what? This house that I didn't want? Because I don't like spending your money?"

"I try to give you everything and you always pretended like you didn't want it. You played me."

"I didn't play you. I don't care about your money. And this?" I picked up the picture he had of Austin kissing me. "I trusted you when you kissed Isabella. All I'm asking is for you to do the same. She orchestrated the pictures. You can't believe anything she says."

"But the money? Explain that to me. Just tell me who's blackmailing us." He put the word blackmail in air quotes.

My phone buzzed. I pulled it out of my purse and looked down at the text:

"Don't you dare. All I have to do is press enter."

"What could possibly be more important than this conversation, Penny? Unless it's him?"

"It's not Tyler." *Isabella must have cameras in here. She's been watching us this whole time.* "You know this isn't about Tyler. You know that. We're just friends."

He shook his head. "You stole from me. For him. And you don't even have an explanation."

"I didn't steal. You said what's yours is mine."

"Come on, Penny. That's just something people say. And I don't know what love is. Obviously. We're calling the wedding off just in time. Because I just liked fucking you. That's all I know. I need another drink."

"You don't mean that."

"I do. You have a great body. But clearly you're a shitty person. You're ugly on the inside. I see that now." He grabbed a glass from the cabinet. "I'll find another ten to keep the bed warm. Don't you worry about that."

"You're just lashing out. Stop saying things just because you're upset..."

"I mean every word that I've said. Go to hell, Penny."

"You're such an asshole." Yes, I couldn't explain the missing money to him. But there was no reason for him to say that he never loved me. That I was ugly on the inside.

"Sure." He unscrewed the cap to the scotch and took a sip straight from the bottle. "I'm the asshole."

"Yeah, you are." I pulled off the lid to the box I had left on the counter. "Because you still talk to Rachel." I threw the pictures at him. "And cheated on me during your bachelor party." I threw the rest of the pictures at him, the ones of him fucking some random girl and kissing Isabella in his office. "And you loved Isabella. You lied to me. And maybe you still do love her.

You left her millions of notes saying how much you loved her. You never left me love letters. You told me you were forced to marry her. That you never loved her. And talking about having children with her? Jesus, James. You never wanted that life with me. So now I know why. Because you just liked fucking me. You never loved me. You're a liar and a cheat."

"Have you been following me?" He held up the picture of Rachel. "What is wrong with you?"

"That's all you have to say to me? After everything I just said? God, you did cheat on me."

"I didn't fucking cheat on you! I already told you that when I got back from my bachelor party. I would never cheat on you. I'm not the one who fucked this up. You are. This is on you."

"Fine. Throw the blame on me. I'll take it, if that's what you need. But, James..."

"What I need is for you to either tell me why you stole from me or get the hell out of my house."

"I already told you! You won't believe me. Because you trust your ex wife more than you trust me."

"Because she never needed my money! God, my parents were right the whole time. You can't trust someone who comes from nothing. All they'll want is your money."

From nothing? I didn't come from nothing. I had a family that loved me. That meant more than all the money in the world. And I thought that's what he wanted from me, to be my family. I was so wrong.

"You kept telling me not to trust Isabella and that I shouldn't talk to her. And I was too naive to see that you were the one I shouldn't trust. So take the money you got your hands on. But you'll never get another dime from me. I'll blacklist your name so you can never get a marketing job in this entire city. I'm done giving you my handouts. I'm done with you. I never want to see your face again."

"Screw you, James." My whole body was trembling. Every venomous word that came out of his mouth broke me a little more. "I'm giving you what you want. I'm leaving." I walked away from him and opened up the front door. "Have fun finding a ten to keep your bed warm." I slammed the door behind me. Part of me wanted him to come after me. To tell me he was sorry. But I knew he wouldn't. He thought I was a gold digger. He thought I was in love with Tyler. And he didn't trust me. I pressed the button to close the doors of the elevator. Apparently he never had.

Ian was leaning against the car when I stepped off the elevator.

I looked down at the ground, hoping he wouldn't look up as I passed him.

"Penny? Do you need a lift?"

"No, I'm good." I kept walking.

"Are you okay?" He put his hand on my shoulder.

"I'm fine." I wiped my tears away.

"What happened?"

"Nothing."

"Let me drive you wherever you're going."

I didn't want to go to my parents' hotel room crying. I didn't want to go to Melissa and Tyler's. Not when James thought I still had feelings for him. I couldn't go to Bee and Mason's. "You don't work for me, Ian. You made that clear the other day." I pulled away from him.

"And I said I was sorry. Please, just let me take you."

"I don't have anywhere to go. And you need to be here in case James comes down. He's drunk. So, don't let him go anywhere. I don't want him to hurt himself."

Ian frowned. "Is everything okay between you two?"

I couldn't tell James that Isabella was the one who had given me Tyler's bank account number. That she had orchestrated this fight between us perfectly. And even if I did, he wouldn't believe me. He trusted her way more than he trusted me. She had him wrapped around her finger. And James had said some awful things to me. He was drunk, but that didn't excuse it. It was like I was hearing how he really felt about me for the first time. And it wasn't what I had wanted to hear. James and I certainly weren't going to fix this overnight. The wedding wasn't going to happen. I grabbed my key out of my purse and the credit card that James had given me and handed them to Ian. I didn't need James' money. I never needed it. I only needed him. "Can you give these to him for me please?"

"Penny, what's going on?"

"We're done." I shook my head. "I'm done. Just don't let him go anywhere while he's drunk. I don't want anything to happen to him."

Ian nodded his head. "I'll still take you wherever you want to go. As a friend."

"It's okay, Ian. I just...I'll walk." Where the hell was I going to go?

"Where will you stay?"

"I'll figure it out. Just don't let anything happen to him." I walked away before he could ask me any more questions.

CHAPTER 29
Thursday

I knew I'd love James until the day I died. That's what hurt the most. He could say as many horrible things as he wanted to me. It didn't change the way I felt about him. And I still wanted him to be happy. Even if I wasn't the one that could make him happy.

Sex. That's what it came back to. That was my biggest fear. That he was addicted to sex. I was just a good lay. Did he really mean that? I felt so cheap. James had lashed out at me before. He was good at pushing people away because he didn't think anyone could love him. So he didn't want to fall for anyone.

I hated that I was walking through the city streets of New York, a city that wasn't my home, feeling bad for the person who had just dumped me. But I did feel bad for him. He was so broken. I thought I could heal that wound. I thought I was enough. But I was just a good lay. I was just an escape from his reality. I was a drug. And he was ready to move on to the next thing.

The most ironic part was that Isabella had warned me it would happen. She had actually been right. Isabella had acted like a good friend to him the whole time she was torturing me. She won. And I didn't want to spend my whole life fighting her. I had a sick feeling that James was running to her right now, falling into her trap. Hopefully Ian would listen to me and not take him anywhere. If he wasn't going to be with me, he needed to find someone that actually made him happy. I didn't want him to revert back to her because it's all he knew.

I pulled out my phone and called Rob who was in town for the wedding. He could take care of James and make sure he didn't get back with Isabella. Rob hated her just as much as I did.

"Cashing in on your last lay as a single woman?" Rob said. "I thought you might call."

"Rob, can you go check on James?" I asked, ignoring him.

"Absolutely. I was just on my way over to hang out with you guys. Are you not there?"

"No. I'm...James can explain. Just take care of him okay? Promise to take care of him for me?" It suddenly hit me hard that I was losing all of James' family and friends too. Rob really had become one of my best friends. More like the brother I never had. I wouldn't be able to hang out with Bee and Mason anymore either. I'd never get to see Jen again. I was losing the love of my life and my new family.

"What's going on?" Rob suddenly seemed to understand that I was serious.

"I'm...the wedding's off, Rob."

"What?"

"He doesn't love me."

Rob laughed. "Yes he does. You're just getting cold feet."

"No. We're done." My voice caught. "It's over. Please just go take care of your brother. He's drunk. And he needs you."

"He doesn't need me. He needs you. Penny..."

I hung up the phone. There was a text message waiting for me from Isabella:

"You did the right thing, Penny. You're both better off this way. You're free to do whatever you want now. Go back to Wilmington. Go home. Live your life. And don't worry about James. I'll take good care of him."

A person passing me on the street gave me a strange look. I quickly wiped away my tears. I was aware of the fact that I looked like a crazy person, but I didn't really care. If James didn't want me anymore, it didn't change my feelings for him. I'd always love him. And I needed to do one last thing for him before it was too late.

I looked in my purse. I had about thirty dollars in cash. That could at least get me there. I'd figure out what to do next later. It was time to finally take Zach's advice. I needed to fight fire with fire. If I couldn't have James, I had to make sure Isabella didn't end up with him either. I put my hand out and hailed down a taxi.

***

I looked up at the Hunter's huge mansion. It seemed strange that this is what James thought I was after. I never cared about his money. I didn't know he still had doubts about that. But his parents had ingrained that thought into his head. If he had just trusted me, the wedding would still be on. I had trusted him. I was going to marry him despite the pictures Isabella sent. But James hadn't given me the same courtesy. What happened between us was just as much his stubbornness as it was Isabella's fault. And she knew him. She knew that he was sensitive about someone being with him for his money. She won.

What life did I have to live without James? I didn't have a home to go back to. New York was my home. Wherever James was, that was my home. He was home to me. I quickly wiped away the tears that had started to roll down my cheeks. I just wanted him to be happy.

I walked up the steps to James' parents' house and pressed the doorbell. A moment later, Eric opened up the door. He was the person that had been nicest to me at the engagement party. I fit in better with their help than with any of them. *Because I came from nothing.*

"Hi, Penny."

"Hi, Eric. I need to talk to James' parents."

"Are they expecting you?"

"No. But it's urgent. Can you please tell them that? I wouldn't be here if it wasn't."

"Of course." He stepped aside and I walked into their huge foyer. "The sitting room is to your left. Please take a seat while I go tell them."

"Thank you." I walked into the room he had pointed to as he disappeared down a hallway. The room was like every other room I had seen in here. It was way too ornate for my taste. Simple people liked simple things. This wasn't a life I wanted. I'd be okay.

No. I sat down and put my face in my hands. It didn't matter what I told myself. I'd never be okay. I bit the inside of my cheek. I wasn't going to cry in front of James' parents. As far as I knew, they were part of Isabella's scheming. If that was the case, I wasn't going to give them the satisfaction of seeing me cry. But I really hoped they weren't. They had said that they'd do anything to protect their son. I just needed to make them see that I wasn't the one that they should be worried about.

Isabella had taken everything from me. And all I could do was make sure she didn't get to take my place in James' life. He needed someone good and kind. Maybe that wasn't me. Good, kind people didn't have sex in their fiancé's office. That's what got us in this mess in the first place. Good, kind people also didn't touch strangers abs during their bachelorette parties. But I didn't want to. I had wanted to stay in and watch a movie. I thought I was a good person. And it hurt that James didn't think so. It felt like no one had ever truly seen me before I met him. But he thought I was ugly on the inside. My chest hadn't stopped hurting since I had left our apartment. *His apartment.* He had made that very clear. *He never loved me.*

James' father cleared his throat. I immediately stood up. "Mr. and Mrs. Hunter, I'm sorry to just stop by."

"A little notice would have been nice," James' mother said.

"It's okay," Mr. Hunter said and walked into the room. "Eric said you had something urgent to discuss?"

James' mother sighed and walked into the room.

"Yes, it's about Isabella..."

"Isabella is a dear friend of the family. She'll always be our daughter in law. If you're here to complain about her, you've come to the wrong place. You'll never replace her."

"Enough." James' father's voice made me jump. He sounded like James when he was upset. "Let the girl speak."

I swallowed hard. "I'm not trying to replace her. And I'm not going to be marrying your son."

"Thank heavens." His mother sighed and sat down in one of the chairs.

James' father lowered his eyebrows. Again, it reminded me of James. "What happened? Where is he?"

"He's fine. He's with Rob." It was the first time that it actually seemed like one of James' parents cared about his well being.

"Okay, well, Eric will see you out," James' mother said. She snapped her fingers and Eric appeared at the door.

"No. I'm not here to tell you about that. I got an email from Isabella this morning, blackmailing me and James. She had pictures of..." right now wasn't the time to be discreet. And I didn't care if Isabella was listening. She had never said I couldn't tell his parents. "Of James and I having sex in his office. She planted a camera in his office or something. And she said she'd leak the photos to some tabloids if I didn't agree to transfer 20 million dollars into her bank account. I didn't want the pictures to be leaked. I was trying to protect your son. I love him so much, I..." I was getting off topic. I blinked away the tears that were starting to well in my eyes. "I did what she asked. And she said I couldn't tell James that she made me do it. So I didn't. But she actually gave me the bank account of this guy I used to date. I couldn't tell James that she tricked me. I couldn't risk it. So he broke up with me. Because he doesn't trust me. I just thought you'd like to know that your perfect daughter in law just stole 20 million dollars from the son that you claim to care about."

"You're lying," his mother said.

I pulled out the bank slip that I had gotten and handed it to her.

"This doesn't prove anything. All it proves is that you transferred money out of James' bank account. That *you* stole from him. Which is exactly what we tried to warn him about. No wonder he broke up with you. Eric, please show Miss Taylor out."

I wasn't sure who I hated more, Isabella or Mrs. Hunter. I handed her a sheet of paper filled with the texts that Isabella had sent me throughout the day. I had stopped and had them printed out. "Isabella was watching me somehow. It was like she could hear everything I was saying and see what I was doing. I just thought that you'd both like to know. Maybe she's not the girl you thought she was." I walked past his mother and toward the door before I could start crying.

"Wait," his dad said.

I stopped and turned around.

"Let me see your cell phone."

"I'm not lying. Those texts are from her. That's all the proof I have. I know it'll be my word against hers and..."

"I believe you."

That's what I had wanted James to say to me. His dad believed me? He didn't even know me. Maybe James would believe me if I could have told him the whole story. I pulled out my phone and handed it to him.

He ran his fingers along the back of it and peeled off what looked like a clear sticker.

"What is that?"

"The thinnest camera and recording device in the world. It was the last technology Blive Tech International came out with before James sold the company. She was watching you. And listening to you." He looked over at his wife.

She shrugged her shoulders. It looked like she was in shock.

Maybe Austin had slipped it on my phone when he had kissed me. That was the only thing I could think of. Which meant Isabella had been watching me all week. I felt a chill run down my spine. My phone was always near me. She wasn't lying when she said she had more pictures. *Oh God.* "Maybe you could get the pictures from her? Ask her not to leak them? I don't want..."

"We'll take care of it." He handed my phone back to me. "And we'll talk to James. None of this is your fault."

"No." I shook my head. "It's deeper than that. We're not...it's over." It pained me to say it. But it was true. I couldn't marry James. He didn't love me. It didn't matter how much I loved him.

If he didn't trust me after everything we had been through, he never would.

"I'm sorry to hear that," his dad said.

"Your son is wonderful. He's not weak. He just needs you both in his life. Show him how much you care. Because I can tell that you do. You should be so proud of him. He's the most amazing person I've ever met."

"You really love him?" James' mom asked.

"So much that it hurts." My voice caught. "I'm sorry, I have to go." I turned around and walked as quickly as I could out of the room.

***

I didn't care if pictures of me having sex were all over the internet. Scandals blew over. I knew that better than anyone. I was such an idiot. I should have just told him.

A raindrop landed on the top of my head. I looked up as a light drizzle started. I didn't have a jacket or umbrella. But I didn't care. The cool rain felt good against my skin. Rain had always been comforting to me ever since I met James. It reminded me of him. Walking under his umbrella back from the party that I hadn't wanted to go to. I wanted to go back to that moment. I wanted to do things differently. The rain wasn't comforting tonight. It just reminded me of what I had lost.

I took off my high heels and continued walking, letting my feet splash in the puddles that were forming on the sidewalk. It was only a matter of minutes until I was completely soaked. My tears had quickly mixed into the rain.

He shouldn't have given up on me. He shouldn't have said those things to me. All I had ever done was love him. *Uncondition-*

ally. That's what love was. It was unconditional. James didn't love me. He had never loved me.

I was holding on to something that had never existed. It felt like I was melting into the rain.

James was wrong. I could take care of myself. I didn't need his handouts. I had my debit card with a few thousand dollars left in my bank account. It was all the money I had saved up working stupid summer jobs in high school and in college before meeting James. And it was all I needed. It was all I had ever needed. I'd use it to leave. That's what he wanted. He didn't want to see me ever again.

I would have followed James to the ends of the earth. I pulled my phone out of my purse and looked down at it. There were no missed calls or messages. He wanted me to leave. So I'd do that for him too. I'd disappear. It felt like I already had. I wasn't me without him.

I wasn't sure when my tears stopped. It was hard to tell in the rain. But eventually I was numb. All James had to do was ask me to stay. If there was anything I could hold on to I would. But he wanted me to leave. I wasn't the one that needed saving. He did. He needed someone stronger than me. Better than me.

I kept walking, like I knew where I was going. But I was completely lost. The truth was, I had nowhere to go. I hadn't come from nothing, but I felt like I was nothing now. Nothing without him. I just needed to get to the airport. I needed to get as far away from New York as two thousand dollars would take me.

A car beeping pulled me out of my thoughts. Water splashed onto my legs as it came to a stop next to me on the road. I didn't recognize the car. I picked up my pace. A car door slammed.

"Penny!" Rob called after me.

"Rob?" I turned around. "What are you doing here? I asked you to take care of..."

"Penny, get in the car."

I had never seen Rob upset before. But he was clearly distressed. "I don't need your help, Rob. I'm fine."

"You're walking in the middle of a storm without a coat, or umbrella, or...shoes?" He looked at my high heels in my hand. "What the hell are you doing?"

"Please, just leave me alone."

"And you're clearly lost. The city is that way," he said and pointed over his shoulder. "I'm taking you home. So, get in the car."

"Rob, James broke up with me. I don't have a home to go to. And I'm not your problem anymore." That's what James had said to me. That I was no longer his problem. That extended to his family too.

"Even if you two did break up, that doesn't mean that we're not still friends. Get in the car, Penny."

"I don't need James' handouts."

"I came after you by myself. Just get in the car. Please."

"How did you find me?"

"You have a GPS in your phone."

"James tracks me?"

"He worries about you."

"He's not worried about me anymore."

"That's not true. He loves you. You know that."

"Did he say that to you?" I let a small spark of hope run through me.

Rob slowly shook his head. The spark died before it had even lit. "Please, Penny. Just let me drive you wherever it is you're going. He'll want to know that you're safe."

He doesn't care if I'm safe or not. He wants me to disappear. "Will you take me to the airport?" I pressed my lips together. This was it. I was really going.

"If that's what you really want, then yes."

I had no idea where I was. I didn't want James' help, but I needed it. Maybe I was a nuisance. He'd be rid of me soon enough, though. "Okay." I walked around to the passenger's side of the car and got in. My wet legs squeaked against the leather seats. I wasn't even sure they'd let me on a plane like this. "I'm sorry, I feel like..."

"It's fine, Penny. You know, you've been walking in the opposite direction of the city," Rob said as he started the car. "The J.F.K. airport is 45 minutes away without traffic. So, it'll be at least an hour." He gave me a smile as he pulled the car away from the curb. There was always traffic in New York. But his joke didn't make me laugh.

It would have taken me forever to walk to the airport. "Thanks, Rob. For helping me when you didn't have to."

Rob shook his head. "Penny, I care about you. You're like a little sister to me. An annoying little sister who likes putting herself in danger. What were you thinking?"

I looked out the window. We really were in the middle of nowhere. It was strange how once you left the city, you couldn't tell you were close to it. I didn't want to disappear. I just wanted to see something familiar. "I wasn't thinking. I just...it's not like I have anything worth mugging anyway."

Rob didn't laugh.

"Can you take me to Newark instead?"

He looked over at me, but didn't say anything.

"Rob, did you go see him?"

He nodded.

I looked down at my hands. That's why Rob wasn't joking around with me. He thought I was a horrible person too. "It's not what you think."

"So you didn't steal 20 million dollars from James and give it to your ex?"

"I think I actually did do that. But I didn't know that's what I was doing. And I didn't have a choice."

"And you told James that?"

"I tried to. Rob, I..." I put my face in my hands and started crying again. "He doesn't believe me. I thought he trusted me. I thought...I mean, we were going to get married. It was all a lie. He never loved me."

"I believe you. I know you wouldn't hurt him. But he's hurting anyway. He's..." his voice trailed off. "You need to go talk to him..."

"Did you leave him alone?"

"Mason's with him."

I nodded my head. "I can't see him, Rob. He made it very clear that he doesn't want anything to do with me."

"That's not what it looked like to me. It looked like he was fucked up and needed you more than ever."

"If you're going to make me feel guilty, you can just let me off here. James kicked me out. Do you think I don't want to be there for him? That's not fair, Rob. You don't know the whole story. And he might need me, but he sure as hell doesn't want me."

"Okay. Newark it is then." He put on his turn signal and drove toward the highway. He put his hand on my shoulder. "How about you start from the beginning?"

***

The elevator doors opened into Rob's apartment. He had changed a lot of things from when it used to be James'. James and I had visited a lot, but not that recently. I ran my hand along the marble countertop.

Rob seemed to believe everything I had told him. He was wondering why I hadn't come to him sooner, since Isabella had never mentioned going to James' friends. And I didn't have an answer. It all happened so fast.

"If you want to take a shower, just use the master. I don't have any shampoo or anything in the guest bathroom."

"Actually, a shower sounds great." My clothes were still a little damp. "Do you have something I could change into after while my dress dries?"

"Yeah."

I followed him into the master bedroom. The bed was in a different spot and the sheets were black instead of white. It hadn't felt like a bachelor pad when James lived here, but it did now.

"Here," Rob said and tossed me a pair of black yoga pants and a white tank top. "Those should fit."

I looked up at him. "I don't even want to know why you have these clothes."

"Women sleep over a lot. I'm a snuggler." He shrugged. "They leave things."

"I never pictured you as the type of guy that let women spend the night."

"I'm letting you spend the night."

I laughed. "Fair enough. Thanks for these." I walked into the master bathroom and closed the door. I tried not to picture James in here with me as I turned on the water. Or as I lathered up my body with soap. I tried not to picture him pushing me against the cold tiles. *Fuck*. Luckily Rob didn't used the same body wash as James or I probably would have lost it again. I quickly got out and dried off.

Looking through Rob's drawers for a comb reminded me of doing the same when it was James' place. When I was a student and he was my professor. I loved spending the night with him. I loved the way he made me feel. For the first time in my life, I had felt alive. I looked at my reflection in the mirror and then quickly looked away. I didn't want to think about him. Especially if he was back home upset about something I didn't really do. Or worse, getting over it with Mason's help. Just like Mason had helped him find a great location for a bachelor party. James cheated on me.

I found a comb and quickly brushed out my hair before getting dressed. The outfit fit perfectly. It was good that Rob hooked up with tons of random women. I hung up my wet clothes and towel to dry and made my way out of the bathroom. I kept my arms folded in front of my chest. My bra had been too wet to put back on and I didn't want to have to ask Rob for one.

He looked up at me as I came out of his bedroom, and then he immediately looked away. "Do you want something to drink?" He opened up the fridge. "I think I have a bottle of wine somewhere..."

"A beer is fine." I sat down cross-legged on his couch.

Rob laughed. "And that's why I love you." He grabbed two beers from the fridge and popped off the tops. He handed one to me before sitting down next to me on the couch. "Are you hungry or anything?"

"No, I'm good." We had gotten some fast food at a drive through on the way here. I wasn't hungry then either, but I had eaten a few fries.

"You're seriously turning down Grottos?"

I laughed. "I'm not hungry."

"Geez, you are upset."

I took a sip of my beer. "Yeah. You know, this might be the last time we ever get to hang out."

"James gets me in the breakup, huh?"

"As his brother, yeah, I think so. And Mason and therefore Bee. And Matt. And Jen."

"If he lets you go, he's a fucking idiot."

"He already did."

Rob shook his head. "James still wants to marry you. You have to know that."

"He said he never wanted to see me again."

"Because he was drunk and upset and..."

"He still said it." I took another sip of my beer. "He said it was only ever about sex."

Rob shook his head again. "He showed me the pictures that you threw at him. That one of him having sex was from college. He hasn't had a beard that long since he was strung out on drugs. He was a dumb kid."

Oh. That made sense. But it didn't change anything. "He was probably the same age there as I was when I met him."

"But you had your shit together."

"I didn't. I fell in love with my professor."

Rob laughed.

"What about the other pictures? The ones of Rachel?"

Rob stared at me for a second before speaking. "My parents were awful to James growing up. You knew that, right? They ignored me and Jen. We definitely got the better end of the deal. But James was the prodigal son. Nothing he did was ever good enough. Living like that...it's a lot of pressure."

I was an only child. I knew what it felt like to want to please your parents. I was always worried that I would disappoint them. But they had never pressured me to do anything in particular. They always seemed proud of me no matter what I did. "I don't know that much about his childhood. He doesn't really talk about it."

"He wanted to play football. Did you know that? That was his dream."

I shook my head. He had never told me that. He loved watching the Giants games with Rob. That was one of their favorite things to do together. But I never knew he wanted to be playing. "He never told me."

"My parents made him quit the team in high school because they thought it was a waste of time. They had this way of sucking out all the joy from his life. Like they found pleasure in it. No matter what James did, he wasn't good enough for them. He was always wrong. They beat him down. I played baseball in high school and college and Jen was into drama club. And James had to watch us do whatever we wanted to. I think that hurt him too. It wasn't just that my parents didn't let him do the stuff he loved, it's that they always made it seem like they liked him the least, you know? By not letting him do anything he wanted. But they got what they wanted, I guess. A genius techie who doesn't speak to them. Their loss right?" Rob set his empty beer down on the coffee table.

I remembered the first speech that James had given in my Comm class. He had said he had wished he could be more like his sister...fearless. "Didn't he ever stand up to them?" I thought about the paper I had seen in his copy of Harry Potter. He was trying to get emancipated.

"Yeah. With Rachel. I lied to you the other day when you asked about Rachel. It wasn't just young love. He was obsessed with her. I think she felt the same about him. They spent every second they could together. So of course, my parents wanted to ruin that too. Even after they told him he had to choose between her and them paying for college, he held on to that relationship. They still talked in private. He promised her that once he got enough money, they could be together again. But then halfway through college, she just stopped talking to him. She refused to take his calls. She said it was over, without any explanation. That's when he really lost it. I think he saw a way out of his life with her. An escape or something. I don't really know. He was a mess. He just snapped. He hit rock bottom. He gave up on life."

That wasn't the story James had told me. He said their relationship had stopped when he had to choose between her and college. "And when he went to see her last week?"

"Did my parents really try to pay you five million dollars to walk away from James?"

I was surprised that James had told him that. "Yeah."

Rob shook his head. "I don't think James realized how far they'd go to get what they want."

I shrugged. "What does this have to do with him visiting Rachel?"

"When you told James that they tried to pay you off...he thought maybe the same thing had happened with her. He thought they had paid her off too. That's why she suddenly didn't care about him anymore."

I remembered James' reaction when I had told him about his parents trying to pay me off. It kind of looked like he was realizing something for the first time. I thought he was just realizing how evil his parents really were. But he was realizing why Rachel abandoned him. "Why wouldn't he tell me that?"

"I don't know. He only went to go see her to confirm his suspicion. That was it. It wasn't because he still has feelings for her. He would never cheat on you, Penny."

"And? Was he right?"

Rob nodded. "They only offered her one million to walk away. She took the money without a second thought."

"That's awful."

"It's certainly fucked up."

I took another sip of my beer. No wonder James felt like no one ever loved him. The love of his life chose money over him. Maybe she had only ever been with him for his money. *The love of his life*. Was she? Was Isabella? It didn't feel like I was anymore. "He looked so happy to see her."

"He just needed closure."

"Maybe."

"Penny, he loved her once, but not as much as he loves you now. Tonight was the only time I've ever seen him more upset than the day Rachel called things off. I know he probably said some stuff he didn't mean, but he needs you, Penny. I don't want to see him hit rock bottom again. You fixed him."

"I didn't. This place did. Teaching. He should be a professor again. He loved teaching."

"If you think that's what saved him, you're lying to yourself. I've never seen him happier than when he's with you. He was even agitated during his bachelor party because you two weren't together. He needs you and only you."

"So, he's addicted to me. I can't..."

"No, Penny. He's devoted to you. There is a huge difference."

I bit my lip. I wanted James to be here telling me these things. But Rob was right, there was a huge difference. If it was true though, James wouldn't have said those things to me. He wouldn't have told me to leave. "I'm not sure he is anymore."

"Look, if I didn't think what you had was real, you'd already be naked in my bed."

I laughed.

"Seriously. I know it's because you're cold, but your nipples are so hard right now and I'm having trouble not staring."

"Shit." I put my beer down and crossed my arms in front of my chest again.

Rob laughed. "And if James wasn't a fucking mess tonight, I also wouldn't have..." Rob picked up his phone "...17 missed calls from him."

"Does he know you're with me?"

"I haven't told him. Do you want me to?"

I swallowed hard. "No. Not yet. I just need some time."

Rob slid his phone back into his pocket. "Then I won't. But time is one thing you don't have much of. I already rented my tux for the wedding and I hate wasting money."

"I thought James paid for the tux rentals?"

"That's beside the point. Now, how about that pizza? And I'm sure I have a bra that's your size. 32 B, right?"

"Why do you know that?"

"I know things." He got up off the couch. "By the way, I saw you staring at the kitchen counter like you were remembering being fucked against it. I've always wondered...exactly how many places in this apartment did you bang my brother?"

I looked around the apartment. "None of the guest bedrooms."

"You're both disgusting." He laughed and disappeared into his room.

I pulled out my phone. James hadn't called me at all. I wasn't mad at him anymore. I was just sad. If he called, I'd answer it in a heartbeat. *Call me. Say something. Anything. Give me something to hold on to.*

CHAPTER 30
Friday

When I woke up, I had almost forgotten where I was. I expected to open my eyes and be in my apartment with James. Instead, my head was resting on Rob's shoulder on the couch. We were both sitting up and his arm was wrapped around my shoulders. He always joked around about sexual stuff, but Rob really was like a brother to me. And he had been there for me when I needed him. I quietly ducked out from under his arm.

He groaned in his sleep. His ankles were crossed and his feet were on the coffee table. He must have been uncomfortable but he had stayed with me instead of going to his bed. I really hoped this wasn't the last time I'd get to see him.

I grabbed my phone. There were still no calls from James. If he hadn't meant what he said, wouldn't he have contacted me by now? The reality seemed even more alarming than it had last night. Rain was pounding against the windows, somehow reminding me of what I had just lost. I wanted to see James, but I knew I couldn't. He had to be the one to reach out to me. He was the one that had told me to disappear. So instead of going to him, I'd go to a place where it would feel like I was close to him.

I walked into Rob's closet. I had been wearing high heels last night and I didn't want to change back into my dress. There were a pair of girly flip flops in Rob's closet. Those would do. I slid them on even though they were a little too big. Taking something from Rob's closet reminded me of when I had run back to my dorm in just one of James' t-shirts. I would never forget those memories. Even the bad ones just seemed good now. Because they were with him.

Rob groaned in his sleep again. I didn't want to be here when he woke up. He needed to go back to New York. James was the one that needed him right now. Not me. I was stronger than James seemed to realize.

I glanced at the clock on the oven as I walked toward the elevator doors. It was only 6 a.m. The coffee shop wouldn't be open for another hour. But I didn't care. I'd just stand outside. I just needed to be there. It felt like I was being drawn to it. I needed to remember the best day of my life.

Before I pressed the elevator button, I froze. I'd do anything for James. If he asked me to jump, I'd jump. He knew that. He knew how much I cared. And he had asked me to disappear. He knew I'd do it for him. I looked down at the ring on my finger. He hadn't called. He hadn't reached out to me at all. This was what he wanted. I loved him. I loved him so much. And if this was what he wanted, I'd give it to him. I pulled the ring off my finger and set it down on the kitchen counter. If James needed me to disappear, I'd disappear.

PROFESSOR HUNTER

Want to know what Professor Hunter was thinking when he first met Penny?

Find out in *Professor Hunter - Temptation* from James' point-of-view!

To get your free copy of *Professor Hunter*, go to:

www.ivysmoak.com/eruption-hb

WHAT'S NEXT?

James and Penny are tying the knot in 24 hours. But Isabella is still out there plotting…

See if they make it to the altar in book 4 of the The Hunted Series, *Devotion*…available now!

A NOTE FROM IVY

I'm broken. I am. I live and breathe these characters and leaving them in pain hurts me.

Before I started writing, I didn't know what I wanted to do with my life. But after I wrote Penny and James' meet cute, I knew. It's always been about Penny and James for me. But not every story is so easy. They've been through so much and it hurts to write this piece of their journey. But life isn't meant to be easy. It's about fighting for what you believe in.

And I truly think that love is worth the pain.

Ivy Smoak

Ivy Smoak
Wilmington, DE
www.ivysmoak.com

Recommend *Eruption* for your next book club!

Book club questions available at:
www.ivysmoak.com/bookclub

Printed in the USA
CPSIA information can be obtained
at www.ICGtesting.com
LVHW051652300124
770120LV00024B/422/J